SCARLET HUNGER

A NILE GHOST STORY

CRISTINE COURCY

SMASHED HOUSE PUBLISHING LLC

For MyFr0zenHeart.

CONTENTS

EPISODE 1: MADDISON ROSE

I lied.

That was my first mistake. Christopher Vantine, newly minted junior Nile deputy, National Guard corporal, and all-around perfect All-American guy, was the last person to take kindly to something as dishonest as...well, dishonesty.

My second mistake was counting on my disarmingly enchanting smile, bewitching hazel eyes, and camellia body oil from the Nile Witch to persuade Chris into letting me slip underneath the police caution tape to see the body...or rather, the remains...of Maddison Rose.

There'd be no body.

I knew this.

Based on my research, and from what I could get out of Chris the other night—*and* if Chris's twin brother, Joey, was to be believed—which, honestly could be counted on a coin toss—Maddie was dead. From a suspected "dog" attack. And I knew that if Maddie *had* been attacked—it wasn't by a dog. And the only thing left identifiable would be her face.

"Please, Chris?" I flashed a sweet smile with my eyes wide and hopeful. "I was all over Lilyriver Road last night. As soon as we got off the phone." I winced at the admission and looked up at him in sincere apology. Of all the guys sniffing around me like creepy vampires straight out of a crappy romance novel, Chris was the only one I knew who deserved better than me. He just didn't know it yet. So, I made sure to keep him at arm's length until that time came. "I know I shouldn't have told you I was working...and I'm so sorry for that—"

Chris took a tentative step forward. "Yeah, I was really looking forward to taking you out. And after seeing Maddie...everywhere..." His face paled and he looked a little sick. He swallowed with a wince. "I just really wanted to see you and—"

"There was nightshade on all four corners," I blurted, despite myself. As much as I needed to play on Chris's affection for me...I needed to get to the point. And him rambling on about date nights was wasting time. "And the ground was scorched."

"And that means...what? Dragons? Or magic salamanders?" Chris hooked his thumbs on his duty belt as he cocked his head to the side and studied my face, his forehead crinkled with uncertainty.

I poked his chest with a giggle. "I see you've been talking to Lacey." The warmth faded from my face as I flipped my long honey hair over my shoulder. "But no. Nightshade at a crossroads is a clear indication of demonic activity. As is the scorched earth."

Chris opened his mouth to argue, but I kept going, speaking through the patient smile held firmly in place between my dimples. "And before you ask—the nightshade at the crossroads, just *feet* from the home of Aubrey's stepsister, Daphne Collins, where Maddison had had a sleepover last weekend—coupled with numerous reports of her increasingly erratic behavior over the last few days...in addition to the fact that her little sister made a *literally* miraculous recovery exactly three days after said sleepover... and now the rumored state of her remains...can I hazard a guess as to the manner of death?"

Chris shifted where he stood, dropping his hands to his sides and then hooking them back on his belt. "Uhhh..."

I winced. "Mhmm. I'd say she was flayed. *Game of Thrones*-esque. Death by a thousand cuts?"

Chris blinked. "How did you know—"

I nodded grimly, my face set and sober. "It's how hellcats get to the soul. Which explains why her head was left untouched. The hellcats localize their work around the torso...and don't stop until they rip out the—"

Chris flinched and held up his hand. "Okay, okay, I got it."

I gave him a sympathetic nod. "It's horrific. Which is why I'd really appreciate it if you could just let me look around. No pictures of her, of course." I bit my lip as the lie left me. "If anything, I'd just take a few shots of the landscape so that my viewers can get a feel for the location..."

Chris glanced over my head at the group of men convening up the bank at the edge of the roadside as he massaged the back of his neck. He looked down at me with a reluctant wince. I could visibly see the internal struggle as he wrestled with the morality of the situation. "I don't know, Jacqueline...I really shouldn't..."

I shook my head as I tried to get him to understand. "Chris, you know why I do what I do. It's not about me. It's about the truth. It's about Maddie. She was my friend. It's not like I'm going to exploit her."

Chris looked away, his jaw pulsing as he squinted into the distance. "Yeah."

"Remember when she helped me throw that Captain America themed graduation party for you? Before you went off to basic? What was it, two years ago? And—"

He smiled at that, his left dimple pressing deep into his cheek. He pulled out his phone, flashing the Captain America shield on the back. "I still have the phone case you gave me."

I blushed. If any superhero suited Chris, it was Captain America. And he had the good looks to match. Though his wide nose and wide mouth were soft and almost sensual, the square shape of his face set the lines of his jaw with just enough edge to convey his masculine strength. And though he wasn't particularly tall, he still had enough inches on me to be imposing. And don't get me started on his hair. Dark, perfectly faded undercut, with the top slicked back like he was straight out of Peaky Blinders. "Yeah... Maddison lent me the money for it. I was waiting on my payday."

"She was sweet like that..."

I scoffed. "More than. She gave her life for her sister." Discreetly, I pushed up on my tiptoes to see over his shoulder at the orchard. "People need to know. Especially when you all insist on covering up the evil," I added sharply. "With the Rousseaus? How your daddy said that they were attacked by yet another dog... a dog that they didn't own. You know that's wrong."

My hazel eyes met his, and I had to fight myself to not look away. The cobalt-blue Vantine eyes were always a bit unnerving. Fortunately, Chris looked away first, for he had the decency to look abashed. He shifted where he stood before his eyes found mine again. His voice broke slightly as he spoke earnestly, "Jacqueline, you know we can't go around suggesting things like demons and—"

I put a hand on his arm. "I know, Chris. I get it. That's why *I* need to. First the Rousseaus, and now Maddie? People need to start waking up. And if I have to be the one to do it, then I will."

Chris hesitated, then he smiled slowly as though seeing me for the first time—though like all islanders, we'd known each other our whole lives. "You're something else, Jacqueline Charlebois."

I returned his praise with a rueful simper and playful push. "That's what they all say..." I licked my lips and cast a sideways glance at the huddle of officers up the grassy bank at the edge of Martin Road. Chris's daddy, Sheriff Vantine, was standing tall beside Chris's twin, Joey, as they talked with several men in suits— mainlanders, by the look of them. I had maybe five minutes before they all trekked back to see what was left of Maddison Rose.

I peeked back at Chris. "Is your mom home?"

Chris sighed heavily with the twitch of an indulgent smirk at the corner of his mouth. "No."

I grabbed his hand and squeezed with a girlish squeal, "Thanks, Chris! I owe you big time."

"Yeah, like *dinner*," he grumbled moodily. "At Liberty Tree!" he called after me. "On you!"

Without looking back, I laughed as I ran across the grass, slick with early morning dew, past the barn and pastures toward the pretty white farmhouse in the distance. Then I cut through the maple trees and slipped behind the barn back around toward the orchard.

Combat boots slipping on damp leaves and wet grass, I bobbed beneath branches heavy with apples and ducked around trunks, constantly flicking my gaze in the direction of the road to gauge the possible position of Maddison's remains.

I tried to keep my tummy clenched and tight. But in the quiet of my own mind, even thinking her name set my stomach churning. I took a deep breath, inhaling deeply through my nose, the chilly October air prickled the inside of each nostril. I had to get through this. As Nile's official (unofficial) paranormal investigative journalist, it was my job to report the truth. And part of that truth often required field documentation...because people weren't always eager to believe things they couldn't see themselves. So, if I had to see sweet 16-year-old Maddison Rose shredded like apple peels all over the orchard to get them to believe, then I would.

And as I reminded Chris, it was for Maddie, too. She was a victim of evil. It was a disservice to her memory to suggest anything else.

I stopped short just before the right row. Despite all my tough talk, my heart palpated in my chest and my lungs couldn't seem to catch a breath. I'd never seen a dead body before...much less a mutilated one...and Maddie had been my friend.

I swallowed, my tongue thick and dry in my mouth. And I stepped between the trees and looked up the grassy lane.

It was just like they say—the world seemed to slow, the birds stopped chirping, time paused, and it was just the cold wind hissing through the branches and blowing back my blonde hair as I moved along the path. Blankly, I stared ahead, unseeing the horror before me, and I held up my phone and snapped a picture of Maddison Rose, her oval face looking up at the gray October sky with her glassy hazel eyes wide, her dark hair splayed out around her head like a black halo. And her body torn to pieces—fleshy, bloody ribbons all over the grass and dangling from the branches.

It was like I'd left my own body.

It wasn't me taking picture after picture of the grisly scene.

It wasn't me scanning her remains with the video light on the phone shining.

It wasn't me.

Dissociation.

The human brain's a frightening thing. The tricks it plays, the lies it tells, all in the name of keeping you sane.

I couldn't tell how many pictures I took. I couldn't even remember how I got back to my car. Something about seeing the sweetest girl I'd ever met sliced up like slits on a pie crust...cast a thick fog over the rest of the day.

EPISODE 2: THE WEIRD, UNSOCIALIZED HOMESCHOOLER

"You really think this is a good idea, Jacqueline?"

I pulled my eyes from the upload page and blinked at my best friend, Patricia White, in a slight daze. "Hmm? What?"

Patty smiled slightly and nodded at the computer screen. "This is a lot more...graphic...than your usual content. I mean, it's—"

My stomach twisted, and I winced. "I know. But I've been as respectful as possible—while still maintaining journalistic integrity." I jutted my chin toward the screen. "I've blurred out her face and all the...carnage. It's not sensationalizing anything. I swear. Or exploiting her," I added firmly as I went back to my work. "It's about the truth."

That entire morning I'd work on the episode. I'd put together the video, spliced it with the photos of the orchard and the footage from the crossroads, and blurred out the gore. Added in some personal pictures of Maddie and a few statements from those closest to her. Recorded the voice over and filmed my coverage. It was thirteen minutes of respectable, irreproachable journalism. And it was ready.

I moved the mouse to click the upload button, but stopped, finger raised as her next question made me hesitate.

"But what's wrong with your usual stuff?" Patty prompted meekly.

I frowned. Well, nothing...aside from the fact that no one cared about it except me. My YouTube channel, Inside My Frozen Heart, with a modest following of 222 viewers, focused on monsters and ghosts, primarily the legends of Martin Isle—Nile, as us islanders called it—the most haunted town in America. My videos were all mini-documentaries—episodes as I called them— featuring new "monsters of the week." Nile had enough stories to fill several sagas of books, let alone a few thirteen minute video clips. And I loved each and every story. Why not tell them to the world?

But I couldn't *help* but love them. Darkness and depravity were kind of my thing. And as a homeschooled kid, I was free to let those interests lead my learning, *and*, thanks to my grandmother, Joy Charlebois, owner of the (cursed) Charlebois Inn, I'd developed a passion for the macabre and bizarre. Nothing more so than legends of ghosts and monsters. It was our heritage, she'd say. In our blood. Literally, if she was to be believed, because according to her, we were descended from witches. And she'd told me, as her grandmother had told her, everything she knew about the paranormal activity hidden within the shadows of society. But now, thanks to dark web searches and internet chat rooms I was *definitely* too young to be lurking in...I knew more. So much more. So, I made half my high school courses dedicated to just that: the study of the supernatural...well, that and filmmaking.

And though some of my videos were simply me sharing my research on well-known monsters and ghosts found all over the world, I also did many episodes documenting our *local* Nile legends—on location. Just last year I'd covered the wolfman of Bell Hill Road (not a wolfman), last spring I did one on the haunted Mirror of Rosecrest (with an exclusive interview with Desiree

Lapierre), then I did a special with Charlotte Grey (the infamous Nile Witch, herself) on the history of witch burnings and hangings on Bird Island, and I still had plans on looking into the Creepy Cow Man...I was waiting on summer for that one. But mostly? I featured content on the illusive Scarlet Witch...whom my grandmother said was the last witch in our family. My passion project, you could say. That story was (is) everything to me.

And *nothing* to anyone else.

To be honest, the Scarlet Witch uploads were always the episodes with the fewest views. I'd be lying if I said that didn't hurt.

"Jacqueline?" Patty put a light hand on my shoulder.

I squinted my eyes shut and then opened them wide. "Sorry. Screen-eyes...my *usual* content?"

Patty blushed down to the roots of her auburn hair. "You know, the Martin Isle stuff...not..." She gestured vaguely at the computer, barely able to look at it.

"Patricia, this *is* Nile stuff. Maddie was an islander. She was killed on the island. And her story needs to be told. People need to know the truth. Otherwise, they'll keep herding themselves like sheep to the slaughterhouse."

Patty swallowed, a loud gulping sound as she scrunched up her face. "But all your other episodes—they didn't have dead girls in them..."

"No one from this decade anyway, no. But the Nile witch burnings of the 17th century? Twenty-seven deaths. At least. And the Bell Hill Road accidents? Three deaths. One disappearance. And Desiree Lapierre, remember her? She was next. The only reason I didn't cover the Rosecrest House again was because I was on vacation—with you," I added with an affectionate smile. "Fortunately, Lacey—you remember Lacey McGregor? She made friends with the newest owner, Hannah Green. Lacey won't give me any details, but she said that the girl is considering an interview." I waved my hand as though to clear my head of the distractions. "Anyways, point made." I turned back to the screen and clicked upload without a second thought.

Patty let out a little gasp. And for some reason, I flinched as the upload progress bar began to fill. I licked my lips and nodded firmly. "Okay. Let's get this over with."

Patricia gave a nervous giggle as her body relaxed a little. "Get what over? You mean co-op? You break into haunted houses and hunt down werewolves, but *co-op* is too much for you?"

I pushed up from the chair, almost as eager as Patty to get away from the computer. "Yeah. You know I hate people. The only reason I go is for you."

Patty slipped her arm through mine and squeezed me in a sideways hug as we left her bedroom. "And you know I'm grateful. I'd be lost without you."

I smiled to myself. The feeling was mutual. We'd been best friends since kindergarten when we met at the mainland Green Mountain Homeschool Association. At the time, GMHA was a brand-new co-op created for the rapidly growing homeschooling community in upstate Vermont. As soon as we stepped inside the building, our mothers pushed us together with an instant commonality—Patty's second cousins once removed were also *my* second cousins once removed...which essentially meant that my grandfather's sister was married to her grandfather's brother. Which, if you think about it, literally means nothing, but to anxious little five-year-olds...nothing was everything. We weren't blood, but that didn't matter. The moms said we were related. Good enough for me. Plus, it didn't hurt that we looked similar enough to be sisters. So, I took her hand and claimed her as my best friend. We had to be. Her cousins were my cousins. Just makes sense...right?

And from then on, it was us against everyone else...while all the other kids were lost and looking to form bonds, we already had one. We were *best friends*. And we were also outsiders—even in the homeschooling community, which was saying something. Well, *I* was the outsider. And because Patricia was my best friend, she became one, too. Even though she was just like the rest of them: rich with happily married parents and tons of siblings.

The only thing that made Patricia different from the pack (and teenagers in general) was her highly introverted personality type and incredibly secure sense of self—both of which she used like a superpower in the world of mean girls and jerkfaces. Patty wasn't shy, she just didn't care that we didn't fit in with the rest of the kids because she much preferred to be alone anyway. *And* unlike literally every other teenage girl in the world, she didn't care about the opinions of others, much less her peers. I envied her for that, and I'd be lying if I said it didn't matter to me just a little.

The co-op was once a week and alternated between homes. Well— alternated between everyone's house but mine. Because I lived on the island, they excused my mom from the rotation...plus, my mom worked. Like all the time. Because unlike the other families, we didn't have a stay-at-home parent who could host a pack of kids inside our massive mansion. But since I'd been essentially adopted into Patricia's family...her co-op days kind of counted as mine, too.

We made our way downstairs and were instantly met with stares. The younger siblings had all gone with Allison's mom to the neighborhood playground to give us high schoolers time to work on our research projects. Erica, a short girl with wide, round azure eyes, blinked at us as we approached the kitchen table. A cool smile slid into place on her pretty face. "What were you two doing up there? You've been gone for hours..." She exchanged a pointed look with Allison who didn't bother to hide her smirk.

I felt my cheeks burn. The lesbian insinuations were getting old. It was taunts like this that shoved people in the closet in the first place. Gross.

Patty placed her books down and took a seat at the table, completely oblivious to the joke. She pulled her things out and got right down to work without a word to anyone else.

Everyone's eyes were still fused to me. It wasn't fun to make fun of someone if they didn't care. So, no one ever cared about Patricia. I was the focus. It was always me. If I wasn't entertaining them, they made me their entertainment.

But I knew how to play the game. I forced a kind smile as I lied, "Just last-minute research."

None of the co-op kids, nor their parents, knew about my YouTube channel. The demons and beasts would be too much for their weak, WASPy constitutions. And I didn't want to deal with the goth jokes that they'd pepper me with.

The first time I'd tried to wear my black lipstick to co-op, my mom had made one of her comments...the kind that sound like a compliment but are actually an insult...suggesting that although I should feel free to express myself through fashion at home—co-op is like my place of work, and I should dress "appropriately." "Appropriately" being code for L. L. Bean and Old Navy. But, in hindsight, I was grateful she'd said what she'd said, because if I wore what I liked to wear to co-op...I'd never hear the end of it. Let's just say the deafening laughter that would follow me would obstruct my education.

There was a reason I didn't use my name on my channel.

And I only shot from the throat down.

And that there were only three people IRL who knew Inside My Frozen Heart was run by Joy Charlebois's weird, unsocialized, homeschooled granddaughter: Chris Vantine (a good journalist needs her police insider...even if he is a baby deputy coasting on nepotism), Lacey McGregor (my lovely assistant), and Patricia White (as Maddie would say, every superhero needs a BFF sidekick).

Okay, so it was technically four if you count my grandmother...

And then obviously Rosalind Grunberg the Nile Historian and her grandniece/assistant...but that was it. Six people out of billions. And I was going to keep it that way. I got enough weird looks from people. I didn't need to encourage any more.

"Last minute research," Natalie scoffed suspiciously.

I gave her an easy shrug. "Got sidetracked by a few YouTube shorts. That new mailbox trend is hilarious."

Benji whooped and shoved Kenneth. "Dude, yes! Did you see the one with the old lady? She ran out buck naked, chasing those girls with a spoon!!"

Ted snickered. "And what was on that *spoon*?"

"Don't even want to think about it. Please. No." Kenneth gagged.

The girls relaxed and allowed me to sit at the table without further comment. In typical girl clique fashion, they assembled behind the alpha female, (me) just waiting to stab her (me) in the back. Which is why they constantly tested me for weakness. But kill them with kindness as my grandmother always said. And I did. No one can hate a happy, bubbly, blonde with a kind, kick-butt smile. I played the part well. So, although I was an outsider, I managed to fit in at the front of the pack.

Erica cleared her throat and scooted her chair closer as she slid her notebook over to me. "So, Jackie..."

I gritted my teeth at the nickname. I didn't do nicknames. There was only one nickname for me and only one person who had permission to use it. But I didn't bother correcting her.

"The girls and I were discussing the fall senior field trip...As you know, the Moms gave Allison and I the assignment of planning the location. And yes, it's a little last minute...*but*..."

I glanced over at Allison who nodded enthusiastically. I looked down at the notebook and my heart sank.

"And we were thinking...Martin Isle. The Charlebois Inn! *Your* Inn!" Erica gushed with a bounce in her seat. "You talk about how awesome it is living on an island and all about your estate! Now we can all finally see your house—sorry, Manor. I can't believe your house has a name. Charlebois Manor." She giggled with delight. "And it's perfect for Halloween! A week there with a historical tour around the island? Unforgettable! As you know," She gave me a coy wink. "there's a discounted package for school groups and—well," She smiled eagerly at Natalie who then took over the pitch: "Since your family owns the Inn. And you literally *live* in the Manor. I mean, we figured you could work in some special behind the scenes access, as well."

I forced another smile. "Right. So, I'm assuming you mean you want to stay in..."

"*Charlebois Manor*. It's the only part of the property that is actually cursed, right? Not the Inn, but the family home. *Your* home."

Right. My home. My stomach sloshed, sour in my gut.

"*Actually* cursed, Erica?" Natalie snickered.

Erica waved away her skepticism. "Jackie knows what I mean."

I stared down at the notebook, my mind working overtime to think up an excuse.

"So, what do you think?" Erica reached for the notebook and ripped off the page with all her itinerary notes. "Just make the reservations and then give the Moms the bill."

"And then we can all finally see your library!" Allison shook her head as her dark, perfectly curled hair swayed around her face. "I've been dying to see it. I couldn't imagine having a whole library in my house. All I have is a study."

"You can show us your room with the widow's walk that you always talk about!" Natalie added, her brown eyes bright. "I couldn't imagine the history behind that. A staircase in your bedroom leading up to a view of the entire lake! It must be beautiful."

"A spooky balcony made solely for suicidal sailor wives? On top of a cursed mansion?" Allison giggled from across the table. "For-get *that*. I'm heading straight for the horses. Jacqueline said she has enough for all of us to ride. And on the website, I saw there's a private family trail that the Inn guests can't access. *That's* where I'll be."

Erica held up a hand cutting off the excited chatter. "So, Jackie—can you get us all the exclusive extras and access?"

"Sure. I'll talk to my grandmother and see what she can do." I heard myself answer brightly.

But inside I was screaming.

EPISODE 3: REALITY BITES

S o…

I may or may not have given everyone the impression that I lived in the enchanting Charlebois Manor, a massive estate atop a rocky cliff on the east coast of the island overlooking Lake Champlain on one side and the Charlebois Inn on the other, surrounded by lush, dense forest.

Charlebois Manor.

My grandmother's manor.

My grandmother's Inn.

And soon to be my *aunt's* manor.

And my *aunt's* Inn.

None of it would go to me. None of it was mine.

Even though…my father was the heir. He was the eldest. But that didn't matter…because my grandfather had put in a morality clause in the will before he died. And my father? Well, he was a degenerate, drowning himself in a bottle somewhere in a leaking sailboat off the coast of Florida last I heard. Which was at least a decade ago. Who knew whether he was even still alive. And if he was? Well, he'd be the farthest you could get from the moral code of any ethical creed. Now, my aunt on the other hand had the temperament of a harpy, but she knew how to behave.

But, yeah...so, to save myself a massive amount of social ridicule—I played up the Charlebois Manor angle instead of letting all the little legacies sneer and pity where I really lived... smack dab in the middle of Nile, in the woods beside a cow pasture (that stank like...yeah...that...), in a run-down old hunter's shack. Yes. Shack.

Poor as the dirt floor my cat slept on.

And now, in less than twenty-four hours...everyone would know.

Well, maybe they wouldn't.

Technically, I *did* have a bedroom in my grandmother's house. And it would always be *my* room...at least until she died and my aunt took over. As soon as that happened, I wouldn't be surprised if Aunt April not only kicked me out of Charlebois Manor but banned me from the property entirely.

These thoughts consumed me the entire forty-five-minute drive (counting the fifteen-minute ferry ride) back home.

I turned off Apple Shore Road and drove the car through the trees along the twisty, bumpy makeshift driveway to the shack. Then I shoved the car in park and sat for a moment, glaring at my sorry excuse of a house. I didn't always hate it. I mean, it *was* my home. But today I did. I kicked open the car door and slammed it shut, rolling my eyes as I marched across the short gravel path toward the porch.

The shack itself was gray, the wood weathered from the sun and rain and time. Honestly, I was just grateful it was still standing. The ice storm last year had nearly flattened it. We were lucky we didn't lose power or heat. Elijah Grunvald had stopped by to check on me and brought his generator. And Chris had hiked through the ice and rain to bring us some fresh firewood for the woodstove.

I shivered at the memory as I neared the door. I was not looking forward to this winter. I yanked open the creaky screen door and jammed my key in the lock. The screen slapped wide with the wind, banging hard against the side of the shack. I flinched at the sound, fiddling with the lock and then thrusting the door open, before I stomped inside.

Okay, so it wasn't a *dirt* floor.

But might as well be.

I tossed my bag onto the dinky kitchen table and crossed the house in a few steps to get to my room.

It was maybe a quarter the size of Patricia's bedroom. Filled to capacity with my twin bed and dresser that doubled as a computer desk. I snatched my laptop off the dresser, dropped onto my bed, and fired it up.

Time to check the stats on the Maddison Rose episode.

I crossed my legs with a little bounce on the bed, reached behind me for my pillow and flopped it down in front of my knees like a little table, and then plopped the laptop on top of it. I pursed my lips as the internet loaded. It'd been a few hours. I should have at least a hundred views. Maybe twenty thumbs up.

Before the website could buffer, an instant message popped up on the screen.

GHOSTFACEWASFRAMED

Congratulations, Jax.

A smile twitched at the corner of my lips. Keirian Cullen. It wasn't the compliment that made me smile. I was used to male attention. It was the curse of the Woodville women, my mother liked to say—after her second bottle of wine. Something about Woodville women made men fawn. We had a "peculiarity." A light about us. A certain sparkle in our eyes. An enchanting, spell-binding magic in our smiles. And even though we were admittedly barely above average in attractiveness, somehow, we could still silence a room.

That's what *she* said. But my mother had a habit of deluding reality to fit her version of it.

All *I* knew was: boys were quick to help me and desperate to date me. And I'd be lying if I said I didn't enjoy the attention now and again. But with Keirian?

With Keirian, it felt different.

He was different. And maybe it was because he wasn't just another guy trying to get me to go out with him...I mean, he had initially, and I'd turned him down, of course. (I didn't do relation-ships—much less long-distance ones) but he was my *friend*. Genuinely. Which wasn't something I was used to with guys.

Or anyone, really.

I tended to keep everyone at arm's length. Never letting anyone close enough to see all of me. Only ever letting them see the parts of me I knew they wanted to see. Like the co-op girls—they got the bright, fun Jacqueline...sorry, *"Jackie."* (Ew.) The co-op guys? They got the cool, mysterious Jacqueline. Chris Vantine and the rest of the island boys got the giggly, girly Jacqueline. Patricia got the nerdy, silly Jacqueline. And my YouTube subscribers and the rest of the internet got the dark, serious Jacqueline. I showed everyone just enough to keep them happy. Just enough to make them love me. Not enough to make them uncomfortable. Not enough to let them know me. Not enough to make them leave.

But Keirian? I showed him everything. He was the only person in the world who *truly* knew me. And I still had no idea why I let him in. Something about the anonymity of the internet, maybe. Online friendships tended to become so much deeper because the screen acted like a buffer. A shield between the words you say and the response of the people beyond. I wouldn't say it gives you courage. But rather, just an illusion of inexistence. The internet isn't real...so you can say things. Be honest. Because it doesn't count.

And I was completely honest with Keirian. Because somehow, I never feared his rejection or judgment...and I'd like to say it was because he lived in my computer screen. Just a tiny anime avatar of Ghostface and a stream of generated words...well, he was a voice, too. But I didn't have many minutes on my phone. I only really used it for my work—the camera and the video.

But no. It wasn't the online thing.

I never worried about Keirian's rejection because I simply knew he wouldn't reject me. And again, it really wasn't a romantic thing, either. It was a kinship.

There was something between us.

A connection beyond the internet, beyond the bond of friendship.

A *peculiarity*, as my mom would say.

Something that neither one of us could explain.

But it was there.

And I told him everything, shared with him every piece of myself—well, almost everything—comfortable in the safety and consistency of his presence.

Usually if you let people get too close, they leave. It was the first life lesson I learned. (Thanks, Dad.)

But not Keirian.

He would never leave me.

I bit my lip on the smile as I reread his message.

MYFROZENHEART

Did you watch it? I haven't checked the stats… it's still loading. Darn internet. Might as well still be the old dial-up.

GHOSTFACEWASFRAMED

I did. You did good, Jax.

My heart fluttered against my ribs with my rising excitement. I grinned down at the screen, wiggling closer on the bed.

MYFROZENHEART

Really??? How many v

Before I could finish typing, the page loaded, and my heart hiccupped in my chest.

The count kept going. Up and up. By the thousands. It was almost at 50k. Five hundred thousand views. I clicked over. Hundreds of comments. And a thousand new subscribers. I couldn't believe it.

A new message binged on the screen.

GHOSTFACEWASFRAMED

You went viral, girl. And not in a gross way.

I stared blankly. Completely stunned.

GHOSTFACEWASFRAMED

Get in the chat. You're famous.

I grinned and clicked over to the Blood Farm Beep.

The Blood Farm Beep was an online server Keirian had started as a little kid when he'd first gotten serious about paranormal investigation. The name was a joke between him and his friend, Rory Meeks. See, Keirian's grandma had a thing about swears. Like a jar and everything. So, being the cool, rebellious eight-year-olds they were—they called it 'Beep'...instead of the other thing. Please, insert eye roll here. Anyway, initially he'd just wanted a safe space for people to come whisper about what went bump in the night, but over time it evolved into a server for other supernatural seekers and content creators.

It was how I first met him. His focus was on their local legend of the Blood Farm Witch. He dabbled in other areas but unfortunately for him, he didn't live in Nile, the most haunted town in America. Like me.

I signed in and checked the new posts. Rory had made one entitled: Jack's Out of the Box.

I giggled, my whole body warm from the rush of endorphins and dopamine. I clicked open his post and read the stream of comments.

ChampIsReal posted—the pressure's on now. How are you

going to top a demonic soul reaping? Would've been better if you'd caught the demon on camera.

ReaperGuardian posted—don't read the comments. Now they see you, they'll target you. No one wants to hear the truth. Truth speakers are the first to die.

There were many of the same flavor: "*How am I going to top that?*" and "*Don't feed the trolls.*" But most were words of admiration and encouragement. Complimenting my coverage, my content, my editing, and my angles.

It was overwhelming. Too much.

MYFR0ZENHEART

I've gotta go to Memé's. I'll call you later.

GHOSTFACEWASFRAMED

Tell her I said hey.

I shut the laptop, heart flighty in my chest. I took a moment in the stillness of my room, the birds chirping in the trees outside. I had their attention. Now maybe they'd listen. Now I could finally find the Scarlet Witch.

EPISODE 4: ROSALIND GRUNBERG, NILE HISTORIAN

My grandmother was the authority. The only true authority on the legend of the Scarlet Witch. Not even the local historian Rosalind Grunberg knew more about her than "the witch that haunts the woods of Nile." Literally that's all. In the Martin Isle Historical Society, Ms. Grunberg had a small room dedicated to the legends of Nile and the only thing she had on the Scarlet Witch was a little plaque beside a ratty old red robe and a basket that read, "Somewhere in the woods of Martin Isle, the Scarlet Witch haunts the trees in search for something unknown to all." Pathetic, really. But as my grandmother said, the Scarlet Witch was family business. Not Nile business.

I drove down the many backroads toward the southern east shore. The Charlebois Inn was just past the east shore ferry, down Apple Shore Road which ran along the water's edge. It didn't take long to get there. The dirt road ended in a fork, left toward the Blanchard's house and a right toward the Inn. I barely slowed down as I cranked the car right and the Inn came into view through the forest of fall-faded trees. Sitting half-way up a grassy hill, cut into a clearing, the Inn was constructed in a kind of L-shape, the dark, gray wood of the old Colonial almost black against the stark white trim of the narrow windows lining the sides. It was old but polished, like an architectural antique set on a display in such a way it could've been featured in an upscale travel magazine.

Up the hill to the left were little cabins snuggled sweetly in between the trees, down the hill to the right were the stables and firepits, and farther down hidden out of sight by the wall of woods at the bottom of the hill, was the beach and the quaint little boat launch for the canoes and paddle boats.

But I didn't stop at the Inn.

There was a side drive off the Inn's gravel parking lot with an archway that read *Charlebois Manor*. I passed under it and drove up the long winding dirt road to the Manor.

Crossing my fingers as I gripped the wheel, I sighed as the empty driveway came into view. My aunt wasn't there. I'd at least get a few minutes with Memé free of Aunt April's interference. She'd moved back into the Manor when Memé first got sick. Well, not *sick*. Her mind had started failing her. Forgetting things. Mixing up time and space. It was just something that happened to the women of our family. It skipped a generation, she said. The doctors called it Alzheimer's disease, but Memé didn't accept that. She said it was in the blood of our women. Not the mind. And she'd often argue with her nurses to leach her like some kind of medieval witch doctor. But they refused. And when she had tried to order some off the internet, my aunt had put a password on the Wi-Fi.

I switched off the car and checked my make-up. Modest eyeliner and a light touch of strawberry ChapStick. Like my mother, Memé didn't like my usual gothic aesthetic, so—like when I went to co-op—I made sure to dress in preppy pastels whenever I came to the Inn or the Manor. But unlike my mother, it wasn't because she cared what other people thought, she said it made her feel like I was waiting for her funeral. And she wasn't ready to die yet.

I scooped up my oversized satchel purse and heaved it over my shoulder. It was heavy. I hoarded too much junk.

I shut the car door and stared up at the Manor for a moment, taking it in as though I'd never seen it before, trying to imagine what the co-op kids might think. There were two sets of stone stairs, both of which curved around a mess of tangled garden in the middle and back up toward another set of stone stairs that lead up the center toward the house. Even before you made it to the Manor doors, it was pretentious. They'd love it. The Manor itself was "shingle-style" as my aunt liked to sniff to anyone who'd listen. The wood siding, a deep, chocolate brown, the porch, covered by a stone archway, the roofs, sweeping and asymmetrical, the windows, varying in shapes and sizes, with three stories and even a few turrets and towers, it was every inch *American* architecture, she liked to snip. And if anyone cared, it'd be the co-op kids.

My combat boots crunched in the gravel drive as I headed toward the left stone staircase, closest to where I'd parked. I scowled as I hiked up the middle staircase. *American* architecture aside, we were lucky there'd never been an emergency or something. It'd take an hour for EMTs to just get to the front door. Nearly out of breath, I bent down, digging around in my purse for my keys, as I reached the top. I stopped underneath the stone archway in front of the double doors, still looking for my keys, when one door flew open.

"Jacqueline Jay! Where *have* you been?"

I blinked, heart stalled in my chest. Rosalind Grunberg. Or "Zan" as she preferred to be called. The Nile historian. She swooped down on me, in a whirl of color and patterns and scarves, bangles clanging on her wrists, pulling me into a tight hug.

As the shock of her sudden appearance subsided and my pulse returned to normal, I smiled and hugged her back just as tight. She pushed me away, holding me at arm's length as she always did. A tall, willowy, old woman, draped in soft paisley fabric and her wavy silver hair pulled back with bright scarves, she always gave off an air of sixties Hollywood. Like a hippie Barbra Streisand.

Her sharp golden eyes looked down her hooked nose as she surveyed the length of me and studied my face. "You look a little flushed, dear. Have you had dinner yet? Your grandmother's been ravenous lately. I'm sure she wouldn't mind if I whipped up something for the two of you?"

I grinned. "No, I just stopped by for a quick visit before work."

Zan, one hand on my back, guided me inside the house and shut the door behind us. "Joy invited me for an evening tea... seemed to forget we'd had a visit this morning. But it all worked out because I had to discuss the Historical Haunt with her...it starts tomorrow as I'm sure you know."

My heart dipped. "They called you, huh?"

Zan's warm smile faltered as she saw my face. "They did, indeed. The Green Mountain Homeschool Association has signed up with all the extras. Those friends of yours have extravagant tastes, don't they?"

I scoffed, barely tempering my disgust. "Yeah. And now I get to ask Aunt April about some kind of exclusive all-access package... that doesn't exist." But I'd have to *make* it exist...if I was going to keep up appearances. There was a loud bang from somewhere in the depths of the manor, and we both jumped. I glanced toward the noise. "How's she doing?"

Zan crinkled her nose. Then she shook her head sadly. "I don't know...she's hit or miss. A bit moody. Keeps mumbling about her scarlet hunger—or, hanger, as you kids say these days, or is it hangry?" She waved an exasperated hand. "Whatever it is."

I smiled slightly but could barely find the humor in it.

"Though she might perk up a bit for you, dear. You know you're her favorite...but be warned: she's been fighting the nurse." Zan met my eyes as she made a silly face and chomped her teeth. "Trying to bite her."

I groaned, torn between horror and amusement. "*Again?*"

Zan's golden eyes glittered. "Joy was always a biter. You should've seen the marks she left on me in preschool."

I chuckled at that as Zan went to fetch her shawl from the coat closet off to the side. "I'll be going then, my girl. Gotta check on that grandson of mine before I head home."

"How *is* Elijah? I haven't seen him lately."

Zan slipped her shawl around her shoulders with a loving smile. "That boy. He's running wild with that new girl of his. Plans for a mountain getaway this weekend." She chuckled affectionately at the idea.

"He's got another girlfriend already?" I scoffed with a laugh. It felt like he'd just broken up with Desiree Lapierre a few weeks ago...but I supposed it'd been months. Last spring...before her break down.

"Well, you didn't expect him to wait around for *you*, did you?" Zan gave me a cheeky wink as she headed out the door with a little wave.

I smiled to myself and made my way up the grand sweeping staircase and down several halls and up another staircase until I got to my grandmother's wing.

As soon as she'd gotten sick, she'd moved into the north wing. Like she wanted to quarantine herself from the rest of the house. Keep herself locked away and hidden. The north wing was the farthest removed from the rest of the Manor. The farthest corner of it, overlooking the lake and several tiny private islands that surrounded Nile. Zan actually lived on one of them—the tiny private islands—but one on the west side. Most of the little islands on the east side weren't inhabited. Their rich owners had bought them only to hoard them. They didn't bother doing anything with the land. What a waste. Keirian was right—rich people did the weirdest things with their money.

I knocked lightly on the door and let myself inside. I paused in the doorway as I took in the sight unfolding before my eyes.

The nurse, Carol Anne, was racing around the room, ducking

around end tables and the plush couch and hurrying around the old piano as my eighty-three-year-old grandmother chased her with an oversized pillar candle shouting for matches.

At the sight of me, Carol Anne burst into grateful tears and pointed dramatically in my direction as she shrieked, "Ms. Charlebois, look, it's Jacqueline!"

Memé stopped short and whirled around to look at me, blinking curiously as though struggling to remember me. But Carol Anne didn't hesitate. Taking her chance while Memé was frozen, lost in her foggy mind, she ran for her purse and pushed past me through the door.

"She's been nicking things. Watch your purse. I'll be back in an hour," Carol Anne blurted breathlessly as she passed. And she didn't bother to wait for confirmation as she made a mad dash down the hall. Just before she disappeared around the corridor, I saw the ugly red circle of my grandmother's bite on her arm.

I turned back to Memé with a soft smile. "Hey, Memé."

That did it. The blank face of Alzheimer's slipped and there she was, albeit still confused. She lowered her hand still gripping the pillar candle to her side, almost defeated, and she murmured, "My darling girl, do we have anything to eat? I've got the scarlet hunger."

EPISODE 5: THE MATRIARCH

My grandmother was nothing if not superstitious. And with her Alzheimer's, it was increasingly hard to determine when she was lucid and when she was just being herself: Joy Jacqueline Charlebois, paramour of the paranormal. But one thing was certain, either way, lucid or lost, I always kept her calm...no matter what I had to do, or what I had to say. Because it was easy for her, even more so than most dementia patients given her supernatural superstitions, to get fearful. And scaring my memé wasn't something I let happen. Ever.

So, as I did during every visit, I sat her down in her favorite plush chair by the window overlooking the lake and the several tiny islands dotting the horizon between us and the mainland of Vermont. The view out her window was beautiful, and I couldn't help but pause to take it in: the crisp and dreary dying October day, the gray water churning almost black below, and the trees of the little isles in the distance were deep olive and brown like mossy rocks.

Tearing my eyes from the islands, I tucked her into the chair with the large Afghan she'd crocheted years ago, pressing the sides around her small, frail frame. Then I reached for the book she'd left on her bedside table. Leather-bound and pages gilded, the tiny tome was a rare first edition of local Nile fairy tales written by the rumored witch Cecily Blackwell. Like our very own Brothers Grimm, the book contained Nile stories of everything from yobas to Champ. I cradled it gingerly as I carried it over to Memé and placed it in her hands, and I sank reverently to the floor by her feet.

Memé's fingers stroked the pages so they fluttered like wings beneath her fingertips. "I was reading late last night." She touched her head lightly. "I must be tired." Her eyes stared out the window for a moment, then she looked down at me with a rueful smile. "I've missed you, my girl. How long's it been? A week? What took you so long?"

I squinted hard, struggling to hold back the blur of tears welling up in my eyes. I'd seen her just yesterday. And every other day before that. But the cruelest thing you could do for Alzheimer's patients—in *my* opinion—was correct them. You needed to let them believe what they believed. Allow them to be wherever their minds placed them. And lie. I made a face as I grinned back up at her. "Oh, you know me, Memé. I've been out searching for the Witch."

Memé inclined her head with loving interest. "You still haven't found her yet?"

I shook my head with a downturned smirk. "I've tried Black-well Woods, the woods by the Tracks, and in the woods around Hyde Road. No luck."

Memé shifted the book to one hand and put the other on my head. She smoothed my long hair, running her thin fingers through the blonde strands. "You'll find her. She's your aunt, you know. She's your blood."

I scoffed. "So, *you* say..."

Memé chuckled at that and patted my cheek, the rings on her fingers cold against my flushed face. "Tell me about your TV channel."

I perked up at that. It always warmed my heart when she

remembered something...well, *sort of* remembered something. She didn't understand the internet past online shopping, even when she was lucid. She was under the impression that I recorded movies. Like *VHS* tapes. For a television station. Or something. Whatever. Point was: she remembered.

"I filmed a new doc on a demonic soul sacrifice. Right here in Nile. And the response was great. Lots of viewers."

Memé smiled sadly. "The truth must be told, no matter how hard it is for us to hear. Who was the victim?"

My stomach twisted as her oval face flashed behind my eyes. "Maddison Rose."

"Lillian Rose's grandbaby? Poor dear. Such a shame." Memé was quiet for a second, the both of us lost in the morose gloom of grief. Then she cleared her throat. "The Roses are a distant relation, you know...though all the old Nile families are connected if you go back far enough...Poor little Rose..." Then she lowered her voice to a thoughtful murmur as she continued, "A soul sacrifice... why I haven't heard of that in years...the last time there was a soul sacrifice around here...well, it was nearly the end of the world. Hopefully this one isn't the same."

I frowned. "When was the last time?"

But Memé changed the subject as though she hadn't heard my question, but more than likely, she'd forgotten it as soon as I'd asked it, "Zan told me your friends are coming to stay at the Inn for the Historical Haunt!"

I grinned and sat up a bit on my knees. "You remembered?"

Memé crinkled her nose as she cocked her head to the side. "Well, of course, sweet girl; she was just here. Are you excited? You're always the one running the show—now you'll be able to sit back and enjoy it with all your little girlfriends. That'll be nice, hmm?"

My face fell a bit, but I kept my eyes bright and cheerful. "Definitely. They are all looking forward to coming. They were actually hoping to stay here in the manor...but I know April won't allow that."

Memé gave my hand a light slap. "Oh, hush. Don't you worry about April. She may think she runs this place, but it is still my name on the darn thing, isn't it?"

"Do you think we could set up some of the guest rooms?" I asked, my voice light and breathless with hope. "We'd only need about—" I counted quickly in my head. "Maybe four? And then they could have a tour of the library and the archives. I could even do a mini presentation of the Charlebois curse!"

"Why, that'd be lovely, wouldn't it, dear?" Memé asked softly, her voice almost dreamy.

I couldn't stop myself from blurting out more questions, "And we could set up a movie in the theater!"

"Yes, my dear. Anything you want..." Her hazel eyes sparkled with mischief as she leaned down close to me and whispered loudly, "And is that boy of yours coming? The one with the weird name...Key-ron?"

"Memé..." My face burned at the question. "Keirian lives in New York..."

Memé waved away her hand. "Oh, half of our ancestors came from New York. Why, the story goes that my great-grandmother settled on one of the isles...not as grand as Zan's, of course, but! If a colonial woman could journey across the lake and start a new life, I'm sure a young man of today can hop on the ferry to come visit."

"Memé—"

She patted my head gently with her gnarled hand. "Oh, don't you worry. If not him, we can always depend on Frances Vantine's grandbaby...Christopher. That boy is always here when I need him."

I scoffed as I cocked an incredulous eyebrow. "You see him often, Memé?"

She gave a slow exaggerated nod. "Now he is a good boy."

"Too good," I muttered with a smirk.

Memé shook her head, closing her eyes peacefully. "He's the one for us. I'm sure of it." Then she sighed heavily and shifted a bit in the chair. After a moment, Memé touched my cheek again as her eyes blinked almost confused. And then my heart dipped a bit in my chest as she asked the same question she asked every day, "Jacqueline, have I ever told you the story of the Scarlet Witch?"

And I had to lie like I always did. I blinked back the tears and gifted her with a gentle smile and a little white lie, "No, Memé."

Memé giggled and nodded toward the fireplace. "Go on, Jacqueline."

Obediently, I went to the fireplace and, with my back to her, I pulled out the long matchbox and lit a fire in the hearth. The warmth from the flames ebbed into the room and Memé gestured toward the window beside her chair as she put the book off to the side. Habitually, almost ritually, I unlocked the window and slid it open wide, allowing a gust of cold lake air to blow through the room. Memé shivered underneath the Afghan and took my hands in hers and pulled me onto the arm of the chair. Her thin, spindly arms wrapped me in a hug. I tucked down into the hollow of her neck, and she nuzzled my head with hers and began as she always did...

"Once upon a time, many years ago, there lived a young girl named Epona. Her family was the last of an ancient line of witches, and they settled on Martin Isle."

"The Grey family," I muttered, unable to keep the bitterness out of my voice. It was hard to believe Memé's claims of our ancestry when the Grey family literally lived a few miles away. And we weren't related to them. I'd already checked the genealogy in the archives of the Martin Isle Historical Society, independently and with Zan's help.

Memé continued, as though she hadn't heard my comment. "The islanders were distrustful, hateful of the family, and cursed them away; so, the father—Charles—took his mother, his wife, and his two daughters (Epona, and her sister, Brigid) deep into the woods, far away from the other settlers. But life was hard...and the family was haunted by a mysterious wolf...who, by night, stalked the family whenever they left the small cabin the father had built. And then, one day, the grandmother fell ill...and there was nothing to eat, for it was winter and the wolf had scared away all the game. The girls were sent to the village to get food and medicine for the grandmother. But when they returned to the woods, they were attacked by the wolf. And only one sister—your grandmother, Brigid,—"

I mouthed the words with her. It was her favorite part of the story.

"—survived. And she ran all the way through the woods to the cabin...only to find her entire family ripped to pieces." Memé lowered her voice for dramatic effect. "Eaten by the wolf. So, Brigid, ran from the cabin, ran from the wolf, and never entered the woods again...and now, the ghost of her sister, Epona, haunts the woods of Nile, forever searching for her grandmother with her basket full of food and medicine."

I smiled as she ended the story the same as she always did. And waited for her to brush my hair from my face and finish with, *"And if anyone is unlucky enough to cross her path...they are never seen again."*

But...she didn't.

Instead, she stared deep into my eyes, almost sadly, and her voice broke with sudden emotion, "And now, my dear, we need to talk about the curse."

I inclined my head as I tried to process what she was saying. Hundreds of times since she'd gotten sick, she'd told the story of the Scarlet Witch the same way. Word for word. What was going on? "Memé, what—you mean the curse of the Manor?"

She forced a rueful smile and shook her head. She fluttered her long lashes as tears spilled down her wrinkled cheeks. Then she cupped my face in her weathered hand. "We need to talk about the scarlet hunger..."

Before I could question her, Memé wrapped her arms around me in a thin hug and rocked me back and forth in a way she hadn't since I was little. "A long time ago…"

"*What in the world is going on in here?*"

Memé's grip on me tightened, her bones digging into me sharply, as the both of us flinched at the shrill bark of my aunt April. I jumped up off the arm of the chair and stood up straight, in between them, shielding my grandmother from the apathetic wrath of her daughter. An up-tight, prickly, pinched woman, I always found it hard to believe this person was related to me, let alone my grandmother.

Even then I struggled to meet her piercing eyes. Her mousy brown hair was yanked back so high it pulled all her thin features up with it, making her look even more severe than usual. Her bony arms were crossed against her chest as she bristled in her pantsuit.

Memé struggled up from the chair and, with an arm shaky with her age, pulled me close to her. "Who are you? What are you doing in my room?"

April's thin mouth flattened into a pinched scowl. "It's me, Ma. April."

Memé sputtered at that and began to protest, growing increasingly agitated. I turned to her and held her arms gingerly. "Memé, can you find me a book?"

Memé tore her fearful eyes from her daughter and stared into mine. Hazel to hazel. "A book, Jacqueline?"

I grinned and nodded encouragingly. "I need you to look for one that will help me find the forest."

Memé's blank face broke into a sly smile, her eyes bright. "The forest."

I gave her a cheeky wink. "You know the one."

Memé pulled me into a tight hug, her bones digging into me uncomfortably. Then she hurried off toward the far corner of the room to the bookshelf.

Confident that Memé was happy with her snipe hunting assignment, I turned back to Aunt April.

It was hard for me to speak to her. At least, speak *up* to her. Maybe it was the disdain in her cold eyes or maybe it was the fact that she'd interrupted yet another precious lucid moment with Memé. But I'd had enough. I swallowed, my tongue thick and dry in my mouth. "You should try to pretend with her...it hurts her when you tell her that what she knows...isn't true..."

"Fortunately, not all of us have your talent for *lies*." April spat with a curl of her thin lips. "Shouldn't you be down at the Inn scrubbing toilets?"

I flinched. She might as well have struck me. The venom in her words was just as stinging as a slap across the face. Eyes burning with unshed tears, I dropped my gaze to the floor. Then, pointedly avoiding April's sharp stare, I took one last look at Memé, who was still scanning the bookshelves, humming to herself. And, satisfied that she was happy, I left the room without a goodbye and practically ran from Charlebois Manor and headed for my work as a maid for my ancestral estate.

I couldn't imagine how tomorrow would go with the kids at co-op. When they all learned I wasn't an island heiress, princess of a sprawling Nile castle, but rather a servant. Why, I might as well be Cinderella, for everyone knew chivalry was dead... Clearly, I was out of luck in the prince department and doomed to scrub the castle floors forever.

As I turned into the gravel parking lot of the Inn and slammed the car in park, Lacey McGregor loped down the grassy hill from the guest cabins nestled in the scattered trees to meet me, in the hopping, uneven gait that was uniquely hers. Lacey was a small, wisp of a girl with blonde hair so fine it sometimes looked white. Unassuming and gentle, she displayed her eccentricity not only in her behavior and mannerisms but in her fashion sense, as well, often clashing colors and textures with random abandon, and this evening was no exception. From her pink jelly shoes to her lemon-yellow leggings to her jean jacket splattered with hand-painted planets to homemade beanie with two googly frog eyes stuck on the sides was shoved over her long lily-blonde hair, each eye rolling dizzily as she bounced down the hill, she was one of a kind, and I loved her for it. She waved as I rolled down the window, engine still rumbling.

"Hey, Jacqueline, are you—"

"Get in, Lacey; we're going water witching."

EPISODE 6: MAKE-BELIEVE

"Where did you want to try today?" Lacey eyed the passing scenery and then added, "It will get dark soon."

I didn't have an answer. Between the two of us, we'd literally walked through every wooded area on the entire island...and the most we'd found was an old witching well deep in the Blackwell Woods.

No sign of the Scarlet Witch.

Lacey nodded somberly. "It's hard, but we have to believe. If we don't, no one else will. And that would be sad."

"How's the mother-sister mission coming? Have you found anything to convince your dad yet?"

Lacey sighed. "No."

I nodded sympathetically. "You know what I keep telling you..."

"Yes. But Cassandra seemed so sure..."

I rolled my eyes at that. "Cassandra is a glorified circus performer. Literally, she ran off with the circus or something. She's just an actress."

Lacey frowned as she fixed me with a wide hazel-eyed stare.

"Oh, no, Jacqueline. Cassandra has the Sight. She is a true Seer. You haven't met her. If you'd come with me for a reading, you'd understand."

"Lily and your mom both went on to Heaven," I murmured as patiently as I could manage. "That means they can visit you... That's why you've felt them. But they aren't ghosts, so you aren't going to pick them up on an EMF machine. Even one designed by the brilliant Elijah Grunvald himself."

Lacey was silent for a moment and then nodded. "You're probably right."

"It doesn't mean you still can't convince him. We'll think of something. And you homeschool now, so—make it a class. It's what I do with the YouTube stuff."

Lacey sat thoughtfully for a moment as I turned down Allen School Road and bumped down Bakers Road toward my house. "You enjoy it," she said simply. "The attention."

A laugh burst loud from deep in my belly. "I enjoy the work. And the attention is what is going to help me get monetized. Which means...well, money. These content creators, like Aubrey's stepsister? Daphne Collins? She makes bank. Aubrey told me that's how her dad bought that house in town. *Daphne* bought it."

"There's something wrong with her."

"Narcissism?" I scoffed and rolled my eyes as I took the hidden turn, overgrown with trees and scraggly brush, onto our little dirt drive.

I shoved the car in park and looked over at Lacey, who shook her head. "Not Daphne Collins. Aubrey. She's been acting strange. I don't like to be near her now."

I frowned at that and then shrugged. "It's probably Damien. You know what he did to her."

Lacey didn't answer. She just turned her head toward the car window and stared silently for a minute.

I gave her her moment. Sometimes Lacey went quiet as she sorted through her thoughts. I always tried to give her time, but today I didn't have the patience. So, I gave her a little nudge. "You ready?"

She looked back at me. "Don't forget to change your clothes this time."

As soon as we made it inside, Dog came darting through the door behind us and threaded himself through Lacey's feet. She giggled in delight and scooped up the fat ginger cat, nuzzling her face in his dirty fur. Dog was a miserable beast. He tolerated me. Ignored my mother. But Lacey was his human. I tried to tell her to take him home with her, but she always refused. "Oh, no. You need him here. And you never know, he could be your familiar. They find their person, you know."

I snorted. "Only witches have familiars. And familiars help. Dog does nothing but glare at me until I feed him."

"He chases the spreegles away. That's very helpful."

I smiled despite myself and held my tongue. Then, satisfied that she'd settled the matter, Lacey took a seat at the kitchen table with Dog in her arms, and I headed for my bedroom and shut the door so I could change. Lacey wasn't wrong to remind me. Last time we'd done Witch footage, I didn't realize until I started editing that I was wearing a pink sweater and Uggs. Not exactly my brand. So, I'd had to scrap most of it and reshoot the next day. I stripped off the pastels and preppy stripes and dug through my dresser for my favorite pair of baggy black pants, crisscrossed with chains, and *The Devil's Rejects* top with fishnet sleeves. I slipped on my pleather black jacket without bothering to zip it shut. Then I drew on some eyeliner, pulled my hair into a high ponytail, and that was it. I shimmied through the tight space between bed and dresser and yanked my backpack out from underneath the bedspread. I flopped it on my bed and started packing, mumbling my list in my head as I grabbed each item: oversized makeup bag, stuffed with healing potions and tonics carefully curated over the years from the Nile witch, the total cost of which amounted to hundreds of dollars; EMF meter; a few reference books; emergency iron blade; salt; holy water. Then I grabbed my old camcorder and went for the door.

But I paused in the doorway. I should check the stats. For collating data—analytical purposes only, of course.

And it was good that was the only reason. Because if I'd wanted to check the channel to stroke my ego with my sudden internet fame and adoration...I'd have been devastated.

First, they love you. Then they destroy you. Everyone knows this. But it doesn't stop it from blindsiding you like a Mack truck straight out of *Joy Ride*.

My heart plummeted into the pit of my stomach, sending shockwaves through my body.

> She used a dead girl for clicks. Enough said. She's canceled.

> It's all fake.

> So pathetic. Look how serious she acts. It's hilarious. Like she's some kind of CNN reporter? Faux News more like…

> @DaphneCollins needs to see this. Keep her name out of your mouth.

> Who does she think she is??

> I knew Maddy. She would be so furious.

> It's so gross. How desperate for attention can you be?

Constant comments. Over and over.

I flinched as the laptop binged loudly with a message from Keirian.

GHOSTFACEWASFRAMED

Don't feed the trolls.

I blinked furiously as fresh tears spilled down my cheeks.

MYFROZENHEART

I didn't use her for clicks.

GHOSTFACEWASFRAMED

I know. But I know you. Nobody else does. You can't blame the masses for mobbing. It's their mentality. Lol

I rolled my eyes.

MYFROZENHEART

You aren't as witty as you think.

GHOSTFACEWASFRAMED

And you aren't as perfect as you think.

I scowled at the screen.

MYFROZENHEART

Clearly. Thanks for gutting me while I'm down.

GHOSTFACEWASFRAMED IS TYPING...

I shut the laptop before I had to listen to any more of his stupid sage advice.

I swallowed thickly and dropped my bag off my shoulder. It landed on the floor with a hard crunching thump on impact, and I gave it a good kick sending it back underneath my bed. Then I went to the grimy old mirror and smoothed the tear-smudged eyeliner back into place before I headed back out to tell Lacey, change of plans. I'd had enough evil for one evening. No desire to go hunting for more. I was done for the night.

But honestly, I wasn't. Not even close. The comments of the mobbing masses kept churning in my head, and I couldn't get them out. Over and over. They were watching me now. And not because they loved watching my content. But because it was so much more fun to watch as they tore me apart. I knew how it worked. I'd seen it happen to Tory Spears. And again to Mischa Markle. And we all know what happened when they canceled Bryan Cooper. But what would happen to me when I posted yet another Scarlet Witch episode featuring an empty forest full of trees? I had searched all over Nile. For years. And nothing.

If I was being honest, now there was an itch of doubt creeping into the recesses of my mind, scratching at the back of my brain. Doubt in the story Memé had made me so ardently believe. The legend that I had trusted to be my past and had used to form so much of myself and my purpose. The story that I whole-heartedly knew could make my future.

One way or another.

Real...or not.

Because if an old lady could make me believe in the Scarlet Witch for seventeen years, I could make everyone else believe in her, too.

EPISODE 7: THE SCARLET WITCH
PROJECT

"Did you guys see this?" Natalie shoved her phone under my nose as all eight of us, plus two of the Moms who were acting as chaperones, all hopped out of various vehicles and huddled together in the gravel parking lot of the Charlebois Inn.

Patricia glanced down and then her eyes darted to me. Instinctively, she took a step back and kept her eyes on the Inn.

I stared down at the phone as the video began to play, and the voice crackled loudly through the speakers as the camera trained on a pair of black combat boots and fishnet-stocking legs as they hiked through the woods. "There's truth buried deep in the heart of every story. And here *Inside My Frozen Heart*, we will always dig it up. You can't skip a stone across Lake Champlain without hitting a Nile legend. Some you have to hunt down...but some end up hunting you. And this one...well, it's going to keep you up at night..."

I swallowed and snatched the phone from Natalie, locking the screen and cutting the episode before it began.

"Well?" Erica looked at me expectantly. "Do you know this

girl? She's supposedly from Martin Isle. Can you believe this? We have to check this out!"

"Uh, no!" Allison snapped with a toss of her dark curls. "I barely can handle a creepy tour with a guide. I'm not going hiking out in some freaky forest looking for some psycho Red Riding Hood!"

"But—"

"All right, ladies…let's head in," Erica's mom called as she led the guys up the walkway and into the Inn.

Natalie locked her phone and tucked it in her back pocket with an angry scoff at Allison. And the five of us girls headed in after them. Inside, the place was cozy and quiet in an old-fashioned empty-tavern type of way, with dark antique oak furniture and low lantern lights adorning the walls and accenting wooden-wheel chandeliers. Sometimes it made me feel like I'd stepped into a pirate ship, and I loved it.

As all of us grouped up around the Moms, I kept to the outskirts and hidden from view of the receptionist, Tree. Tree was the classic Vermont hippie from the roots of her crunchy, strawberry-blonde hair down to the tips of her socked and sandaled feet. She was a natural beauty with a sprinkling of copper freckles across her nose and the apples of her cheeks that darkened ever so slightly when she smiled. She had a calming presence that somehow managed to put everyone around her at ease, including animals. I still remember the first time I met her. Lacey and I were crossing some fields in search of flummox fairies and there she was, sitting on an old fence sweet-talking a squirrel. And now here she was, sweet-talking co-op monkeys. The last thing I needed was for her to notice me. Her voice may be soft, but that didn't mean she didn't enjoy using it. And I wasn't about to stumble into an awkward conversation this soon into the trip. I wasn't ready for that.

I could feel Patty's eyes on me, and I gave her a warning squint and slight shake of my head. She nodded her understanding and pointedly pursed her lips together. One of the best things about her, she'd take my secrets to the grave. And that quality in a friend was priceless.

They set us up in the Red Wing, a long hallway on the second floor consisting of four family suites decorated in all different shades of red, black, and gold. The Moms each had one, the boys shared, and then us five girls shared the fourth.

Our suite was charming, yet posh, opening into a sitting room with a kitchenette to the right of the door and a little space at the back for the large television and big, cushy couch. Across from the sitting area was a half-hallway that led to each of the bedrooms, one to the left one to the right.

Patricia and I took the main bedroom, and the other three girls ducked into the second bedroom, dropping their bags on each bunk and claiming their beds. I put my bag down on our dresser and glanced over at Patty who had sat down on the bed, her eyes on me.

I cocked an eyebrow expectantly.

She bit her lip and then asked, "Did that really happen?"

Ouch. Her question cut, like paper slicing into the meat of my heart. But could I blame her for it? No. "Patricia, my whole channel depends on my reputation. And that is—honest, researched journalism."

Patty didn't question me again. She was loyal...to a fault. And I knew it.

"It was a really great episode. And if Nat found it—"

I grinned despite myself. "I know, it's really taking off. I just gotta make sure I keep my head down...and off camera." I gave her a cheeky wink as I leaned back against the dresser.

Erica stuck her head in the room, and I flinched guiltily. "Get ready. We head down to breakfast in five."

"I'll be a bit late," I murmured more to myself than Patty. "I forgot something back home at the Manor."

. . .

I opened the door almost tentatively. The last thing I wanted to walk in on was Memé chasing Carol Anne and chomping her teeth. I smiled slightly, relieved at the sight of Memé in her armchair reading quietly with Carol Anne relaxing on the loveseat across from her, scrolling on her phone.

"Hey, Memé..." I murmured, approaching her slowly so as not to disturb her.

Carol Anne locked the phone and pushed up from the couch. "I'll be back in twenty." As she passed me, she paused to touch my shoulder and leaned in close. "Remember, watch your purse."

I ignored her and went to my grandmother. I sank down by her feet, leaning back against her chair.

"Ah, Jacqueline. You're late." She smiled down at me warmly as she cupped my head in her hand with a gentle caress.

I blinked.

Before she'd gotten sick, I'd visit her every morning for breakfast. For two reasons; one because I loved starting my day with her. She'd be reading the paper, holding it out with one hand as she sipped coffee from a blue and white china teacup and saucer in the other. Occasionally swapping the coffee for a bite out of her peanut buttered slice of toast (sometimes English Muffin). I loved watching her in the morning, with her long dressing gown and her hair like silver waves tumbling freely all around her. She was beautiful. And two...my mom wasn't big on breakfast, and she worked. All the time. And in the morning, if she wasn't working, she was sleeping off the shift...or a bottle. So, it was either cold cereal with the cat...or alone if Dog wasn't around either.

But whatever. The point was: she remembered. I took a second to get over the shock. "I am. I'm sorry, Memé. I had to help the co-op kids check in down at the Inn."

She nodded her understanding. "Well, you may have missed breakfast...but it doesn't do for an old woman to miss a meal. Can you fetch me some eggs with some fruit on the side, dear? You know I've got the scarlet hunger something terrible these days. Carol Anne is absolutely awful about nutrition. That girl is constantly forgetting to eat. Sometimes I wonder whether she isn't a wraith. Eating my brains in the night." Memé made a face and stuck out her tongue.

I laughed, shaking my head at her. "All right, I'll be back." I pushed up from the floor and made to leave but hesitated. There was a breakfast tray beside her seat on the side table, full of neatly stacked, dirtied dishes. I glanced at Memé. She'd returned to her book without looking up. Clearly it wasn't Carol Anne who was forgetting about meals. I bit my cheek and scooped up the tray and headed for the door, but Memé's next question stopped me. "Do you have any matches, my dear?"

I turned slowly. Something inside me went cold as Memé twisted in her chair to smile at me. I glanced at the empty hearth. "Uh, are you cold, Memé? I can light the fire if you want..."

Her face suddenly went blank. The Alzheimer's had her again. She tilted her head as though she were considering something. Then she said, "The scarlet hunger is catching."

My hands tightened on the tray, and I took a step back into the room, closing the distance between us. "Memé, what is the scarlet hunger? I thought that was just something you used to say...like people talk about eating horses...but—" I bit my lip as I struggled to word my question...to articulate my concern. "You mentioned it the other day...that you wanted to talk to me about it. Does the scarlet hunger have to do with the Witch?"

She laughed as though I'd told a joke. "You don't worry about that, my dear. It's too late. I'll find those matches on my own. Run along, Jacqueline. You shouldn't be here now."

By the time I got back to the Inn, everyone was assembled outside and waiting for Willis, the old farmhand who drove the tractor wagon for the tour, to show up. The first stop on the tour was the Rosecrest House. I switched off the car and pocketed the keys, my eyes on the girls grouped around none other than Lacey McGregor. They all turned as one, watching me as I sat in the car. They whispered together and then Erica smiled a wolfish grin that made my heart dip uncomfortably. Great. What now?

I scooped up my oversized purse and got out of the car, ready to face whatever disturbance Lacey's presence had caused.

I approached the group, and the girls all grinned. "Well, well, Jackie...you've got a lot of explaining to do."

I ignored them and gave Lacey a kind smile. "Hey, Lace. I see you've met the co-op. I told you it wouldn't be worth joining."

Natalie made a face. Allison inclined her head at Erica wondering whether she'd been insulted. Erica's grin twitched but she still managed to hold it in place.

Lacey didn't notice the tension brewing between us. Instead, she reached into the oversized satchel hanging diagonally across her pompom plastered neon-green sweater. "Here. I knew you'd be gone on the tour most of the afternoon. I wanted to make sure you had this."

She passed me her dowsing rod. The girls all snickered as they eyed the forked stick. Then Kenneth shoved forward and pointed at the dowsing rod almost accusatory. "Wait! That's a witching rod. I saw it on that freaky goth girl's channel! It's for finding dead bodies."

Lacey looked at Kenneth with a blank stare. My heart dropped and I opened my mouth, but before I could cut her off, Lacey said simply, "Are you all fans of Jacqueline's internet documentary?"

The girls all froze and then their eyes moved as one to stare at me. I steeled myself against the weight of their eyes heavy with their judgment, keeping my focus on Lacey. I forced a kind smile. "Thanks, Lacey. This will really help."

"Uh, hold on." Erica closed her eyes for a moment. "You're

telling me that that goth freak who had some kind of creepy Red Riding Hood ghost encounter is *Jackie*?!"

Allison, always quick to miss the point, blurted out breathlessly, "You have, like, a million subscribers!"

Lacey looked at me with a perplexed crease in her brow. "You found the Scarlet Witch?"

I took a breath.

"So, she *says*. It looked fake to me," Erica snapped.

"Totally faked! And stupid. Ooo, the ghost of Little Red Riding Hood." Natalie rolled her eyes. "Lame."

"How do you have more subscribers than Daphne Collins?!" Allison whined. The knowledge that I'd outdone Allison's own subscriber count by hundreds of thousands apparently turned her fifty shades of envy. She could barely contain the jealousy from spewing from every orifice. "How?! You don't even show your face!"

"Because she's a liar," Erica replied icily.

Lacey frowned. "Jacqueline doesn't lie." Then she looked at me very seriously. "You're right. I wouldn't like to join this co-op." Then she leaned forward and gave me a light, airy hug. "Enjoy the Haunt."

I forced another smile. "I'll find you later."

Lacey gave me a serene smile and a small wave before she turned on her heel and headed back up the grassy hill toward the cabins scattered around the woods. Allison and Natalie burst out into fits of giggles they'd apparently been holding inside since they'd encountered Lacey.

I gritted my teeth as I watched them laugh at her. My hands tightened on the dowsing rod, and I had the strong urge to stab Natalie with it...at the very least poke Allison with it. Erica, though, had eyes only for me. She popped her hip and crossed her arms over her chest. "So, you want to explain. Or should we just assume you're a liar."

I tore my eyes from Natalie and Allison and fixed Erica with a cool stare. "Honestly, Erica, I really don't care what you think of me."

"So, you don't live here." Erica glanced back at the Inn with her lip curled in disgust. "You *work* here."

"As a maid," Natalie spat as though it were a dirty word.

"Gross," Allison muttered.

Before I could snap a retort, Benji looped his arm around me. "So, you're the hot emo girl?"

"No, Benji. She's just a pathetic liar pretending to be something she's not for attention. A cliche at best. A joke at worst."

"Gross." Allison, ever inventive, muttered again.

Benji ignored them. "But aren't girls supposed to like serial killers?"

I fixed Erica with a deadpan stare and said coolly, "Humans bore me."

Then without wasting any more time or any more breath, I pushed between Allison and Natalie and headed inside to the Inn. I went straight for the Red Wing and shoved open the door to our suite. Resisting the urge to slam it behind me and to kick furniture as I moved through the sitting room, I went for the master bedroom and chucked the dowsing rod onto the bed. It bounced off and landed on the floor. It wasn't Lacey's fault. I didn't blame her, but, in that moment? I definitely blamed the dowsing rod.

I grabbed my backpack from the top of the oversized dark oak dresser and dug out my laptop. I slammed it down onto the mattress and tossed myself onto the bed after it. Sprawled out on my stomach, I opened the computer and woke it up. I went to check my stats, and my stomach twisted as I saw the comments. The girls had already gotten to work. Comment after comment on every single episode. The three of them working together in a quickly constructed smear campaign. Calling me a liar. A fake.

But that wasn't all.

Several other people had tagged me in a video from none other than Vermont local YouTube sensation, Daphne Collins, who apparently now had taken issue with me and had uploaded a 'response' video to my Maddison Rose episode.

And that? That was the kill shot. In the four minutes and thirty-six seconds it took to stream her video, my reputation as a trusted paranormal investigator reporting the truth about the supernatural died.

EPISODE 8: TRUTH OR DARE?

Before I could bring myself to click play, a message popped up from Keirian.

GHOSTFACEWASFRAMED

Did you watch it?

MYFR0ZENHEART

No. More liar talk?

GHOSTFACEWASFRAMED

Everyone's a liar. And if they think they aren't,
they're lying to themselves.

I snorted. Wasn't that the truth? My eyes shifted from the message box to the video thumbnail. Daphne Collins, with her perfect dark hair flowing down her shoulders in soft waves, stared back at me with eyes so dark they could've been black, with a smirk and dubiously cocked eyebrow. Word graphics shouting on the screen: "Truth or Dare?"

I clicked play. And then the reaction video from Daphne Collins blared metallic and staticky over the cheap laptop speakers:

"Mmkay. I didn't want to do this. I really didn't want to waste my time, but I was told that my name was dropped, so here I am. Wasting hours of my life watching stupid, like, what? 'Mockumentaries?' Of some dumb goth chick who's so ugly she won't show her face." Daphne rolled her dark eyes as she tossed her hair. She held up a finger, flashing elaborate rings and a French tip. "Now, I've watched all her crap, so you all don't have to...seriously, you owe me. But now I can confidently—and *truthfully*—say that Inside My Frozen Heart is nothing more than a rag. That's literally what that channel is." She smirked nastily and then licked her lips as though savoring her next verbal assault.

"First, I'll address the episode in which my name was mentioned—yes, Maddison Rose was at my house." She nodded, black eyes wide and expression sarcastic. Then she leaned close to the camera. "Big deal. She went to my school. Was friends with my stepsister. I know Goth Girl is probably a loser with no friends, so I'll explain this to her slowly: that's what you *do* with your friends...you let them stay at your house. And sometimes...*all night*." She covered her mouth as though she'd said something scandalous. Then she rolled her eyes again and shook her head. Her voice dropped low and cool as she continued, "That doesn't mean she picked up a demon on the way home. Like, seriously? Now, back to the fact that Goth Girl is a lying sociopath..." A slow, coy smile slid across her beautiful face. She was enjoying this way too much. Pot...kettle anyone? My jaw tightened as I forced myself to keep listening.

"All you have to do is look at her content *prior* to Maddison Rose to see it. All that garbage about a 'Scarlet Witch?' *Nobody cared*." Daphne giggled wickedly. "Not a single person. Oh, I'm sorry, what was it? 202? 202 paranoid, Cheeto-stuffing, neckbeards. Who likely only followed her for her below-the-neck body shots and weird little girl voice...I mean—camera angles are everything. And the fact that she'll show everything *but* her face...puts a lot into question." Daphne waved away her last statement. "But that's beside the point. Which is: she *used* Maddison Rose.

Exploited her death. For clicks. It's disgusting. And all of you who subscribed to her channel after that? You all should be ashamed and unfollow her now. Because what did *you* do?" Daphne bobbed her head closer to the camera. "You fed her craving for attention. So then what did *she* do?" Daphne forced a cold, sardonic laugh. "Like, *the next day*, she posted a new video for you all. In which, she supposedly has an *encounter with a ghost*. The same freaking ghost she'd previously been unable to find and whining about for years? *Years*! Pretty convenient to find the thing immediately after amassing all the eyes...nope. Doesn't do it for me. Fake. Hoax. Liar.

"And all you groupies in the chat sticking up for the little freak, why don't you put it to Goth Girl? You know what? *I'll do it for you*...Goth Girl...or whatever your name is...since I can't trust you to tell the truth, I dare you to livestream it. Livestream your Scarlet Witch, or you're a liar, and it didn't happen."

The video ended.

I stared at her frozen sneer for a moment. My head blurred with a stream of panicked thoughts. The bing from another message cleared the mess in my mind.

GHOSTFACEWASFRAMED

So, what are you going to do?

I didn't bother typing. I didn't know. What *could* I do?

There was a knock at the door. I jumped and slapped my laptop shut as though I'd been watching something shameful... which I guess I had been...and turned. It was Patricia.

"Hey. Are you okay? The historian's here...everyone's waiting."

"Tell them to go ahead. That I'm sick or something."

Patty gave me a sympathetic wince. "Okay."

"Yeah. I think I'm going to just head home. Tell the Moms I'm heading home with the flu...or something."

"The flu, huh?"

I forced a smile. "Or something."

"You know they won't believe that."

My smile slipped. Ouch.

"Erica was quick to tell me all about your secret YouTube identity...and job at the Inn." Patricia commented softly.

I nodded with a grim shrug.

"I'm sorry they found out."

I sighed heavily and opened the laptop, revealing Daphne Collins's sneer. "It's worse."

Patricia crossed the room and leaned beside me on the bed as I clicked play. I didn't need to watch it again. I pushed up off the bed, and I went to the dresser to pack my things with Daphne Collins's cynical cackle grating in my ear.

At the end of it, Patty shut the laptop.

I turned, leaning back against the dresser, arms across my chest. "So, there's that."

Patty bit her lip, her forehead creasing with uncertainty. "You're not going to let her bully you like that, are you?"

I scoffed. "I've had a lot worse." And that was true. Just ask Aunt April.

Patricia straightened off the bed and glanced down at the laptop. "But—"

I shrugged again, irritation increasing and eyes burning with unshed tears. "It's not like I can livestream anything. You know if I get another data overage charge my mom takes the phone. Plus," I bit my lip on the truth. I scoffed and shook my head. I couldn't meet her soft-hearted gaze without losing it. Everything I'd worked for with the channel—I finally had the viewership to really *do* something. And now I'd screwed it up. My hand went to my forehead, and I squeezed my temples as though I might push back the tears threatening to spill.

"Jacqueline...you can use *my* phone. We can do this. We have to clear your name."

My hand fell to my side again, and I took a deep shaky breath. I studied her for a moment as she gave me a small smile and the simple, trusting stare of a true friend that I didn't deserve.

Crap.

I took another breath. "Okay."

Patricia's grin broadened and lit up her whole face. She closed the distance between us and gave me a tight hug. "It'll all work out. Trust me."

And I did. I only wished I could say the same.

She pulled away and held me at arm's length. "So, what's the plan?" Patty released me and dropped onto the bed with a little bounce as she watched my mind work.

"Well..." I licked my lips and thought for a moment. I started pacing the length of the room. "If you're really all right with me using your phone...I can sneak out tonight and film it. The Moms are always out by nine, and you know Ted's mom takes sleep meds..."

Patricia nearly squeaked. "Sneak out?"

I looked at her with an amused smirk as she practically squirmed at the idea of breaking the rules. "I don't know, Jacqueline. Do we have to *sneak out*? I mean—"

"Patty, relax." I laughed. "You aren't coming with me. You're—"

Patricia opened her mouth to argue, but someone beat her to it: "You better make room for us in your little plan."

My heart slammed into my stomach. Great. I turned slowly just in time to see Erica, Allison, and Natalie lurking in the doorway.

"Don't you know what happened to the cat when it listened at the wrong keyhole?" I asked wryly with an air of boredom.

The three of them exchanged stupid sneers of confusion.

"It was skinned alive," I finished, my eyes wide and insane.

Erica made a face. "Whatever. You've both been up here for forever. The Moms sent us after you guys to make sure you weren't up here kissing or something."

I took a step toward her as though I might hit her. I was so freaking close.

Erica instinctively sidestepped toward Natalie to use as a human shield before continuing with her hasty explanation. "But *whatever*. Point is, we are coming, too. Otherwise, we'll tell the Moms. And the Moms will tell *your* mom. And then you'll probably get kicked out of the co-op...which means fines. And," Erica sniffed as she waved a careless arm around the room. "Considering you clean rooms and scrub toilets for a living, I'm guessing you can't afford it."

I wanted to slap her. Or throw Dog at her face and watch as he ripped off her cakey makeup with his claws. But she was right. If I dropped out of co-op...there was a penalty. And if I was kicked out of co-op for breaking rules...there was a fine. And these weren't normal, Nile, live-in-a-hunter-shack kind of prices. These were mainland, mansion, lake-front property kind of payments.

She had me and, judging by the evil glint in her azure eyes, she knew it. Everyone did. I was Cinderella. And they were the ugly co-op sisters.

Fine.

Before I could concede, the boys burst in rowdy and loud as only boys can and bumbled their way like neanderthals toward the main bedroom where we stood.

"Hey, what's taking you guys so long?" Benji leaned his head over Allison's shoulder, literally inserting himself into their semicircle. "We've been waiting for, like, a half hour."

"Yeah," Kenneth nodded as he wedged in between Natalie and Erica. "I want to see the Wolfman. And the Horror House!"

Natalie rolled her eyes. "Who comes up with these names?"

"Thirty minutes?" Ted scoffed. "Benji, chill. It's been, like, two."

"We were just making plans for our late-night ghost hunt," Erica murmured with a coy smirk.

"Seriously?" Benji asked.

Kenneth whooped. "We want in!"

Erica looked from Kenneth back to me with a wolfish grin. "Looks like we've got the full senior class…"

"We could make it a prank!" Natalie squealed.

"What?" Allison scrunched up her face. "How?"

"Nat, that doesn't make any sense," Erica muttered coolly.

I shifted my gaze from face to face, hating each one more than the other. Forget about clearing my name. This was serious to me. It wasn't some sort of game or slumber party activity. And they were mocking it. Making a joke of it.

"You realize ghosts can kill people, right? Like, it's literally been documented. Fatal ghost encounters are common. And the Scarlet Witch is an old spirit. Centuries old. With minimal human exposure."

"Ooo…" Ted wiggled his hands at Allison who slapped his fingers away with a squeal.

"So?" Erica asked, her hip popped defiantly.

"So, that means she's as nasty and violent as they come. And if you all insist on tagging along…" I surveyed them again with my mouth in a grim line. "Well, at least the odds of my survival exponentially increase."

Allison scrunched up her face and cocked her head to the side, looking remarkably like Natalie's puppy when you hide her ball behind your back. "Wait, what?"

"She's saying the ghost is going to pick us off one by one like the kids in *Texas Chainsaw*." Benji chuckled appreciatively. "And you know the hottest girl is always first to die, so that means— Erica?" Benji slapped a hand on her shoulder as he stared deep into her eyes. "You'll be totally safe."

Erica's smug smirk slipped, and her eyes narrowed. She slapped him off her. "Wait, *what*?!" she snapped again.

I sighed inwardly, struggling to find patience and pretense that had been lost since the moment my worlds collided. "This is serious. Whatever you think about my channel and whatever you think about paranormal activity—"

"Excellent movie," Kenneth quipped.

I rolled my eyes and continued, "This is dangerous. And I don't want anyone coming that's going to get me killed by being an idiot. So, if you're coming, you're going to listen to me. Do what I say. Or else I'm ditching you in the woods with the Witch, and I wouldn't lose any sleep over it."

Amused chuckles rippled through the group, but I didn't smile. "I'm not kidding. I will leave your dumb butt in the woods if you cause me even a twitch of a headache. So, I'm going to put it into words you will all understand...and burn them into your brain: No child left behind, *unless they freaking deserve it.*"

"So, when do we leave?" Kenneth asked eagerly.

"I have some stuff to prep—"

"Like what?" Erica sniffed.

"—so I'm ditching the tour today," I continued forcefully as though I couldn't hear her (stupid) question. "You all cover me. I'll be back to the Inn by dinner. So, don't let the Moms get suspicious. About two hours after curfew, I'll send a mass text with instructions. Don't be stupid. Stay awake. Put your phones on silent and keep them in your hands."

They all began talking together as the excitement began to bubble and ripple through them at the idea of sneaking out to hunt a ghost in the most haunted town in America. Great for them. This wasn't anything new to me. I actually had work to do while they were all tagging along for a joyride into Halloweentown.

I had to get enough iron and salt and flashlights...

But first...

I still had to find the Scarlet Witch.

EPISODE 9: WHAT LIES AHEAD

I waited for everyone to leave, watching through the curtains as the oversized tractor pulled the wagon behind it and drove onto the road loaded with the Moms, the kids, and Zan at the helm like a ship captain. I had only a few hours until dinner. And I was going to take advantage of every second of every minute of them. I had to. Because I'd be damned if I let everything I'd worked for die. I scooped up my laptop and shoved it in my backpack and hurried out the door.

By the time I made it to my car, Lacey was hopping down the grassy hill from her cabin. I smiled at her, but didn't stop to talk. I yanked open the car door and hopped in.

"You didn't go on the Haunt," Lacey stated bluntly as she stopped directly in the way of me closing the door.

I resisted the urge to roll my eyes at the obvious. "No. I've got things to do."

"You found the Witch." Lacey inclined her head, her lily-blonde hair falling to one side like white silk. "Why didn't you tell me?"

I pursed my lips and looked away from the hurt in her wide, hazel eyes. "Get in, Lacey."

Obediently, she skipped around the car and slipped in the passenger seat without another word. If she had any question about what we were doing, she didn't ask it. And like so many things about Lacey, I was grateful.

But I knew I'd hurt her feelings. And I had to explain...at least a little. "I haven't found the Scarlet Witch."

Lacey frowned thoughtfully. "But those girls said—"

"They're all idiots. But that's not why I'm upset...you know my films? How I post them on the internet?"

"Your-Tube, right?"

I snorted as my hands twisted on the wheel. "Yeah. Well, a lot of people are saying my work is all a hoax."

"That you're lying?"

"Basically."

"Even the one we did on gullums? Maddison helped us with that one."

I gave her a terse nod as I cut down a backroad to avoid the tractor trailer hauling the co-op tour.

"I'm sorry, Jacqueline. I know how hard you work on those episodes."

"Yeah."

A pensive quiet settled around us in the car as I drove through the island. Off Route 2, down backroads and dirt drives, through farmland and woodland, all paths leading to the lake whichever way we took. I had no leads. No direction. No hope of finding the Witch. Growing increasingly agitated, I ripped it into the Vantine boating access. And slammed on the breaks, tires spitting stones and digging up dirt in a cold cloud around the car. Lacey and I jerked back in our seats as I shoved the stick in park.

We sat still for a moment staring out at the tossing gray lake ahead of us through scraggly bare branches of the dying trees.

"Road rage causes two thirds of all traffic fatalities." Lacey paused thoughtfully and then added, "And statistically, female drivers are the more likely to be injured in a crash."

I laughed despite myself and covered my face in my hands. I groaned, my frustration boiling over into one loud growl. "I know. I'm sorry, Lace. It's just—you know better than anyone how it is... to know deep in your bones that something's true and not be able to help people see that it's real."

Lacey nodded solemnly. "Mrs. Molley is a gullum. No one will listen."

I smiled and patted her hand. "Exactly."

We both stared out ahead watching the waves crash against each other as they rolled into the rocky shore. Then Lacey murmured, "Bird Island looks lonely. They all do. The isles."

I nodded, only half listening. Then her words registered. "Wait, what?"

"The isles. They look lonely. Don't you think? I try to visit them when I can...but—"

I turned sharply in my seat. "The isles! We haven't checked the isles!"

Lacey blinked at me but didn't speak.

"That would explain why there is literally no information on the Witch's story! She's haunting one of the isles *surrounding* Nile!"

Lacey frowned thoughtfully. "But doesn't the story say the family was shunned to the woods? Not off the island."

I revved the car to life and whipped it out of the access and onto the main road. "There are woods on every isle surrounding Nile except Bird Island. And you know stories get mixed up over the years! This explains everything! I just need to check the deeds first. Zan has everything at the Historical Society. We find the isle, and then we just have to borrow a boat."

I sped along the roads and turned on to Route 2. I should've listened to Lacey about my driving...because I totally forgot the speed limit. That is, until blue lights and the woop-woop of the cop car refreshed my memory.

I cursed under my breath and pulled over...into the Martin Isle Historical Society.

The shiny cop car parked behind my old junker. And Lacey looked at me with grim disapproval. She didn't need to tell me she told me so...but she told Chris—as soon as I rolled down the window, and he poked his handsome face down to smirk at us.

Chris laughed and shook his head, his eyes on me. "This is— what, your *second* speeding ticket in a week? Joey told me how he caught you ripping it over the hill by the east ferry after midnight."

"It's not my second ticket if you don't give me one." I smiled coyly with a shameless flutter of my lashes.

Chris grinned. "My God, Jacqueline Jay. You're gonna be the death of me..."

"All the more reason to let me off with a warning." I bit back my smile as my eyes moved across his face.

A small pinch of red tinged his cheeks as Chris glanced at the Martin Isle Historical Society. "What was the rush this time?"

"We are going water witching. Would you like to join us, Chris?" Then Lacey looked at me. "Chris has a boat."

My eyes widened with delight, and I gave her leg a gentle pat. Then my gaze slid sideways toward Chris. "I forgot all about *Steggy*...how about that date, Chris?" I bit my lip on my sly smile. "When do you get off?"

Chris cleared his throat and smoothed a hand over his gelled hair. Then he leaned his arms on the side of the car, nearly bent half inside my vehicle. "Well...I could call Joey and get him to cover for me..."

I touched his arm and gave him a squeeze. "I'll call you when we're ready."

Chris's eyes flicked from my hand on his arm to meet my suggestive gaze. "You think I've forgotten about that ticket?"

I giggled. "No. But I know you aren't going to give it to me anyway."

Chris shook his head, unable to hide the amused smirk

pressing a dimple in his cheek and crinkling his cobalt eyes. Then he leaned back, out of the vehicle, and straightened, his hands on hips, surveying the road as though making sure his daddy wasn't watching. He turned back to me and pointed his finger at my nose. "Don't make me regret this. But here's your warning. No more reckless driving, or I'll rack you with so many points you'll lose your license until you graduate."

I nodded furiously, unable to stop the smile from spreading across my face. "Yes, sir, Officer Vantine." I lowered my voice to a husky whisper, "Although, that would give me an excellent excuse to guilt-trip you for rides in that old Chevy you keep tucked away in the barn..."

Chris rolled his eyes and laughed. Then he put his hand on the edge of the door, as though holding me there with him a moment longer. He met my eyes, held them gently, as he gave me a warm, sincere smile. "Congratulations on the Witch, Jacqueline. That's huge."

His words hit me hard in the heart. Not at all in the way he'd intended. I looked away as I tried to catch my breath, gnawing the inside of my cheek as my face burned hot in the cold October air. Lacey may not be online, but Chris certainly was...and he'd have seen my latest episode along with the rest of the world. "Yeah. I guess I went viral." I shrugged almost sheepishly and struggled for something to say to change the subject.

Chris made a face. "I'm not talking about your followers. I'm talking about the Witch. I can't believe you finally—"

My eyes darted to Lacey who was staring at us politely. Before he could say any more, I put my hand over his and blurted, "Sorry, Chris, but I totally lied."

EPISODE 10: THE COLORFUL ONE

C hris hesitated and then narrowed his eyes. "What do you mean?"

I winced and screwed up my face in an innocent wince. "I wasn't speeding because we're working on an episode...I just really, *really* have to pee." I did a little leg jiggle to illustrate my point as I flashed a cheesy smile.

Chris raised his eyebrows in surprise, and then he laughed. "Well, go on then. I'll catch you two ladies later."

Then he gave us a little wave and headed for his car. Before he had a chance to pull out of the Historical Society parking lot, I jumped out of the car, backpack slung over my shoulder, and ran for the old brick building, Lacey hurrying after me.

Because Zan was leading the Historical Haunt, Missa Martin's —Zan's grandniece and part-time assistant—pink corvette was the only car in the parking lot. But that was normal. Not many people even bothered with the Historical Society. Honestly, I was probably the only one who ever visited.

But the Historical Society really was a hidden gem of Nile. Most islanders didn't care for their history; they loved the legends and relished in the infamy of their homeland...but they didn't bother looking into the factual details. Like any other small town, rumor and gossip were all they needed. Forget the truth behind any of the whispers. Lies and hyperbole were way more fun.

The two of us headed up the steps together and hurried inside, the cold of October biting at our heels. I closed the door hard behind us, shutting out the gust of lake air billowing in at our backs, as the small brass bell clanged overhead. Immediately, I dug into my purse for my phone and switched on the Wi-Fi connection. As I slipped it back inside my bag, I noticed Lacey, small in her pompom sweater, shivering in her thin rainbow-striped leggings and yellow galoshes.

I scoffed affectionately and gave her shoulders a rough rub as Missa appeared through the archway on the left with a curious smile. "Hey, guys. What can I do for you?"

I did a double take. Today her hair was a deep swirl of purples, blues, and greens when only just—was it last week? It'd been blonde with ribbons of pastel rainbow all throughout. I smiled at the sight of her corset laced tightly over her long-sleeved shirt. "I love that choker," I murmured appreciatively at the dog collar chain tight on her neck. Missa always was the picture of millennial emo aesthetic, and I'd be lying if I said I didn't take a lot of inspiration from her. And honestly, I was envious of her ability to express herself so freely. Between my grandmother, and my mother who wrung her hands if my lips looked too black, and the co-op, I saved my self-expression for my channel.

Missa grinned as a rogue blush spread across her olive skin. Her amber eyes sparkled with pleasure as her aquiline nose crinkled. "Really? I wasn't sure..." She did a little spin. "You should've seen the look Daddy Ed shot me as I headed out for work this morning..." She rolled her eyes and laughed at the memory of her stepdad's face. Missa hadn't always been a Martin...the Martins were old Nile. Descendants of the founders, thus the namesake of the island. Her mother, Catherine, a Grunberg, had married her high school sweetheart, Austin Tyler, and when he'd joined the army, they'd left Nile. Which was big news. Because no one ever left Nile. And then she'd come back several years later—without him, but with four small kids and no wedding ring. The *real* scandal was what happened after: she reconnected with his former best friend, the quiet, steady Edwin Martin, and she married him five years and two more kids later. Missa, being the oldest at eighteen, had changed her last name to match her stepdad's. It'd been the first thing she'd done as an 'adult.' I couldn't imagine changing my name to match someone else's...no matter how much I loved them.

And no matter how disgusted I was with my father.

Names meant something. And I'd like to keep mine, thanks.

"So, what's up?" Missa scrunched up her face. "I'm surprised you aren't helping Aunt Zan with the Haunt this week!"

"Jacqueline had to use the bathroom," Lacey stated serenely as she moved to study a Lake Champlain painting on the wall.

Missa blinked. "Oh, well—"

"It's okay; I know where it is." I waved a careless hand. "What I really need is to look at the land deeds. In particular, the private isles surrounding Nile."

Missa frowned, her forehead creasing beneath her purple and turquoise bangs. "Well, you might need the Town Clerk for that...I don't think—"

"The deeds from the founding. Like the earliest owners...they should be with the—"

Missa's amber eyes widened as she smiled. "The genealogy records, right, okay! Give me a minute."

I forced a kind smile. As much as I loved Missa, it was always a bit of a pain to work with her. Especially when I was on a deadline. She wasn't an expert like Zan, who literally knew what I needed before I did, most days. But I couldn't fault Missa for that. She was volunteering. Her actual job was at the antique shop with her mother. I nodded my thanks to Missa and then turned to Lacey. "I'll meet you in the archives in a minute?"

The Historical Society was really just a giant colonial house, and it was furnished as such. Like stepping into Colonial Williamsburg. I crossed the old creaky wood floor, the groans muffled by the thick paisley patterned carpet, and down a snug side hall to the bathroom. As I shut the door, I took the time to check my phone. The trolling had grown to classic cancel culture levels. Hundreds of comments under all the episodes spewing hate and hoax accusations. And worse, the episode on Maddison Rose had been reported to YouTube. They were reviewing it for TOS violations now.

It wouldn't be taken down forever. I was always careful to follow TOS.

But the fact that it was even put into question...I gritted my teeth as my hands tightened around the phone. I locked it and shoved it back into my backpack. I flushed the toilet and ran the sink and stomped out of the bathroom, just barely able to keep myself from slamming the door behind me.

I found Lacey and Missa in the archives, going through stacks of browning old documents stained with age and who knew what else. They both looked up as I walked in and smiled.

"Okay, so there are thirteen isles surrounding Nile. And we've got the owners of all of them during the 17th century." She waved a hand at the documents preserved in plastic page protectors. "Have fun."

I bit my lip at the amount of papers. There had to be a way to narrow it down. I approached the table across from Lacey and the two of us began scanning the documents for the names Perrault, Sullivan, White, or Mann. Years ago, I'd already traced my grandmother's maternal line. These were the names most likely to be the origin of the Scarlet Witch...if it was true. And Memé wasn't... I closed my eyes briefly as my fingers pinched the deed in my hands. I would not go there right now. Perrault, Sullivan, White, and Mann.

As Lacey and I combed through the documents, Missa leaned back against the giant copy machine and watched us with her head tilted in quiet interest. Then she blurted the question she'd clearly been biting back. "Did you accept it?"

I took a breath and then glanced at her sideways with my eyebrow cocked in question.

Missa nibbled her lip and then clarified. "The dare. From Daphne Collins...are you going to livestream it? Does this—" She waved a hand around at the papers, her bracelets clanging. "—have to do with the livestream?"

My eyes flitted toward Lacey, who was humming to herself as she swayed back and forth on the balls of her feet, plucking up deeds and placing them back down. I wondered whether she was actually reading them. I looked back at Missa. "We're—"

Missa held up her hand hastily. "You don't have to tell me! I'm sorry, I just...I couldn't believe she did that to you. She really is such a putz. Daddy Ed's nephew, Jack? You know Jack? She was supposed to go on a date with him the night before Apple Fest. Ditched him. Like it was a joke. She climbed out a freaking *window*. Left him waiting outside the girls' bathroom like an idiot." Missa shook her head in disgust. "She's soulless. Like a demon."

Jack Martin was like Lacey in that he was too gentle for the word. A punk-rock emo kid that played up the fact that he looked like a teenage Pete Wentz, he spent most of his time playing drums in his parents' basement. He was self-taught and insanely talented. But kind and soft-spoken like his uncle Edwin. Hurting him was like kicking a puppy. Gross.

I scowled and exhaled deeply, nostrils flaring. "Well, what I *can* tell you is we are looking for an isle." I smiled sheepishly.

Missa laughed. "Thanks, that helps..." She giggled again. "Well, whatever you guys are up to, I hope it doesn't take you to Wolf's Rock."

"Wolf's Rock? Is that one of the isles? I only know Bird Island..." I muttered distractedly as I went back to the documents, my eyes searching for one of four names. "Why's that?"

"Oh, you know. The wolves."

My hands froze above the next deed. I looked at her sharply. Missa's smile faltered underneath the severity of my gaze. She inclined her head. "Just joking..."

I licked my lips as my forehead creased with confusion. "Missa, there aren't any wolves in Nile. Are you talking about another legend, or—?"

Missa waved a hand at my words. "Psh. If it was a legend, *you'd* already know about it."

I snorted in agreement. This was true.

"But I'm surprised you don't know about the wolves on Wolf's Rock..." Missa crinkled her hooked nose as her golden eyes rolled. "Although, I guess it makes sense...you deal with wolfmen and ghosts...not animal rights." She giggled as though she'd made a joke. I wasn't laughing. My brain was too busy working to make the connection I'd missed. Forget the punchline.

I shifted where I stood, my hands releasing the deeds and letting them drop back onto the others. "There are actual wolves on Wolf's Rock?"

Missa nodded slowly, her eyes wide as though I were slow. And in that moment, I was. Missa hesitated before explaining, "Uhuhhh. They are protected by Fish & Wildlife. They don't even let you on the island. I think it's technically abandoned, and the game wardens just keep it safe. Something about albino wolves or something." She shrugged. "Nicky told me about it."

Missa's boyfriend, Nicky Damiani, was a game warden with the Vermont Fish & Wildlife Department. He'd know better than anyone else...

"Are there *a lot* of wolves?" I prompted, my head still dazed from whatever I was missing.

"No idea." Missa frowned thoughtfully. "Honestly, I only know about it because I wrote Nicky's research paper for one of his college classes about the wolf population in Vermont." Missa met my eyes with a wink. "The last one was killed in the mid-

1800s. You know that Wolf's Rock is now the only place they're found in the whole state?" Missa scrunched up her mouth in a pensive pout. "You know, now that I think about it. There wasn't anything actually *on* the wolves on Wolf's Rock. Just that Nile put the isle under protected status after several fishermen kept reporting giant white wolf sightings. They probably have people go in there occasionally to measure the populations. I just don't remember reading anything about the actual wolves, like, specifically."

I stepped away from the table and went for the maps. Pulling the rolls out and spreading them out on the table, I moved my hands across the lake and searched for Wolf's Rock. The Scarlet Witch had been killed by a wolf...along with her entire family...this was a better lead than anything else I'd ever come up with. I found Wolf's Rock; it was just off the shore where Charlebois Manor towered on the cliffside. The same isle Memé was always watching from her chair by the window. This had to be.

Quickly, adrenaline rushing over me like a wave on the rocks, I slapped the map back in a tight roll and went for the deeds. "Who owned Wolf's Rock?"

Missa pushed off the copy machine and hurried for the table. Lacey made a soft "Hmmm." sound as she pawed through the pages. The three of us weeded through the deeds spurred on by my obvious increasing excitement. But I found it first.

I held up the page. My eyes blurred, and I blinked through the tears as I read, "Charles Perrault."

EPISODE 11: WOLVES

It was all there. Charles Perrault. Settled the island with his wife, elderly mother, and two daughters. The daughter, Brigid, left the isle and moved back to Nile and married George Talbot in 1666. Wolf's Rock was abandoned after her death, and no one bothered to claim it after. Probably due to the wolves.

I'd found her. For real. The origin. The truth in the lie. And regardless of whether the ghost was real...at least now I had documented, inked up proof that it wasn't just made up for the fun of it.

The Scarlet Witch was so obscure and dubious because she was haunting an uninhabited isle. A tiny island no one bothered to visit because it was home to wolves.

Great.

I hadn't anticipated that. In all the years I'd hunted for her, I hadn't expected the descendants of the Scarlet Witch's killer to be an issue for me. A ghost encounter was one thing.

But wolves?

Awesome.

What now?

. . .

I had to talk to Nicky. Or at least, the Fish & Wildlife. I got Nicky's number from Missa, and Lacey and I helped her pick up all the page protected documents, returning them to their proper places. As we left, Missa looked a little bummed. So, before we headed outside, I paused in the doorway. "I'll be back for an interview, so, if Zan isn't back yet, you better be ready to answer some questions for the next episode."

Missa grinned at that. "Good. Because if Nicky gets featured over me, I'll be really mad."

I laughed at that and gave her a little wave before shutting the door behind me. I squinted out into the cold as the air bit at my nose. Lacey hopped to the car as I held back, surveying the woods across the road. The sun was cool and pale as it hovered just above the trees. It would be dark soon. I didn't have much time before I had to be back at the Inn for dinner. And there was still so much to do.

Lacey and I met Nicky Damiani at the island ferry dock diner. It was a small boxy shack of a place with dim lighting and a hazy smoke that clung to the place and permeated the air that hadn't seemed to clear from the decades before they'd outlawed smoking in restaurants. The owner was a crusty old crab who spent most of the day barking at his underaged staff as though infuriated by their very presence. There were several ancient booths lining the grimy windows overlooking the parking lot and the lake in the distance, with a counter and barstools opposite for those that wanted a front row seat to the verbal abuse of minors. All and all, I hated the place, but it was one of the only places to eat in Nile.

I eyed the fat owner with cool eyes as Lacey and I took seats in the booth opposite Nicky, flinching despite myself as he shouted at the waitress, Rachel St. Claire, a punk-rock cheerleading junior, who bellowed back at him just as loud, and twice as profane.

I smiled slightly as I held up my phone and switched on the camera. "What can you tell me about Wolf's Rock?"

Nicky scoffed at the question. Then he jutted his chin toward me as I watched him through the phone screen. His dark eyes crinkled as his face broke into a cocky smile. "Missa put you up to this, didn't she?"

My heart dipped slightly. "What do you mean?"

Nicky shook his head, looked off to the side, and then back at me. His eyes kept moving between the phone and up toward my face. A lot of people never knew where to keep their eyes. "Wolf's Rock doesn't really have wolves."

My body relaxed. "Then why is it protected? It *is* protected, isn't it?"

Nicky opened his mouth and then shut it again. He shrugged. "Yeah. Sure. It's protected. Just like Champ is. You realize there's still a law against harassing *him*, right?"

Of course, I knew about the laws protecting Champ...and I also knew that he was real...but I was in journalist mode. I was the observer and inquirer of fact. So, I let him continue to 'educate me.'

Nicky tilted his chin forward again. "Look it up. It's there, in the books; it's just outdated. There are a lot of laws still on paper that aren't ever enforced because they don't make sense anymore."

"So, it is the Fish & Wildlife's official position that there are no wolves on Wolf's Rock?"

Nicky nodded, his eyes wide. "Uh, yeah." He shrugged and ran a hand over his face as he scooted forward in the booth. "I mean, I patrol the lake. We all do. No one's seen any wolf sightings."

I smiled and cocked a skeptical eyebrow. "Just because you haven't seen them from the shore doesn't mean—"

Nicky frowned. "There've been research teams that have tried to collect data on any potential packs. Nothing there. This I'd needed to add to my presentation when Missa conveniently left it out of the paper."

"This is why you should always do your own homework," Lacey murmured as she sipped from her stack of teacups.

Nicky's dark eyes flicked toward Lacey at my left, and he pursed his lips on a smile. "You're right about that, Lacey. I learned my lesson on that one."

I waited for him to take a gulp of his milkshake before I tried again. "There must have been a reason for the law to be put in place...were there *ever* wolves on the island?"

"Sure." Nicky shrugged. "There were mountain lions in Milton, too. But not for, like, a hundred years."

I nodded slowly as though giving him credit for his superior knowledge. "Now you liken this isle's protected status to that of the laws protecting Champ...but something tells me if you saw someone 'harassing' the monster of Lake Champlain, you wouldn't interfere, yet I feel like you are expected to intervene in the event that you were to find someone trespassing on Wolf's Rock, is that correct?"

Nicky scrunched up his nose. "Well, yeah." Then he waved a careless hand at my question. "But that's just because of the fisherman rumors."

Now that was interesting. My eyes moved from the phone screen to meet his dark gaze. "What rumors?"

Nicky snorted into his shake. "It's Nile." He wiped the whipped cream off his mouth with his hand. "Everyone spreads rumors. There's always a new ghost. A new legend. None of it is true."

I raised my eyebrows in question. And he rolled his shoulders impatiently. "The old men whisper at the docks about a giant wolf. Eyes glowing in the woods off the Wolf's Rock shore at night. Apparently, there was a man who got stuck on the island during a storm. He tried to take shelter in an old cabin. The abandoned isles always have crumbling structures—" Nicky snapped his fingers and pointed at me as he added, "like the old church on Bird Island. Anyway, they say he came back with some kind of sickness, talking about a wolf. They say he had rabies."

"Why?" I asked softly. I knew where this was going.

Nicky glanced uneasily at Lacey as though not wanting to upset her. He looked back at me. "He bit his wife. Took a chunk out of her neck."

EPISODE 12: JACQUELINE JAY RESPONDS

I dropped Lacey off at the Inn, so she could change and get her things ready. And I headed to the Manor. I had no intention of livestreaming with a gang of co-op kids tagging along. Honestly, I didn't even want to take Lacey, but I knew she wanted to come which meant I would let her. People tended to ditch Lacey and leave her behind. I wasn't going to be just another jerk to her. But the fact that I would be literally leading her into danger ate away at me.

I hadn't been lying—the Scarlet Witch was centuries old. And ghosts, like I told Lacey over and over, they rotted with age. If we did find her, she'd be feral and twisted. Warped by her unfinished business or emotional trauma. So, though I wouldn't stop Lacey from coming, I planned on doing everything I could to discourage her. But first, I needed to stop at the Manor to film my response video.

I parked beside Carol Anne's minivan, scooped up my backpack, and fished for my keys. I didn't bother ringing the doorbell, I just unlocked the door and let myself in. If Carol Anne knew I was visiting, she'd have me sit with Memé while she gave herself a break...not going to happen this time. I moved through the halls quiet and wary, like a ghost haunting the house. I slipped into my room and slapped on the light. The chandelier overhead switched on, and I flinched as all the pastels punched me in the face.

Like Memé's apartments in the North Wing, my room was huge. I wouldn't have been surprised if my whole house could fit inside. On the left was my computer and gaming setup that any 'influencer' would envy, complete with cat-ear headset and custom keyboard in a cutesy pink and purple dreamy theme that made Memé smile and me tolerate. To the right was my elaborate princess canopy bed with way too many pillows and frilly blankets. At the back of the room was the infamous spiral staircase leading up to the widow's walk, and beautiful bay windows that curved to form the perfect reading bench, plastered with more pastel pillows.

As much as the colors grated at me, I did love my room. Having a place in the Manor meant more to me than anyone could begin to understand. And my favorite part was that Memé had picked out the paintings with me. And every painting hanging along the walls was custom ordered from local artist, Maddison Rose. I took a moment as my eyes moved along each one. At mine and Memé's request, she'd painted all the landscapes and land-marks of Nile. Each featuring one of the legends I loved so dearly. And through the Pepto-Bismol-pink puked all over the room, you could see the stories of Nile all over, and it felt like home.

I set up my tripod on the floor in the middle of the pink fluffy carpet and clipped in the phone. I dug into the back of my dresser for something suitable. I didn't have many choices stashed in the Manor, so a simple pair of tight black pants, dark tank top, and an aesthetically, intentionally ripped and torn, red and black striped knit-sweater would have to do.

I moved to the vanity to check myself. Then I leaned toward the mirror and, out of habit, lined my eyes with eyeliner, but atypically, I glided matte black lipstick across my lips. I only both-ered with it for the channel. Satisfied with my appearance, I dug the black sheet out from underneath my bed and draped it over the canopy, blocking the pinks and pastels and posh from the view of the camera. Then I plugged in the fairy lights and hung them across the black sheet. Then I sank down to the floor so I was eye to eye with the camera lens. Crossing my legs, I placed my hands gently on my knees, as though I might begin to meditate. I took a deep, calming breath, willing my heart to steady. I could do this. Just like any other video. I'd done dozens. I could do this one.

And, just like in all my other videos, I angled the camera just below my nose and pressed record.

"Hello, Insiders..." I held up my hands and gestured to the black sheet and twinkling lights at my back. "As you can see, we're doing a sit-down this time. No editing. No refilming. Just raw and real. So, go ahead and grab your coffee because this'll be a long one." I nibbled my lower lip as I struggled with where to begin. Whatever. I took a breath and then let it out in a stream of verbalized thought. "If you're watching this, chances are you aren't here because you want to learn about flummox fairies, or hear about alion encounters, or anything remotely related to what it is that this channel is for: uncovering and exploring the supernatural hiding among us in the shadows.

"So, *if* you are new here, which, statistically speaking you probably are...I just wanted to take a minute to explain the true purpose of this channel...not my entire backstory. If you want that, go watch *Episode 1: The Charlebois Manor, Curse or Covert Cover-up?*

"The reason I have this channel is to expose the truth of the paranormal to the world. Yes. I take it seriously. It is literally life and death for all of us. But when someone is mauled, or murdered, or taken, they lie. The public covers it up because it sounds crazy. It doesn't make sense. And the victims never get their stories told... and the rest of us are left in the dark like sheep without shepherds awaiting future attacks from the wolves lurking among us. So, I use this channel to tell the truth, no matter how crazy. Because maybe if enough people hear me...it won't sound so crazy...and maybe I won't have to show you a dead girl to get you to finally pay attention."

I paused, teeth gritted hard. My eyes burned and blurred with tears, and I allowed them to spill down my cheeks, dripping from my jaw like raindrops. I swallowed, emotion thick in my throat. Taking a shaky breath, I kept going. "This is why, when Maddison Rose was sacrificed—yes, I say *sacrificed* because that is what it was —I knew I had to figure out what had killed her. Because I didn't believe it was right to allow the false narrative surrounding her death to continue unchallenged. The evidence clearly shows—and go watch the episode for a more detailed, in-depth look at the findings—Maddison Rose encountered a demon...I will not, and *do not*, claim that she summoned one. Now, followers of this channel will understand, and you Insiders all should know, the distinction is an important one.

"If you'd like to educate yourself, please see *Episode 13: Demons Like Mine*.

"In all likelihood, she was targeted, but that is just my conclusion based on my knowledge, research, and evaluation of the evidence. She encountered a demon and sacrificed her soul in exchange for the recovery of her critically injured little sister. Maddison Rose was a *martyr*. A heroine. Selfless, with a heart so full of love, she was willing to be dragged to hell to give her sister a chance at a full life. And despite what people think about me, or about this channel, it would be an insult to the memory of Maddison Rose—and the *sacrifice* of Maddison Rose—to say she died in any other manner than a sixteen-year-old girl giving her life to save her sister's. It's hard to hear, but it's true. And *that* is what this channel is about. The truth."

I inhaled deeply. Almost done. "Now, it has come to my attention that another content creator has challenged the integrity of this channel and demanded a livestream to prove the validity of my content. Normally, I'd ignore her. But I've had enough. Enough of the willful ignorance of the masses. The paranormal is out there. It is coming for us. And if you don't wake up. You're next. Just ask Desiree Lapierre. You can see her exclusive interview featured in *Episode 222: Dark Reflections.*

"Anyways...following my latest episode, *The Scarlet Witch Project,* I'd had plans—and am currently putting together—a brand-new episode on the Scarlet Witch with exclusive interviews, behind the scenes access, and newly uncovered facts, but as an expression of good faith to the *true* believers of the supernatural and the devoted followers of this channel...I *will* do a livestream in the next few hours following the posting of this video...but not in answer to that person, or to satiate the hunger of the gossip-starved cretins of the cyberverse, but as an exclusive special—a teaser of sorts, revealing the location of the elusive Scarlet Witch and hopefully catching her on film for you all to see in real time.

"So, in summary: there will be the livestream teaser, and the episode to follow as soon as possible. And trust me, it'll be a good one. Until then...I'll keep you safe Inside my Frozen Heart." I placed my hands over my heart and then blew a kiss to the camera.

Done. I pressed the record button again, ending the video, and sat quietly for a moment.

Usually, I'd edit the footage prior to upload. But that had taken a lot out of me. The emotional output had drained me and there was no way I was going to sit through it all over again. I pulled out my laptop and sent the video to the computer. As I clicked through the tabs to the upload screen, a message from Keirian binged on the screen.

GHOSTFACEWASFRAMED

You can ghost me all you want. It doesn't make what I said any less true.

MYFROZENHEART

What are you talking about?

GHOSTFACEWASFRAMED

Jax...come on. Don't play stupid. This is what you do. You get upset and you hide until you want attention again.

You're mad at me for saying you weren't perfect.

I pursed my lips as I scowled at the messages. Before I could type a response, Keirian sent another.

GHOSTFACEWASFRAMED

You aren't perfect, Jax. You mess up and do stupid things. Like your last episode. Case and point. But that doesn't mean you aren't amazing and one of the best people I know. And before you post your reaction to Daphne Collins, because I know that's the only reason why you're online right now...you really should think about some of what she said.

A low growl rumbled in my throat as I slammed the backspace on my initial reply and poked out a new message and jammed the enter key.

MYFR0ZENHEART

What is that supposed to mean???

GHOSTFACEWASFRAMED

She's a meathead, but she had a point if you read between the jerky. Your followers—

your real followers—

like me...

we care about your content, but we also care about you. The real you. And you're always careful to be just what everyone wants you to be, but...

well, it wouldn't kill you to be yourself once in a while.

I rolled my eyes at his Hallmark-greeting-esque advice and clicked back over to the upload screen. I prepped the video clip and then submitted it. There. Done. I shut the laptop and exhaled deeply. Now, all I had to do was—

I flinched, my eyes darting toward the bedroom door as a scream shrieked through the Manor.

EPISODE 13: A BITE & A BANISHMENT

"She bit me! She bit me!" Carol Anne shrieked over and over, her voice thin and high with panic. She was in shock. Not accusing Memé or even explaining anything to me. She was just declaring it. As though to herself. To make herself hear and understand that Joy Charlebois had ripped a chunk of flesh out of her wrist.

I stood frozen in the doorway, eyes fluttering, struggling to process what I was seeing. Blood was splattered scarlet all over the loveseat where Carol Anne liked to sit. Memé was hunched over the fireplace, her back curled, the bones of her spine poking through her dressing gown.

"Memé?"

She straightened quickly at the sound of my voice, and she turned with a smile, bright with blood. "Jacqueline!" She frowned. "Your clothes. It's not time for that yet. You should change."

My stomach sloshed like the water churning in the crick.

Carol Anne was still screaming.

Memé didn't seem to hear. But my brain finally started to register, and I hurried over to Carol Anne to help. My boots crunched over smashed pieces of Memé's china blue and white shards all over the hardwood floor. Like small bones grinding underneath my feet. I winced at the sound as I snatched Carol Anne's arm. It wasn't too grisly. At least I couldn't see bone… much of it anyway.

"Okay…" I winced at the sliver of ivory slimy with meat and blood. "Okay. You'll be *okay*." I swallowed the bile bubbling up in my throat and shoved Carol Anne back down on the loveseat. "Just—here…" I slumped my shoulder and dropped my backpack to the floor. Then I unzipped it and quickly slapped through the contents. My hands closed around the makeup bag. I dug it out and fingered through my supernatural first aid. My breathing relaxed as my fingers found the bungleweed. "Here." I popped the little stopper with my teeth and dropped a few precious drops on her wrist.

Instantly, the bleeding stopped and clotted over. I grinned despite myself. The Nile Witch, Charlotte Grey, had sold the bungleweed to me when I was working on the Camp Abnaki case. She'd promised it would help with most supernatural wounds…but (fortunately, I guess) I hadn't needed to test her potion. Until now. And it was working just as advertised. As it should, considering it took me nearly six weeks to earn enough to buy it. And she gave it to me at a discount. I looked at Carol Anne, hoping to see my enthusiasm reflected in her eyes…but she'd fainted. Which I supposed was good considering it'd be hard to explain a paranormal potion to her. Especially when my grandmother had just gone zombie on her. My heart dipped. Memé.

Sometime in between her acknowledgement of me and my nursing Carol Anne back to almost full health, Memé had made her way over to me and was now standing beside me, staring blankly at the equally blank face of her victim. The Alzheimer's had her again.

I corked the potion and gingerly tucked it in the makeup bag, into the backpack, and zipped it shut. Careful not to make any sudden movements, I slipped my pack back on my shoulder and glanced at my grandmother.

"Memé?" I murmured tentatively.

She turned sharply, her hazel eyes wide and curious. She stared at me, her head slightly inclined as though her mind was empty and waiting for instructions.

"Can you sit and read with me?" I breathed.

Memé smiled then and nodded almost shyly. Then she hurried to her chair by the window overlooking the lake, black in the evening light, and the dark, ominous shadow of Wolf's Rock.

In the rush to get to the source of the scream, I'd only grabbed my backpack. My phone was still in my room on the bed beside my laptop. I glanced in vain around the room, knowing full well Aunt April had removed all the phones from the north wing. With Memé's Alzheimer's, it wasn't a good idea to give her instant access to any person she wanted at any time. I looked down at the loveseat. Carol Anne's phone, ever present in her hand, had slipped off the couch and onto the floor in the attack. Thankfully, she'd been watching a video and the phone hadn't locked. I bent down to call Chris and Dr. Damiani, the only doctor in Nile.

I tapped in Chris's number and pressed Send, my eyes on Carol Anne, who had begun to stir and regain consciousness. She blinked and looked down at her wrist and then moaned in disgust, shutting her eyes again.

"Hello?" Chris's voice barked into the phone. He was using his Man Voice like guys did when they didn't know who was calling.

"Hey, Chris, it's—"

There was a sharp smell of smoke curling underneath my nostrils and thick lashes of heat flicking against my back. Gripping the phone, I turned my head toward Memé.

Fire.

Carol Anne shrieked and jumped up from the loveseat and tore from the room. Apparently, she'd had enough of my grandmother...and I didn't blame her. Somehow, Memé had lit the drapes next to her chair on fire, the chair in which she still sat, calmly watching the flames consume the fabric just inches from her dressing gown. Instinctively (and stupidly), I tossed the phone and grabbed Memé by the shoulders, wrenching her out of the chair and throwing her behind me, out of the way of the fire. I watched, horrified, as the flames climbed the drapes and danced on the ceiling. What to do? What could I do? Chris. I scrambled for the phone.

"Chris, get Bobby here. There's a fire in the north wing of the Manor. Hurry!"

"Get out of the house," Chris snapped before hanging up.

Get out? The whole house would burn. I looked around the room, frantic for something to stop it. Water? Where would I get water? I ran for Memé's bathroom, for the first time fully appreciating the massive size of her suite. I snatched the vase of fresh flowers, ripped out the hydrangeas, and, switching on the water, filled the vase to the top. The flames were so big. I'd never get enough water. There'd never be enough. I plugged the sink and let the water run before turning back to the bedroom and dashing for the curtains.

Memé hadn't moved from where I'd shoved her. She simply stared almost serenely at the fire as it ate away at the floral wallpaper. I tossed the water at the flames, and Memé shouted in protest. She pushed in between me and the fire, her back to me and her arms spread wide to the flames. I stared at her confounded in horror. She looked like a witch worshiping a bonfire.

"The fire cleanses, Jacqueline! My grandmother always told me. It's the only way. We need the fire! And we're running out of time. It's hungry! Look at it!" Then she laughed.

It was her laugh that shook me from my shock. I grabbed her and wrenched her from the room, shoving her into the hallway. I slammed the door on the room and hooked my arm through Memé's, dragging her down the hall.

She fought against me for a moment, but as we turned the

corner, she grew still as though defeated and sad. Then she hugged my arm tight to her, and whispered, "Is it time for dinner, Jacqueline? I've got the scarlet hunger, you know."

The Nile Fire Department was all volunteer, and all the boys who showed up, I knew. Bobby Ryder. Freddie Harris. Richard Cole. Preston Evans. Cory Blanchard. Nicky Damiani. Joey Vantine, Chris's twin, even showed up. It was a motley crew of the most recently graduated Nile boys, and I usually found it amusing when they all clumped together. They reminded me of the Lost Boys, running wild and mischievous all over the island.

But not tonight.

Tonight, they charged into Charlebois Manor and saved the historic landmark from ruin at the hands of its matriarch.

As I stood outside in the gravel drive, hugging a blanket around Memé, keeping her tight against me as though I were afraid she might run back into her room and throw herself on the curtains like a pyre, I couldn't help but wonder whether that's what she'd wanted all along.

Chris had beat the rest of the boys here. He'd ripped up the road and tore into the driveway just as I was guiding Memé down the stone staircases. He hadn't even stopped to turn off his patrol car. He kicked open the door and jumped out to meet us. He'd checked us over and grabbed the blanket for Memé out of the back of his car. Then he'd rounded up the boys as they'd come and led them into the Manor himself.

By the time he came back out, the fire was out. Chris had Joey wait with Memé as he pulled me aside. "What happened in there?"

I scoffed, then sniffed as my eyes blurred, and I had to look away from the crinkled, piercing, cobalt stare. "Well, you should be getting a call from Carol Anne Meyers."

I squinted back the tears and met his eyes with a deadpan stare.

His brow furrowed as he shifted his stance. "What do you mean?"

"My grandmother bit her. She *bit* her. Bad enough that she could've needed stitches." I clenched my jaw tight and backed away from him. "Can I borrow your phone? I should call my aunt."

"No need." I flinched at the snap of her voice. Aunt April marched up to the two of us, her pale face purple with her fury, as random strands of hair fell from her bun like antennae.

"How could you be so careless?" She grabbed my shoulder and gave me a shove. I stumbled back, combat boots skidding in the stones.

"Hey! Hey!" Chris stepped between us and put a hand on Aunt April, holding her back from me. She slapped him off her and sidestepped out of his reach. But she kept her hands clenched at her sides as she spat, "Don't tell me Carol Anne didn't warn you about the matches! She could've burnt the whole Manor down!"

"The Manor?" I scoffed, my voice thick with emotion. I flung a hand out in Memé's direction. "She could've *died* in there! And you're worried about the Manor?! At least I was with her! I'm the only one in this broken family that even cares about her!"

Aunt April's lip curled with disdain. "Just like your father—a budding little narcissist. Selfish and self-absorbed. What were you *doing* here, hmm? Judging by that trash all over your face...taking pictures of yourself for the internet? *How could you let her near the matches*!"

I folded my lips tight as though I might hide the black from view. I blinked as a tear bled through my lashes and streaked down my cheek. My lower lip trembled as I struggled to keep myself together. "Carol Anne never said anything about matches! She said she was stealing stuff! She didn't say anything about matches!"

Aunt April rolled her eyes and shook her head. "You are such a pathological liar," she muttered under her breath. Then she let out a little chuckle, and her face went stony and cold as she stuck her finger in my face. "I want you to go inside, collect your things, and never set foot on the estate again."

I swallowed slowly as I digested her words. My eyes slid toward Memé who was making polite conversation with Bobby Ryder. He was always a favorite of hers. He'd volunteered in our stables and worked with the horses since he was little. His daddy was a mean drunk, and whenever he was on one of his benders, Bobby'd sleep in the stall with his favorite horse. But Memé never knew. I kept it a secret. Until one night when he was thirteen, I'd found him nestled in the hay, black-eyed and nursing a busted lip. I ran for Memé, and she'd given him a cabin at the Inn. He stayed there sometimes, and she never again let it be rented out. It was his, she'd say. As I watched her laugh with him, I wondered whether she remembered that.

"She'll want me to visit." My voice was soft and imploring. And I hated myself for it. "You know she will."

Aunt April laughed cold and callous. "So, I will tell her you're on your way...and then she'll forget five minutes later. You of all people can appreciate a little white lie, can't you? Isn't that what you wanted me to do, anyway? Lie to her?"

Chris took a step toward her. "Unless something's changed in the last hour, Joy Charlebois is still the owner of this property. And until I hear otherwise, you can just—"

I put a hand on his chest. "Forget it, Chris. I've got things to do. I don't have time for this. I'll call you when I need your boat."

Aunt April laughed again, but this time full of cruel humor. "A boat? What are you going hunting for now? Champ? Or is it mermaids, like the McGregor girl keeps going on about?"

I kept my eyes on Chris, ignoring her. "Keep your phone on you."

And I didn't look back as I headed back up the stone staircases and up to the Manor for my things.

EPISODE 14: TO WOLF'S ROCK

Back at my house, I got my go-bag ready. I left my laptop on my dresser and double-checked everything. I had the salt, the iron, and the holy water. I moved the makeup bag—or rather, my supernatural first aid kit—containing the tonics and herbs from my backpack to the duffel. And then I added the book on spirits and the book about supernatural maladies. I scanned the others piled up in the small space between the foot of my bed and the wall. Maybe the book on monsters would be helpful, too.

The Scarlet Witch was said to be a ghost, but a lot of paranormal beings were written off as ghosts. And I needed to be prepared for anything. My stomach tightened painfully. And apparently wolves...the story Nicky had told of the sailor played over in my mind. It could've been wolves...but maybe the Scarlet Witch wasn't the only monster inhabiting Wolf's Rock.

And a paranormal entity in the shape of a wolf, well, that could be a lot of things. People often heard 'supernatural wolf' and thought werewolf. But that, again, was an ignorant assumption. There were a lot of other creatures, both corporeal and bodiless, that had wolf-like characteristics. I snatched up the monster book and thumbed through the pages. This was giving me a headache.

Normally the investigation prep was exciting and fascinating and my favorite part of the job. But now with the pressure of the livestream and worries of Memé scratching at the back of my mind, I just felt overwhelmed and stressed.

I took a breath and tossed the book in the open duffel. I'd have to grab silver, just in case. Although, werewolves shouldn't be an issue because the lunar cycle wasn't right—better to be over-prepared than under. I really didn't like going in so blind. I mean, usually I had days, if not weeks, of research before going into a situation. The wolf element was a completely new dynamic I hadn't considered. I checked the time on my phone. I was running out of daylight. And I had to get back to the Inn for dinner. No more time.

I shoved everything back in the duffel with an anxious impatience that sent shivers up and down my arms. I was twitchy and agitated. Not good.

And as I hurried from my room and out the front door, I called Chris to meet me at the docks in ten—"Bring coffee."

Reluctantly, I stopped by the Inn for Lacey. Satchel swinging, she hopped inside the car for the minute drive to the east shore docks just off Apple Shore Road. I glanced at her as I parked. She'd bundled up in an extra puffy orange coat tugged over jean overalls so baggy they could've been snow pants. "Lacey, are you sure you want to come? You know what I keep telling you about old ghosts..."

Lacey looked at me with a blank stare. "You always take me water witching with you."

I pursed my lips together in a tight line and nodded. This was true...but mostly because I'd given up hope of finding the Witch. And this time was different. Now we knew with great certainty she'd be on Wolf's Rock. At least, if she *was* anywhere...that's where she'd be.

Lacey gave me a serene smile. "The last ghost I met was old, and she wasn't that dangerous. The mawkit was, though. I didn't like that."

"And what about the wolves?"

Lacey frowned as she considered this. "I actually thought about it, and I think as long as we aren't bothering them...they will understand we are here to help them...and they'll leave us alone."

I cocked an eyebrow as I stared at her. "You think a pack of wolves will leave us alone because we're hunting a ghost?"

Lacey nodded simply. "They are trapped on the island with her. You know as well as I do that animals don't like tethered spirits. I bet they'll appreciate the assistance in getting rid of her."

"Huh." Like so much that Lacey said, her logic surprised me. "Well, I don't know about getting rid of her. This is purely observation and documentation. I don't do the hunting thing."

Lacey scrunched her lips to the side as she thought this over. "Hannah seems to think we should be saving people from things in the process."

I made a face. "Who's—oh, you mean that girl from the Rosecrest?"

Lacey bobbed her head. "Yes. I told you. She's my best friend."

I grinned at that. "That's right. I forgot. Well, saving people is great."

Lacey inclined her head. "But you don't want to?"

I snorted at that. "I never thought about it before; I guess I'm of the mindset that people should know...but once they do, they should be responsible enough to deal with it. Like—if you know an area has a lot of crime, lock your doors, right?" I shrugged. Maybe I was selfish. But I was a firm believer in personal owner-ship and responsibility. I had enough trouble keeping my own head above water, how could I even think of saving someone else?

"So, we aren't going to help the Scarlet Witch pass on?" Lacey prompted curiously.

I smiled at that. "Not today. I just need to catch her on the livestream and then we're done. I've got to be back in time for dinner at the Inn."

Lacey nodded sympathetically. "I can't imagine how long it would take to find out what a centuries old ghost wanted..."

"Centuries," I joked. I switched off the car and reached for my duffel in the back. "Ready?"

The two of us got out of the car and headed down the grassy hill to the docks. We didn't have to wait long before Chris's red, white, and blue motorboat, *Steggy*, sped around an isle and came into view. He slowed as he neared the dock and pulled it up against the side, tossing us the rope to tie it to the dock.

Chris had changed out of his uniform into his brown leather jacket and a blue checkered flannel shirt, tugged smartly in his khaki Dickies. I had to smile. I'd told him once that his leather jacket made his eyes pierce my soul, and after that he tended to wear it a lot more often than anything else. Chris Vantine had a unique style in that he was the only island guy that dressed like a grandpa...definitely the only guy above the age of eight to still tuck in his shirt...yet somehow, he pulled it off. And I couldn't lie, he looked good. Heart-skipping hot, if I'm being honest.

He held out his hand for Lacey first, who stepped into the boat with surprising grace considering her marshmallow coat and giant jeans, and the awkward height of the boat in relation to the dock. After Lacey hopped safely inside, Chris smiled down at me with an almost curious crinkle in the corners of his cobalt eyes.

"What?" I smiled awkwardly, my cheeks burning.

Chris just shook his head, his freshly gelled hair slicked smartly to the side, his smile broadening, pressing a dimple into his left cheek. "You look good, that's all. I didn't get to tell you before; I like your lips."

I blinked as my heart fluttered. Then I remembered. I was still wearing the black lipstick. Scowling at myself, I rolled my eyes and held out my hand. "Help me in, Vantine."

Chris laughed and hoisted me up. His arms encircled me and

held me fast. I looked up at him, startled at the closeness. We were basically embracing. Chris met my eyes, the blue glittering with mischief like sunlight glinting off the lake. My eyes dropped to his mouth. He smirked with a cocky confidence that made my scowl deepen. But before I could have the satisfaction of shoving him off me, he let me go.

With the loss of his warmth, the cold lake air swirled around me, and I hugged my ratty sweater tight against myself.

"Coffee'll have to wait until we get back." Chris untied the rope anchoring us to the dock and pointed to a huge rucksack and a duffel bag in the corner of the boat. "And you can drop your stuff here or keep it on you. Whatever. And grab a seat, it's a bit choppy this evening." He eyed me, suspiciously. "Didn't you bring a coat?"

Ignoring him, I took the passenger seat beside the—is it a driver's seat? Captain's seat? And swung my duffel off my shoulder so I could hug it in my lap. Lacey took the seat behind me that faced the back of the boat. I looked at Chris with a sarcastic smile. "Is that a sleeping bag I saw rolled up on your ruck?"

Chris, still standing, revved the boat to life and grinned with that same mischievous glint in his eyes. "Don't get any ideas, Charlebois."

I scoffed, my face heating with embarrassment.

Chris laughed. "Relax. I brought a tent, too. Hold on tight, Lace."

My eyes widened as he gunned the boat and sent Lacey and I jolting back, or in her case forward. Through the wind whipping through the boat, I heard Lacey giggle in delight as we zoomed over waves, bumping along the lake like a skipped rock.

"Chris, we aren't going to need a tent!" I shouted over the lake air blasting us from all sides.

Chris chuckled, his eyes on the water as he steered us around the edge of the east shore, his eyes scanning the surrounding isles as we passed. "You of all people must've seen the Blair Witch Project."

I blinked at that. "But you don't believe in any of it!" I bellowed back over the wind.

Chris smiled. "Hey, before today, I'd never believed in a million years you'd ask me out—and here we are."

I laughed at that. "I didn't—"

He tore his eyes from the water just long enough to fix me with an amused smirk.

"Oh." I guess I had.

Chris jutted his chin toward the water ahead. "Wolf's Rock."

I sat up straighter in the seat, bracing myself with each bump of the waves. There it was. I was so close. Closer than I'd ever been to finding the Scarlet Witch. It was like Christmas in October. I was positively giddy, and Chris could see it on my face. The kind of infectious smile that makes everyone within a five-foot radius happy, too. And I was more than glad to share the joy.

There.

I stood up, grabbing Chris's shoulder for support along with the side of the boat. My grip on him tightened, my black nails digging into his muscles. Then I slapped his arm, barely able to contain my excitement.

"That one!" I shouted through the billowing lake spray. "Right over—yes! Eeee!" He pulled into the shore of Wolf's Rock, slowing and cutting the engine. I bounced up and down, shaking Chris along with me. Lacey giggled, and I jumped on her in a big hug.

Chris jumped out first and guided the boat in as close as he dared before he dropped the anchor. Then I passed him his bags, and Lacey and I used the ladder to climb down. I hadn't thought about getting wet. We'd be soaked for a while. And I didn't bring extra shoes or socks.

As we waded into shore, Chris seemed to read my mind. "Don't worry. I've got socks, too."

I smiled despite the urge to shove him into the lake.

"See? Pays to be prepared. What'd *you* pack, huh? Books?"

I pursed my lips on a smirk and didn't answer. Which was answer enough. Chris laughed as we stumbled onto the rocky beach, finding footing over the mossy slippery black slabs littering the shore.

Once we were far enough on the beach that we weren't at risk of getting wet, but not too near the woods, we stopped while Chris dug for fresh socks. He passed me a pair and then Lacey, but she held up a hand with a small smile. "I have my own." But instead of reaching for her satchel, she reached in the pockets of her jeans and pulled out a sock from each.

After our socks were changed, I felt their eyes on me. I swung my bag off my shoulder and fished out my phone. I switched on the data to check sunset time. Then I turned off the data, locked the phone, and dropped it unceremoniously back into my bag. Then I rummaged inside for my tiny iron blade and my dowsing rod. "Don't lose this." I passed Chris the blade, and he pocketed it without question as I gripped the ends of the rod. "We've got to be fast. Two hours until I need to be back to the Inn." I looked between them: Lacey, patient, wide-eyed and dreamy; Chris, smiling slightly, affection crinkled in the corners of his eyes as he waited. This was it. And I felt pretty lucky to share it with them. I took a breath. "Let's find the Scarlet Witch."

EPISODE 15: IT'S TRUE, SHE LIED

"Water witching is an ancient divination technique in which you use a rod of wood carved into a wishbone-like shape to locate not just water, but precious metals, as well. But, in the paranormal investigative world, we use a charmed dowsing rod to locate human remains." I held up the rod, and Chris angled the phone camera closer so the viewers could see the rod and the intricate carvings etched in the wood as I continued, "These charmed rods are extremely rare and hard to find...but fortunately, I have the Nile witch on retainer. And as most of you know, if we can find the witch's body, her ghost should be close by."

I took Chris's phone from him and panned it around the rocky shore and over to the woodline of Wolf Rock. Then I took a deep breath and turned it on myself, finally revealing my face to the world. "Good evening, Insiders. My name is Jacqueline Jay, and I welcome you Inside My Frozen Heart." Then I turned the camera and pointed it at Lacey. "You all know my good friend and part-time assistant on this channel, but until now you've not seen her, nor have you learned her name...this is the brilliant Lacey McGregor."

Lacey blinked and smiled a bit uncertainly. "So, are people watching this now?"

My heart warmed at her naivety. "Yes, Lacey. Remember it's livestream, so it's basically a window for the world to watch us."

Lacey blinked again. "Wow. Hello. I've never met so many people before..."

I turned the phone back on me. "Lacey has been with me in the background since the beginning, filming and researching and doing all the invisible work that often goes without credit. I'm so excited to finally share her with you all. As true Insiders know, without Lacey, I never would've had the faith and courage to get the channel this far."

"And this..." Then I turned the camera on Chris. "This is your eye candy for the evening. Chris Vantine, newly minted Nile deputy, and unofficial cameraman for Inside My Frozen Heart. He has been kind enough to lend his phone for this livestream. So, everyone in the comments, give him a shout out." I checked the stream of comments and hearts flowing in across the screen. I bit my lip on a smirk. "You've got a lot of fangirls in the comments, Chris."

Chris cocked his head to the side as he struggled to keep a straight face.

"God, look at you!" I laughed and took a step closer, the phone high near his face. "Guys, can you see this? He's blushing."

Chris couldn't contain his grin, his dimples pressed into his cheeks as he looked away. "Come on, Jacqueline..."

"Here he is ladies...Single, hardworking, and willing to hike through haunted woods to help a girl find a ghost. What more could you want?" I backed up and panned the phone around as I circled him. "Striking blue eyes. Sensual mouth. Strong jaw. Dark, Peaky Blinder hair with a gypsy-gangster swagger to match."

Chris laughed and shook his head. "Yeah, okay..."

"Strong enough to tip a cow..."

He folded his arms across his chest and did his best to fix me with a disapproving stare, but his eyes still crinkled with amusement.

"I'm 5'4" so he's gotta be *at least* 5'8"..."

"5'9"," Chris corrected sharply.

"Oops. I forgot how you boys are with your height..." I side-stepped next to him and cuddled in close, flipping the camera around like we were taking a selfie. I leaned my head close against his shoulder as I stared up at the camera and gave a little coy smirk.

He looked down at me almost startled and then up at our faces reflected in the phone raised above us, smiling despite himself.

I giggled. "What made you decide to escort Lacey and me through Wolf's Rock?"

"Well..." Chris cleared his throat and looked pointedly at the camera. "Jacqueline has been trying to take me on a date for months. Ever since my boot camp graduation—what was it two years ago, now?" He glanced down at me. Then he shrugged and looked back at the camera. "Anyways, for years she's been throwing herself at me—like take today, for example—she sped past my speed trap just to get my attention. And before I could give her a ticket, she asked me out *again*. So, I decided, why not give her a chance, hmm?"

My eyes slid sideways, and I pursed my lips tight against a grin.

Chris laughed again and addressed the me in the phone screen. "Seriously, though. I've been a fan of the channel for a while and when you told me you needed a boat—and my phone—*and* when I heard that there could be *wolves* on this island that you neglected to mention...I figured you'd need a little back up from the Nile sheriff's department."

I blinked and looked up at him. I licked my lips as I smiled awkwardly. "You heard about that, huh?"

Chris snorted as he met my gaze. "Yeah. You left out that little detail, didn't you?"

I fluttered my eyelashes innocently and gave him a sweet smile.

He rolled his eyes, but still couldn't hide his grin. "Come on.

Let's get this over with." He gave my head a good-natured shove, and I squealed as I stumbled a bit on the rocks, regaining my footing and turning the camera back on my face with a smile. I whispered loudly to the viewers, "For the record...he's been asking me out since, like, the fifth grade."

Off camera Chris shouted, "It was ninth!"

My eyes glittered as I mouthed, "Ninth." I shook my head and then straightened my face. "Okay. Now you've met the crew, it's time to meet the Witch. Lacey will oversee the livestream. She's Luddite, so bear with her if there are any technical difficulties."

I handed Lacey the phone as I explained, "Okay, it's just like every other recording you've helped me with except this time—it's in real time. So, remember: everyone is watching."

"Like reporters on the news." Lacey nodded as she studied the screen. "I like this, Jacqueline. We should do it like this more often. Oh, look at the hearts. That's nice."

I smiled. "Yeah, well—"

"Oh." Lacey's smile slipped into a furrowed frown. "Why are they putting their thumbs down? That's rude."

I laughed and put a gentle hand on her shoulder. "Ready, Lace?"

She nodded, still frowning down at the screen.

"Okay..." My eyes moved up the rocky shore and stopped at the woods of Wolf's Rock.

It was dark.

And not just from the thick curls of black clouds rolling in across Lake Champlain. The sun was setting and had already disappeared behind Nile. The woods of Wolf's Rock were just a thick wall of timber. Tall trees overgrown and tangled together. The sparse leaves left on the gnarled branches, hanging by thin threads, spun wildly in the gusts that pressed against the isle from the lake. How dark would it be inside the trees? I reached over and toggled on the flashlight for the camera. I glanced at Chris, who had pulled out a flashlight of his own. "Let's go."

I took a tentative step forward.

It was cold.

In the shadow of twilight, so close to the icy water carrying wind along with its whitecaps, I clenched my teeth against the shiver that threatened to rattle my body and disturb my concentration.

Chris clicked on his flashlight as he walked on my left. Lacey shined the camera around on my right. We were ready.

Arms out, dowsing rod ahead of me like a sword, I led the way across the rocky beach and ducked underneath the trees into the woods.

It was quiet.

With a stillness to the silence, broken only by the occasional gentle hiss of leaves as the wind forced its way overhead. I was just grateful for the insolation the wall of timber provided against the chill. With each step it felt like we were passing into another world. An eerie, topsy-turvy kind of world where at any moment a tree with a gnarled face of bark and knots might reach out and grab us. This was it. I knew it. I could feel it in my bones. Deep in my core. The wood of the Scarlet Witch.

But I couldn't focus. Thoughts of Daphne Collins and internet trolls and insults and tarnished reputation keep streaming through my consciousness like a bad film reel. I couldn't block them out. I paused mid-step and closed my eyes. Water witching required total focus. And now I couldn't do it. I couldn't stop the thoughts. My brain wouldn't shut up.

"You okay?" Chris's hand rested on my shoulder as Lacey stepped a little way ahead, her lemon-yellow galoshes rustling in the dead fallen leaves as she scanned the trees with the camera and murmured to the viewers.

I nodded curtly as my hands tightened on the rod.

"You don't have to worry about wolves."

I glanced at Chris in surprise. His face was tinted in the

shadow of twilight. The yellow orange glow highlighting the edges of the trees shined in his striking eyes.

His teeth were a blue-white in the dim as he smiled. "There aren't any here. And if they were here, they wouldn't bother back-packers. But...just in case, I brought my firearm, so we're good."

I squeezed my eyes shut and blinked furiously. "No. I just can't focus. Give me a second." I took a few deep breaths and tried to count the trees, but it was too dark. Darkness had fallen over the lake, and we were just a tiny rock in the middle of a giant black pond. I groaned softly, disgusted with myself. "I'm not worried about wolves...I just...I can't get them out of my head."

Chris inclined his head. "Who?"

I sighed, my jaw tight with impatient frustration, and I tugged him off to the side, out of earshot of Lacey and the view-ers. I took a breath, opened my mouth, then shut it with a hard bite to my bottom lip, holding back. I searched his face, struggling with how much to say...how much of myself to share. And I real-ized, in the crinkle of concern in the corners of his cobalt eyes...I felt safe. Maybe Keirian was right? And, in a moment of desperate lunacy, I blurted, "The Scarlet Witch has been everything to me. *Finding* her has been everything. And now it's all..." Tainted. Infected. Desecrated. I sighed again as I searched for the simplest explanation. "Now it's about proving myself to everyone. Rather than—"

"But you found her already, so..." Chris's words trailed off into a question rather than a statement.

My heart ached with shame at the doubt I deserved. I stared at him blankly in the dusk, my mouth set in a grim line. I didn't bother covering up the lie any longer. But I didn't have the courage to come clean.

"That last episode..." Chris took a step back as though I'd shoved him. He leaned his head down close to me and whispered in harsh disbelief, "Jacqueline, you made that all up? You *faked* it?"

My eyes burned and blurred and then spilled, and I had to look away. I licked my lips and tried to answer, but I couldn't get the words out. So, I bit my lips together and nodded.

Chris cursed under his breath as he glanced at Lacey, a slim shadow a few yards away, examining an ancient oak tree through the phone screen. "All that stuff with the red cloak and the dark hair and the running...it was all a lie."

I sniffed and scowled at the disappointment that sharpened his words. "I made a mistake, okay?"

Chris scoffed. "That wasn't a *mistake*, Jacqueline..."

I shook my head, my temper rising like steam from the shame heating my face. I gritted my teeth on the guilt and resentment that coated my tongue.

Chris Vantine: infantryman, sheriff deputy, Nile Golden Boy, and all around good-man-in-a-storm, was now learning the hard lesson that I'd known to be true all along—Chris Vantine was too good for Nile gutter garbage like Jacqueline Charlebois.

But it just hadn't clicked yet. He was still in denial. So, in true 'good man' fashion, he continued his lecture on morality, "A mistake means you didn't intend to do it. But something tells me all that took some planning."

I snorted. And here's where he would leave me. Never look at me the same. Probably never speak to me again. Well, at least, I could give Keirian a sweet and salty told-you-so.

"*Fine*," I conceded, my voice cool. "I—"

"I can't believe you'd do that." Chris cocked his head as though he were seeing me for the first time. And he was. "Lie to everyone about—"

That was it. He flayed a nerve. I closed the distance between us and jutted my chin up high so our faces were but a breath apart. "Didn't you hear my aunt earlier?"

He stared down at me, and I glared up at the judgment in the shadows on his face. "That's what I do. What I am. Jacqueline the Liar." I shrugged as though I didn't care, my voice rising to make my point heard. "My whole *life* is a lie, Chris. Okay? Why are you so surprised? That's how I've freaking made it this long. How I survive. I tell everybody whatever they want to hear just so they'll leave me *alone*." My voice broke, and the tears poured. And I hated myself for it. So, I turned it on him and snapped nastily, "Like I wish you would've."

Chris grabbed my arm and yanked me into him. I tried to fight him, but he held me fast. I looked up at him, my eyes hard and furious, but he wasn't looking at me. His eyes were scanning the woods.

"Chris—"

"Quiet," he murmured, an order somehow both soft and strong at once.

I mirrored his example and searched the trees.

Then my heart dropped as I saw what he saw.

Or rather, what he didn't see.

"*Where's Lacey?*"

"Lacey!" Chris's shout echoed eerily through the empty forest as he tried again to reach her. "Lacey!"

The leaves hissed all around us in response as the wind passed overhead.

He didn't let me go. One hand clamped around me, the other swinging the flashlight around the dark woods, he hurried us through the wispy dead leaves and ducked us under broken branches and weaved us around trees.

My head couldn't connect with what was happening. Just like back in the orchard with Maddison. Everything was slow. Paused in time. I couldn't let it continue because then what would become of Lacey? Rewind. We needed to rewind and go back, cut out the clip of the argument. Back to Lacey.

Where was Lacey?

"She was right here. At this tree." Chris stopped us in front of it and released me to stand on my own. I swayed where he left me as he spun around.

Then I shook my head and snatched at my duffel. "She has your phone."

I grabbed mine and tapped quickly, mindlessly at the screen. I slapped it against my ear, my whole body shaking trying not to think too far ahead. Trying not to imagine...things. The phone rang and rang. Then Chris's voice message beeped on.

"Try again. We'll listen for the ringtone."

I shook my head. "It's on silent. I put it on silent."

"Maybe she turned it on," Chris snapped back as he continued to scan our wooded surroundings.

"Lacey doesn't know enough about phones to figure that out," I muttered coolly. I dialed the number again. "The most she'd be able to do is answer." I tried again. "Which she isn't," I snapped in frustration.

"Lacey! LACEY!" Chris turned to me, his chest rising and falling rapidly as his breathing increased. "Okay. Okay. She wandered off. So, I gotta find her. First, I'm taking you back to the boat. If I'm not back in twenty minutes, call Joey for a search party. And—"

I scoffed. "Chris, think about it. Somehow, Lacey managed to vanish within the two minutes it took for you to lecture me? I don't think—"

"You can get pretty far in two minutes."

"But *she* wouldn't. Lacey's been in the woods with me hundreds of times. She knows not to walk off. Especially not when..." I swallowed thickly and glanced around at the trees that seemed to lean in on us as though listening.

I took a breath and looked back at Chris. I slapped the phone against his chest. "Here. Keep calling her." I picked up the dowsing rod and held it out in front of me. I closed my eyes for a moment and pictured Lacey, just as she was when she was standing by the oak tree. Then I inhaled deeply and exhaled in equal measure. When I opened my eyes, I could feel the tug, the unmistakable pull of the rod. I took a step forward.

Chris snorted in disgust. "Seriously? After all the—"

I lowered the rod as the force faded with my concentration. "Obviously, the Scarlet Witch took her!"

"Obviously," Chris scoffed sarcastically.

"—which means our best chance of finding her is to find the Witch's body!"

Chris muttered under his breath as his eyes looked over my head into the darkness beyond.

I scowled up at him. "Look, I know you're never going to believe *anything* I say ever again, but this is *real*. And this ghost is *old*. Which means it'll *kill* Lacey at the first hint of provocation. *So, I'd appreciate it—*"

Chris started tapping on my phone, ignoring me.

"She's not going to answer! The Scarlet Witch has her, and we—"

Chris looked up, his eyes shining black in the dying light and the glow of my phone. "The camera's not on you anymore, Jacqueline. It's just you and me. So, you can knock it off now." His eyes dropped back to my phone.

"Well, you can just shove that phone right up your butt!" I spun on my heel and marched away in the direction the rod had pointed, but I didn't get far before Chris's voice stopped me.

"Here."

I turned.

He was still staring down at my phone. Then he held it up for me to see. The livestream. I ran back to him and grabbed the phone from his hands. I slid the bar, fast-forwarding to the oak tree. I lifted my thumb and let it play. My heart harried in my chest, I struggled to steady my breathing. Chris stepped closer to look over my shoulder and the warmth from him calmed me ever so slightly as I watched the camera move up and down the length of the tree. Lacey murmured thoughtfully about the loneliness of the oak tree without any lilylarks to sing it to sleep.

My heart dipped as the picture glitched.

There.

There she was.

The picture glitched again, but the sound still carried. There was a small gasp. That was Lacey, and then a low murmur like a breath, which, if we had the tools to enhance it...we'd hear the Witch. And then the stream ended. And that was it.

Chris cursed under his breath, and he marched away from me, his hand raking through his hair as he glared out at the woods, growing blacker by the minute. I stared down at the phone. There was my proof. I'd found her...well, Lacey had. Everything I'd known in my heart. It was true. And now Lacey was gone. But now I knew for certain I could find her.

I turned off the data, locked the phone, and tucked it away in my bag. I took the dowsing rod and looked at Chris. "I know you don't believe me. But she was there on the stream. And now—"

Chris whirled around, now just an angry shadow in the dark. He marched toward me, closing the distance between us as he flung out a hand at the old oak tree. "All that stream showed us was the tree. It cut out before we could even see what direction she took off in!"

"*Not Lacey*," I snapped back, matching his fury with equal anger, heated by my impatience. "I'm talking about the Scarlet Witch. That was her on the stream. The glitch. The static. That's what happens when you catch paranormal activity on film. And if we're going to have any chance of finding Lacey *alive*, you need to trust me, Chris."

Chris shook his head and looked away, wrestling with himself.

I gripped the dowsing rod and looked in the direction it'd pointed. The trees, like dark stilted shadows, seemed to stare back.

I turned to Chris. "Please?"

"Fine." He nodded, a stiff jerk of his head. "But if we don't find her soon, I'm calling Joey."

"Thank you." I hesitated before giving him further instruction, but it was important. "Now...don't make any sudden movements...or shout out for Lacey if you see her...until I tell you it's safe, okay?"

"What do you mean?" Chris grunted, his patience for me completely tapped.

I took a breath. "*Because*, Chris, please, just—"

"Fine."

The icy bark of his voice cut into me, but I shrugged it off and turned back toward the trees and held out the dowsing rod. It took a second, but there was a gentle tug, like someone was pulling on the end, leading me into the heart of the island, and I followed.

My feet moved slowly, allowing the rod to guide my steps, but the sensation was so faint, I couldn't move too quickly, or I'd mistake my movements for the rod. I was so focused on my body, I wasn't paying attention to our surroundings, but Chris was... suddenly, his hand, gentle but strong, cupped my shoulder and held me back.

I lowered the rod and looked up. There was a shadow standing beside a tree a few yards from us. It wasn't moving. It was still. Still and standing awkwardly straight...and if I had to guess...staring directly ahead.

Staring at us.

The wind breathed heavy through the trees overhead, scratching at the leaves and creaking in the branches, and an ominous shiver scurried along my arms.

"That's Lacey...right?" Chris whispered.

I didn't answer. I couldn't. The truth was...I didn't know.

I stared, wide-eyed at the shadow, fear, primal and raw, prickling underneath my skin. If it was Lacey...why was she just standing there staring at us?

Something wasn't right.

Chris must've felt the same because he moved to step in front of me.

I held his arm back. "Wait," I breathed. The word came out in a cloud of hot air. The temperature had plummeted. Like the whole forest had plunged into winter. There was a hiss that carried through the trees, rustling through the leaves, that I no longer trusted to be the wind. My nails dug into his arm as my heart pounded furiously in my chest.

Chris leaned down so his forehead touched mine, both of us still staring at the thing still staring at us. "I trust you, Jacqueline, okay? Tell me what you need me to do."

I licked my lips and swallowed. "Well, it's either Lacey or the Witch...and if it's Lacey. She could be possessed by the Witch. Or she could be hurt. Or have ghost sickness. Or—"

"Okay, so what do we do," Chris murmured gently.

The calm, steadiness of his question, slowed my thoughts and soothed my heartbeat.

"Remember back when I was nine...you were twelve...we were coming back from shooting those pumpkins...and that rabid raccoon came out of the barn?"

"Mhmm."

"Slow movements. Non-threatening. And do you have the iron that I gave you?"

Chris nodded his head, a strand of hair falling out of place, tickling my forehead.

"Let's go."

I lowered the dowsing rod to my side and took a tentative step forward.

The shadow didn't move.

It stayed frozen in place.

I took another step.

And another. Wincing each time I moved, half expecting the thing to charge from the darkness and rip me to pieces. But it never moved.

When we were close enough to see that it was Lacey, without thinking, I hurried to reach her, closing the distance quickly but stopping short just as fast.

Her back was to us. And now I could see she wasn't straight like I'd thought. Her small shoulders were hunched forward. And her head was lowered like she was looking at the ground, her lily-blonde hair like a white veil shrouding her face in the darkness.

Chris came up beside me. I stepped around to face her. She didn't respond. Gently, I touched her shoulder. Her head snapped up. I flinched away from her.

Lacey blinked at me, her features barely distinguishable in the dark of the forest. Then she inclined her head, her hair falling to the side. "She found me, Jacqueline."

I moved closer and gripped her arms. "Did she hurt you, Lacey? Are you okay?"

Lacey straightened, considering my question. "I can't remember. I can't remember anything."

My heart dipped.

Not good. My eyes burned. *Really* not good.

Chris put a protective arm around her and squeezed. "Well, before whatever-it-was shows its face again..." Chris turned with her back the way we came, escorting Lacey through the woods and toward the shore. "Let's get the heck off this island. We'll stop at the Inn before we take you home. Tree will be able to look you over and—"

I hung back, unable to move, as my mind spun in frantic circles. If Lacey couldn't remember anything, then that meant—

"Actually," Lacey's voice, soft and matter-of-fact as always, interrupted Chris. "I'm starving. Can we eat first?"

EPISODE 17: WHAT'S EATING LACEY MCGREGOR?

"She can't go home, Chris. Not tonight. I'll keep her with me at the Inn."

"What do you mean?" Chris muttered back, his eyes, like mine, trained on Lacey as she sat at the diner booth, swinging her legs under the table while she munched on a taco and flipped through a wildlife magazine, waiting for us to return from the counter with her soda. "Why can't she go home?"

I tore my eyes from Lacey and looked at Chris. "She can't remember what happened."

"So?" Chris's scowl marred his face. "Isn't that a good thing? Or are you just mad that you can't interview her for your channel?"

Clearly, he hadn't forgiven me. His impatience with me was so uncharacteristic of his easygoing nature it put a bad taste in my mouth and soured my mood. I pursed my lips together in a tight pout. "If she can't *remember*...that means the encounter has affected her *physically*. Which means—" I rolled my eyes as I stopped myself from going on a tangent. "Well, it could mean a lot of things. But you saw her eyes!" I hissed as I jutted my head toward Lacey.

Chris's stoney stare softened slightly. "Her eyes are a bit red... maybe she got scared and cried a lot when she saw the thing. *I'm* still not seeing what the problem—"

I took a breath and cut him off. "It's a sign of ghost sickness."

"Ghost sickness?" Chris scoffed, the skepticism crinkled in the corners of his cobalt eyes as he struggled between a smirk and another scowl.

"The Native Americans were the first to diagnose it. But, basically, they say it's something that happens to particularly empathetic people who come in contact with spirits."

Chris's gaze searched my face and then shifted toward Lacey. "She seems fine," he muttered defensively.

"She may be, but I want to keep an eye on her just in case."

"Ghost sickness..." Chris shook his head. The gel in his dark hair was failing and strands were falling into his face. He raked a hand through it as he struggled with himself. "You still haven't told me what it is."

"It is what it sounds like. It's an illness." I shrugged and waved a hand dismissively. "Symptoms include bloodshot eyes, which mimic the effect of excessive crying, and paranoia and hallucinations and suicidal ideations."

Chris looked at me stricken at the thought.

My eyes flicked toward Lacey as she munched on a taco. "Fortunately, increased appetite is *not* a symptom," I quipped.

Chris wasn't laughing. "*Suicidal ideation?*"

I frowned. "Yeah. It isn't good."

"Well, if she has it, how do we, you know, cure her?"

I took another breath and exhaled in a weighted sigh. "I'll have to visit Cassandra Sawyer for a passionflower or chasteberry tonic. If she *has* any. Normally, I'd go to Charlotte Grey...but she's out of town last I checked."

Chris blinked at me and then scoffed. He muttered darkly as he shifted away from me and folded his arms across his chest.

"What?" I snapped, my patience dwindling to match his. "Say it."

Chris's jaw tightened and pulsed as he continued to keep his anger in check. I had to admire him for it. I'd seen boys lose their temper over much less. Men, too. Emotional regulation in males was rare these days. Sheriff Vantine had raised good ones. But I'd known that already, hadn't I?

He ran a hand over his eyes and down his face. Then he met my gaze with a hard stare. Hazel hitting cobalt like steel clashing against ice. "I guess I'll be getting a room at the Inn tonight."

I cocked an eyebrow, humor twitching in the corner of my frown. "You can't. You're not even old enough to drink yet." Then I bit my lip on the smirk creeping up my face. "You'd have to have your daddy do it for you..."

"Guess I will." Chris shrugged as though unbothered by my teasing. But he couldn't keep the gravel out of the timbre of his voice when he continued, "Because I'll be damned if I head home and something happens."

I gave him a playful nudge with my elbow into his arm. "I didn't know you still cared so much."

Chris didn't reply. Instead, he snatched Lacey's soda, pushed off the counter, and headed back over to Lacey, who was finishing her third taco. He slid into the seat opposite her and said something that made her giggle through a big bite of taco.

A ghost of a smile passed across my face as I watched the two of them. Maybe it wasn't ghost sickness. I sniffed in amusement as Lacey reached for her fourth taco and took another giant bite.

Then I checked the clock on the diner wall. Great. I was late for dinner. And now I had the co-op to deal with. I walked back over to our booth and nodded to Lacey. "You ready? You're staying with me tonight."

Lacey inclined her head in question as she continued to crunch her taco.

I gave her a soft smile. "We're having a slumber party tonight at the Inn. We can celebrate your incredible livestream."

Lacey swallowed and returned my smile in kind. But then she frowned thoughtfully. "Will we be able to watch it again?" Then she bounced a bit in the booth as she took another bite of taco and spoke around the mouthful. "I'd like to see what I forgot."

I glanced at Chris before I gave a half-lie. "No. We can't watch it again." Whatever Chris's opinion of me, I wasn't about to disappoint her or worse, trigger her by showing her the footage.

"But come on...we have to stop by Cassandra's first."

"All right. I'm almost finished." Lacey reached for her taco, her eyes wide. "I'm so hungry."

Chris laughed at that. And I smiled, but it didn't quite reach my eyes. For some reason, all I could think was what Memé would say if she saw her...

I turned down the long dirt drive that rolled up a hill to the Rosecrest House, an ancient old Victorian, decrepit and deteriorating before our eyes. Decades ago, the house had been hastily split into four apartments by the monster that'd inhabited the landlady in the interest of finding the best souls to suck, with one in the basement, two in the main house, and a final apartment slapped on the side of the attic with a make-shift fire escape and playhouse door.

We made it up to the house in silence, and I shoved the car in park beside Huck Sawyer's old pickup. There were no other cars in the wide gravel drive, despite the fact that last I counted, five people lived in the place. And the old Victorian herself was dark. The only light came from the soft glow emanating from the tiny rectangular windows of the cellar. The Sawyer's apartment.

I glanced in the rearview at Lacey. "Does Cassandra have a car?"

Lacey nodded, her bloodshot eyes on Huck's truck.

"I'll run down and ask Huck when she'll be back. Okay?"

Lacey nodded. "I'll wait here." Lacey started pawing at the pockets of Chris's rucksack. "Chris, do you have any snacks in this thing?"

I kicked the car door open as Chris helped Lacey find something to eat and I shut it quietly behind me, before running around the side of the house to the cellar.

I hesitated at the top of the stairs. Even in the dark of the moonlight, I could see where the cellar doors had been ripped up to reveal the stairs leading down to the apartment, but it didn't give the place any less of a creepy, dungeon-like feel. A perfect place for a psychic. I rolled my eyes and hurried down the stairs. Lacey. Lacey needed help. I knocked sharply on the door and waited.

After a moment, the door opened, and I dropped my gaze to meet the kind, crinkled eyes of Huck Sawyer. A little man with a warm smile, Southern drawl and gentlemanly charm to match, Huck worked with the horses over at the Kennedy farm, but he also helped with ours on occasion. And whatever negative opinions I had of his wife, I held Huck in the greatest of esteem and affection.

"Jacqueline Jay—are you okay?" He frowned, his large forehead creased in concern.

I forced a smile, but it wouldn't reach my eyes. "Can you tell me when your wife will be home?"

Huck nodded knowingly. "I see...she's driving back from South Carolina. She should be home at first light..." He hesitated as my face fell. "Is there anything I can get for you in the meantime?"

I bit my lip on the request. Huck wouldn't know what to look for, and I wasn't about to go rooting through Cassandra's herb stores without her knowledge. Lacey would be okay until morning... "No. We'll be back in the morning."

Huck nodded again. "If you're sure..."

I bowed my head in thanks. "Have a good night."

Heart sinking, I hiked back up the stairs and headed for the car.

I got us a suite on the only empty floor we had left: the Blue Wing. The plan being: Lacey would stay with Chris while I hurried down to meet the co-op for dinner.

At the mention of the campfire hot dogs and smores, Lacey was adamant that she wanted to tag along, but I managed to convince her that it wouldn't be a good idea. The co-op kids might've seen the livestream...and wouldn't be too happy that I'd taken her instead of them.

The explanation seemed to satisfy her...or rather, the bag of trail mix she'd dug out of Chris's rucksack did. With a simple smile, she plopped on the loveseat in front of the TV and clicked on the remote, before shoving her hand inside the bag.

I turned to leave, and Chris walked me to the door.

He held it open for me, but we paused in the doorway.

His eyes were on Lacey. "So, what am I watching her for?"

"Paranoia. Hallucinations. Excessive crying. Really anything odd...just, you know, call me." I closed my eyes briefly and then rolled them to the ceiling as I cursed quietly. Lacey had lost it during her encounter. "Your phone. God, Chris, I'm so sorry."

He shrugged, clearly unbothered. He looked down at me with a small smirk. "Good thing I've had your number memorized since ninth grade, hmm?"

I smiled at his words as much as the small flutter in my heart. I gestured vaguely around the room, my eyes never leaving his face. "Press nine to make an outgoing call...I'll be back in less than twenty. I just need to make an appearance...and then I'll come get her."

Chris jutted his chin toward me. "What room are you in?"

I batted my eyelashes with a coy simper. "Why? You planning on sneaking over after curfew?" I cocked my head to the side as I searched his face, my eyes glittering as a blush colored his cheeks.

He shook his head, unable to hide the dimple that pressed into his left cheek. "Jacqueline..."

I giggled and gave his chest a shove. "Third floor. Room twelve." Then my smile faded as I remembered. "It'll be *me* sneaking out if anything..." I mumbled more to myself than him.

Chris frowned at that. His forehead creased with pending disapproval. "What do you mean?"

I rolled my eyes. "God, Chris, you think I have a hot date, or something?"

The cobalt in his eyes darkened. He raised his eyebrows with a downturned smirk. "Well, knowing you—"

My face hardened at the insulting implication. "Oh, whatever. Just watch Lacey." I snatched the doorknob away from him. "I'll be back." And I slammed the door in his face.

Honestly, I was jealous of Lacey being able to hide inside the Inn with Chris. Somehow, I had a feeling the girls, Erica in particular, would still expect a trek through the woods to find the Scarlet Witch. Of course, I wouldn't really take them to Wolf's Rock. I'd just pick some random patch of Nile forest and take them on a midnight hike. The idea set a permanent scowl on my face as I marched down the grassy slope to the fire pits. I could see the co-op kids crumpled around one fire with the Moms around another.

Everyone turned as I approached, the glow from the fire running over their faces like ripples in the lake, casting shadows along the angles and making their expressions even more menacing.

I checked in with the Moms and then took a seat on the log beside Patty, who scooted to make sure I had enough room and passed me a stick without question or comment, much less judgment. But the others continued to stare. The weight of their eyes made me shift uncomfortably.

No one spoke.

The fire crackled and hissed in the dark.

Patricia offered me the marshmallow bag. I took one and stabbed it pointedly onto the end of the stick and stuck it in the flames. The smoke billowed up and blurred their faces as the wind, rushing up from the lake in the distance, passed through the camp.

Eyes on my marshmallow, tasted by the fire, I said, "So, I take it you all saw the stream."

There was a murmur amongst them, angry like a buzz tickling my ears.

"It was lame," Allison snapped, ever imaginative.

"You're still taking us out there tonight."

My eyes moved slowly from the marshmallow to Erica. I licked my lips, stalling for time and sampling my words. "Sure."

"And you're going to have to stream it..." Erica added. "I don't know if you've checked the comments, but the live was *weak*. No one is convinced. Majority opinion says you faked it. Again."

I lifted the stick straight up and out of the fire. With a quick breath, I blew out the flames charring my marshmallow. "Wow, Erica, I didn't realize you were so concerned with the reputation of my channel." Carefully, I slid the marshmallow, now black and bubbling, off the stick, waited for it to cool just enough, and popped it into my mouth.

Erica scoffed. "I *don't* care."

I smiled as I swallowed the hot gooey mess. "So, then you're more interested in the cross-promo that a cameo on my livestream would give you..." I snapped my finger as I pointed at her. "Now *that* sounds like the Erica we all admire."

Erica opened her mouth, but all that came out was a little huffing sound.

The boys snickered amongst themselves at our exchange. "Forget about the live. I just want to check it out." Benji shrugged as he held out his hand around the fire for the marshmallow bag. I passed it to him, my mind working fast, trying to think of a way out. Nothing. I had nothing.

"Livestream convinced *me*," Ted announced proudly.

And I had to smile at that. "Oh, yeah, Teddy? You're a believer now?"

Ted flashed a cocky, sideways grin at me from across the fire. "You know me, Jacqueline; I've always been a fan."

From across the firepit, hidden by the flames, Kenneth let out a whoop of agreement.

I grinned and held out my hand for the bag. Benji passed it back with a roguish wink. "Jacqueline's had me at hello..."

Erica scoffed, bristling at the inequitable distribution of male attention. "Whatever. Allison's right. It *was* totally lame. Ooo—it's a bunch of trees. Then an oak tree. Then you lost service." She rolled her eyes. "Yeah, *that'll* keep me up all night."

Natalie and Allison giggled, their heads bent together as they split a bag of chips.

There was an awkward silence which I took as an opportunity to make my exit. I promised Patty I'd meet her back at the room, and then I turned to leave, but Erica's voice made me pause...

"Remember, Jackie—if I don't get a text tonight, you can expect a fine in the morning."

I looked back at her over my shoulder.

"Didn't you realize?" Her azure eyes glowed in the fire light, fluorescent and feral. "That livestream is proof you ditched today."

I gritted my teeth on a retort. I had none. None that weren't derogatory anyway.

She laughed. "See you tonight, Jackie."

EPISODE 18: THE WHITE KNIGHT

"She's asleep?"

Chris nodded as he let me in the room with a gentlemanly wave of his hand and quietly shut the door behind me.

"I called her dad. He was still in the shop with Ed. Told me to remind her about her first research project." Chris chuckled softly as he added, "He seemed pretty excited about grading it for her..."

I smiled at that as I moved toward Lacey. She was slumped over on the loveseat, the empty bag of trail mix crushed in between her little arm and the pillow she was snuggling. Chris had draped a blanket over her. Her lily-blonde hair fell sweetly in her peaceful face.

"She doesn't look like she's having nightmares..." I looked at Chris.

He wasn't watching Lacey; his eyes were on me. "No. No nightmares."

"And nothing out of the ordinary?"

Chris smiled slightly. "Well, she eats more than any girl I've ever met but...no, nothing strange."

I hesitated, unsure of what to do. "I hate to wake her...the Moms could be doing a bed check in an hour."

Chris put his hands in his pockets and shrugged. "You could wait here until then...but I doubt she'll wake up."

"Do you mind if she stays here?"

Chris shook his head. "Her dad said it's fine, and I'm not on duty tomorrow...so I can stay up and watch her. When will you know for sure that she's...not infected, or whatever?"

I bit my lip as I considered this, studying Lacey as though she might start seizing at any moment. Like everything with the paranormal, nothing was certain. All I knew was learned from whispers and rumors. It was an underworld, and knowledge was shrouded in mystery. "I'd say twenty-four hours..."

"Okay. Well, I'll watch her, then. And I'll let you know," Chris murmured, his voice soft and quiet.

I looked up at him, eyes searching his face. The warm weight of his cobalt gaze, the gentle slope of his wide nose, the soft stretch of his mouth, and the strong lines of his square jaw. I didn't want to go. I wanted to be there for Lacey, of course, but there was something else holding me back.

Chris moved nearer. It didn't seem to be intentional; I wasn't even sure whether he'd noticed he had. It was instinctual.

We stood so close, I was highly aware of the height of him, the solidness of his frame, overwhelming my shorter stature and slighter build. Almost wonderingly, my eyes traveled the length of his chest, across his blue-checkered shirt, over the brown jacket snug against his broad shoulders, and for some reason it took every ounce of self-control not to touch the leather. Startled at the urge, I stared up into his eyes, hazel met cobalt, and I couldn't look away. "Thank you for helping her," I murmured, my voice low and breathless.

"Of course," he breathed back.

I didn't move for the door. And he didn't open it for me.

I didn't want to leave. And judging by the crinkle in the corners of his eyes, he knew it.

And that broke the spell. I stepped away from him, instantly cold and alone. More alone than I'd ever felt. I reached for the door, but he took my hand and squeezed it. "Jacqueline…"

I looked back at him in surprise. He licked his lips and smiled almost smugly. "I'd like to take you on that date now."

I blinked. My mouth parted, but I didn't answer. I couldn't. He'd struck me dumb.

He grinned as though I'd consented, and I guess I had because without noticing, I'd smiled back. Again, instinct. Then he gave my hand a gentle tug and pulled me through the sitting room to the dining area and the little table by the window. He guided me to the chair, pulled it out, and with his hand on the small of my back, I dipped slowly into the seat.

Then he went to the loveseat and slipped the remote out from underneath Lacey's pillow and switched it to the music stations. I pursed my lips on a smile as he picked the old jazz station and soft sound of smooth, soulful horns drifted around the room.

"Are you trying to impress me?"

He set the remote down on the coffee table and then straightened and met my eyes. He dipped his head as though he were tipping his hat. "And are you impressed, Miss Charlebois?"

I licked my lips, pressing them together, not trusting myself to speak, and nodded almost shyly in response.

He grinned at that, his cobalt eyes glittering. "Just wait until I ask you to dance."

I laughed in genuine surprise and delight at the idea. But before I could offer a sassy response, he walked to the kitchenette and started up the coffee machine. I tried to temper the grin spreading across my face to a simple smile, but I couldn't keep it contained as I watched him move with calm confidence around the space as though it were his own apartment. For all the hundreds of dates I'd been on, I'd never once been asked to dance. Chris

Vantine was a rare breed, a true gentleman in every sense of the world. I didn't even come close to his caliber or character.

He headed for his rucksack and pulled out two MREs and a few spice jars and a small bottle of oil as though it were a pantry. Then he went to the countertop stove, pulled a pan from the cupboard, and started cooking.

I pushed back in the chair. "Here, let me help."

Chris turned and held out a hand. "Sit, woman."

I blinked, cheeks burning and fighting the paradox of pleasure and pique.

"Now, while you're deciding whether to tease me or scold me, why don't you tell me what you're looking for in a guy?"

I giggled despite myself. "I don't know why you're so interested in me...honestly, Chris."

"What do you mean? How could I not be interested?"

"For starters, I'm a liar."

Without turning to look at me, he nodded slowly as he added the contents of the MREs into the pan. "Sure, you lied. But you're not a *liar*. It's a bad thing you did. Not a bad thing you *are*. Like, I nicked a playing card from Miss Fran's daycare when I was three. Doesn't make me a thief."

I cocked a dubious eyebrow at the weak analogy, but I let him have it. "Well, you have to admit: you don't really know me."

Chris snorted at that and shook his head. I couldn't see his face, but I could tell he had that stupid sideways smirk on his face and his left dimple was creased.

"What? It's true."

Without turning around, he said, "Don't worry, Jacqueline. I know enough." He left the stove and slid a cup underneath the coffee machine.

"Only what I let you," I argued pointedly.

He turned at that, leaning against the counter as the coffee machine at his back whirled and hummed, filling a slow stream of hot brew into the cup. His eyes found mine and held them.

"People let their guard down at home. Because they feel safe. And I'd like to think I'm one of the few people you can count on your hand who you feel at home around. There's Lacey. Zan. That mainland girl, Patty, from your co-op. Your grandmother. And me." Chris jutted his chin toward me in challenge. "Tell me I'm wrong."

"You're wrong."

Chris grinned as his eyes darkened. "Fortunately for me, you aren't as good a liar as you think you are, Jacqueline."

I scoffed at that.

"Well, go on then." He folded his arms across his chest with a smirk. "What don't I know about you?"

Before I could blurt out an answer, he continued, "I know where you live. I know where you work. I know your mom. I know your cat. I know that you hate the cat, but gave him a home anyway because he needed one—"

"I gave him *food*...then he wouldn't leave. I never should've done that," I muttered moodily.

"—Which shows you're compassionate. When you were four you made friends with Portia Molley, at Miss Fran's daycare, but when she made fun of Lacey you didn't talk to her again—"

"Well, she wouldn't stop," I mumbled, defensively.

"—and you made friends with Lacey that same day. Which shows you're kind and honorable—"

"*Honorable*?" I scoffed. "Seriously, Chris?"

"You'd rather spend time with your grandmother than do anything else. You visit her every morning for breakfast and try to make her happy...even if it makes you miserable. Which says you're considerate."

I laughed at that. "What do you mean 'miserable?' Like you said, I love spending time with her."

"Pink, preppy clothes make you scowl."

I giggled despite myself.

"You're a shameless flirt. Love the attention, but are scared to death of commitment. Because...well..." He shrugged as though it were obvious.

"Daddy issues?" I offered, drily with an eyebrow raised.

Chris continued as though I hadn't said anything. "You say your life's ambition is to, how do you say it? 'Expose the truth of the paranormal to the world'...but really, I think you're just looking for connection." Chris held up a finger as he snickered, "Which is funny when you think about it because true connection is the one thing you run fastest from...there's gotta be some kind of word for that..."

I crinkled my nose at the assertion. "What do you mean 'connection?'"

"The Scarlet Witch. She's your ancestor. You're really just looking for family."

My smile faded, replaced by a thoughtful frown as I considered this. It made sense. Maybe.

"And love."

I scoffed at that. "What? How do you figure?"

"Your favorite movie is—"

"*The Blair Witch Project*," I blurted quickly.

Chris paused, his lips pursed on a smirk. He held up a finger. "Ahhh, see, you like to *tell* everyone that's your favorite, but it's actually *How to Lose a Guy in Ten Days*..."

Eyes wide and horrified, I stared at him with my mouth agape. "How did you—"

Chris grinned. "Did you forget I used to work at Nile Video? You rented that DVD, like, once a week."

A ghost of a simper flickered across my face. "You used to leave it behind the counter for me..." I blinked at the memory. But then I jerked back to the present, flustered and embarrassed. "Well, *so?*" I snapped defensively as my face began to heat. "It's funny..."

But to my chagrin, he only smiled at me, that cocky, knowing smile that pierced his left cheek. Then he turned his back on me to fix the coffee.

"I bet you don't know how I take my coffee," I snapped lamely.

"Black."

I scoffed in surprise.

He brought it over to me in a delicate teacup balanced on a saucer and placed it gingerly in front of me. Then he went to brew his own. I stared down at the cup with a small, thoughtful smile. Like everything else about the Inn, the guest room china had been hand selected by my grandmother. It was blue and white. Like hers. The smile slipped.

"What's wrong?" Chris set his teacup and saucer down in front of his seat.

I blinked as my eyes blurred, and I shook my head, cementing the smile onto my face. "It's just been a long day."

Chris shifted where he stood and then spoke in a voice low and heavy with sincerity. "I'm sorry for what I said back on the isle."

I crinkled my nose and waved away his apology. "It's fine. I deserved it."

"No. I was out of line, and—"

"Chris, that's not what's bothering me. It's the coffee."

Chris shifted from one foot to the other and then stuck his hands in his pockets, clearly perplexed. "You got all misty-eyed about the coffee?"

I snorted. "No. The cup. My grandmother's china. She...she has the same ones. They broke today. You know, when—"

Chris's face fell. "Oh. Oh, God, Jacqueline, I was so worried about Lacey, I completely forgot about...have you heard from her?"

"No, and, honestly, I'd rather not talk about it."

Chris opened his mouth to argue, but then shut his mouth and nodded.

I fluttered my eyelashes with a coy simper. "So, do you burn the beef on all your dates? Or just with me?"

"Burn the—?" Chris cursed under his breath as he hurried back to the stove.

I giggled as he struggled to salvage the dinner, and the smell of spices, barbecue sauce, and cooking meat seeped through the suite. "You know, Chris, you need to watch your white knight complex. Not only will it distract you from your cooking, but it could get you in trouble."

Chris scoffed as he shot a sideways smirk over his shoulder at me. "Oh, yeah, how's that?"

But before I had time to answer, Lacey stood up from the couch.

"Hey, Lace, how are you feeling?" I murmured gently.

She didn't answer. Her eyes were on Chris, wide and still as red as before. She looked as though she'd been crying for days. Her hair was a bit disheveled from sleep, sticking up in the back but hanging limp along the sides of her face, and, coupled with her bloodshot eyes and blank stare, she looked a bit deranged. And she still didn't answer me.

Instead, she moved toward Chris with stiff, stilted motions, her lips parted and teeth slightly exposed. It was then I noticed the shine of drool on her chin and pool of it in the corner of her mouth.

"Lacey?" Chris switched off the stove and moved the burnt beef off the heat. He looked from Lacey to me and back again. "Lacey, are you okay?"

I stood up from the chair. The movement was instinctive, defensive, as though my body sensed the unnatural state of her. Sensed danger.

"Lacey!"

It was like she couldn't hear me. Then she lunged for Chris.

I shouted in alarm and rushed forward, but then I stopped. It wasn't Chris she'd gone for. It was the pan of barbecue beef. She bent over the stove and started digging at the meat with her hands.

Her fingers scraping the bottom of the still burning hot pan and shoveling hot, steaming strips soaked in sauce into her mouth.

131

EPISODE 19: MORAL COMPASS, LOST MY WAY

"Wait!" Chris grabbed her wrist and held her back. "Lacey, that's hot!"

Lacey blinked, and her face, mouth burnt and raw around the edges and messy with meat, relaxed as though she'd been sleeping. Then I realized, she had. Lacey'd been sleep-walking.

Chris grabbed the pan and tossed it in the sink. Then gingerly, he pulled her hands toward him as Lacey began to cry. And I couldn't tell whether it was the pain of her burnt hands or from the fear of waking up, but whatever it was, Lacey dissolved into small, delicate sobs that vibrated through her tiny frame.

"It's okay, Lacey. Here." Chris guided Lacey to the faucet and held her hand underneath the cold rush of water. I went for my bag and dug out my bottle of seaberry. I'd picked the potion up from the Nile Witch when I'd thought I'd found a salamander... but unfortunately for me, it'd just been a regular one.

"Try this." With a hand on Lacey's shaking shoulder, I popped the top of the tonic and sprinkled it onto her burnt fingers and rubbed a bit around her mouth and on her chin. Instantly, the potion soothed the burns, and I watched as her raw, bubbling red skin slowly faded back to normal.

Then Chris and I helped her back onto the loveseat, and I sat down with her, hugging her sideways as her cries subsided and her body stilled. Chris stood over the two of us, his face stony and his hands on his hips.

"Were you asleep, Lace?" I murmured gently. "Can you tell me what happened?"

Lacey's lower lip trembled, her bloodshot hazel eyes wide and blinking. "I...I was in the Dream Realm..."

"The Dream Realm?" Chris repeated for clarification.

Lacey looked up at him as though noticing him for the first time. "It's one of the several realms of consciousness." She sniffed loudly and then wiped her nose on her sleeve. "Everyone goes there when they sleep. You didn't know?"

Chris cocked his head to the side, his brow furrowed trying to make sense of what he heard as nonsense.

I waved an impatient hand at him. "She just means she was dreaming. Go on, Lace...what happened?"

Lacey frowned as she studied her healed hands. "I was hungry. So, I went into the kitchen. My grandma was visiting. She was cooking, but she was wearing a red, hooded robe."

"Like the one in the Historical Society?"

"Yes." Lacey's head bobbed, and her voice was a whisper when she asked, "Is she haunting me, Jacqueline?"

I gave her a gentle squeeze and a rueful smile. "No. Lacey. She's not haunting you. And you aren't possessed. But you might have ghost sickness."

"Then I need to see Cassandra." Lacey made to stand up, but I held her back.

"Lacey, she's not home until morning..." I searched her eyes. "We stopped by there on the way to the Inn, remember?"

Lacey inclined her head as she blinked at me. "We did."

I glanced at the clock. It was almost curfew. Great. On top of

Lacey, now I had to take the co-op on a midnight field trip. I turned back to Lacey and forced a smile. "But you don't have to worry...because Chris is going to stay up all night, keeping an eye on you. And I'm—"

"I want to stay with you, Jacqueline." Lacey snatched my hand and held it tight. Surprisingly strong for her small hand. I winced as the rings on my fingers crunched against my bones.

"But..." I struggled to think of an excuse to keep her here. One that wouldn't hurt her feelings or freak her out. I had nothing. "I think you should stay with Chris, Lace."

"Why?" Lacey prompted.

"Because..."

I felt Chris's eyes on me. My face burned with embarrassment. It was like I could hear him in my head—no more lying Jacqueline Jay. "Okay. The thing is...Erica, the short troll with freaky eyes? She's basically blackmailing me."

"What?" Chris's snapped so sharply I flinched.

I glared at him sideways as I continued to give Lacey my explanation, "They want me to take them out after curfew for a ghost hunt on a livestream."

"You're taking them a quarter way across the lake for a—" Chris cursed in disgust as he raked a hand through his hair. He stepped away from us and then paced back to tower over me. He jutted his chin out as he demanded, "With whose boat, hmm?"

I scoffed. "Not yours. You realize how much trouble you'd get in? Sailing a group of high schoolers to a prohibited island in the middle of the night? Isn't that like encouraging the delinquency of a minor, or something?"

Chris's jaw pulsed as he glared at me. "And what would happen if I tipped off the chaperones? And crashed this dumba—"

I fixed him with a cool stare to rival his own. "Then Erica would show them the livestream Lacey helped me film and get me kicked out."

"You hate co-op," Chris muttered.

"Expulsion comes with fines. And the continued cost of tuition. And a lot of other things that I can't afford, okay? You think I *want* to go around—"

"Yes."

I scrunched up my face, lip curled in a sneer. "Excuse me?"

Chris nodded, his jaw set and his eyes dark. "I do. I think you love the attention. And you need more footage to save your channel because we both know Lacey's livestream looked like you cut it on purpose and faked that one, too. So, yeah, I think you—"

Horrified, I tore my eyes from him and looked at Lacey, heart high in my chest, hoping she wouldn't...

But she did.

Her face fell, and her eyes blurred as she blinked at me in question. "You said..."

Chris cursed again, realizing his mistake.

Lacey blinked slowly as though she couldn't understand. Her brow furrowed as she frowned. Then her bloodshot eyes hazed with hurt, and her lower lip trembled again as she breathed, "You lied."

My heart tightened at the hurt in her voice and the pain on her face. I opened my mouth but shut it again. Lacey didn't understand the nuances between white lies and mean lies. There'd be no point in defending myself. I took a breath. "I'm sorry, Lacey. I was worried it might upset you to see it. Make whatever aftereffect worse."

Lacey's eyelashes fluttered, spilling fresh tears down her cheeks, as she looked away from me and stared blankly at the carpet. She sniffed as saline slipped down her upturned nose. "I'd like to stay with Chris tonight." She scooted to the side and then stood from the couch. Without addressing either of us, she said softly, "I think I'll go to bed."

Then she headed for the bedroom off to the side of the kitchen and shut the door behind her. Chris made a move to follow her but hung back. "Shouldn't I be watching her?"

I shrugged and snapped with a bit more venom than I'd intended, "Just sit outside the door." Then I tempered my annoyance and added, "You'll hear something if things get weird."

Chris nodded reluctantly and shoved his hands in his pockets. I fiddled with the holes of my loose-knit sleeves. He didn't grab a chair. I didn't get up to leave. It was again that weird stalemate in which neither of us wanted to change the current standings. And our anger and frustration and something else I couldn't name snapped and buzzed between us in the air like the static before a storm.

My eyes flicked toward the clock. I was running out of time.

But I didn't want to leave.

Things seemed unfinished.

So, I pushed up from the couch and made my way to the sink and started to scrub. I couldn't help Lacey. I couldn't save my channel. I couldn't deal with Chris. But I could do the freaking dishes.

Behind me, Chris made his way over to the table to grab the untouched coffees. I held up a finger in warning. "Don't touch my cup."

He scowled. "It's cold."

"I'll drink it cold. Don't waste the bean juice."

He rolled his eyes and marched up to the sink and dumped it down the drain. "I'll make you more. You're not drinking old coffee."

My mouth twitched as I continued to scrub the pan, torn between irritation and amusement.

For all of his obvious annoyance, Chris had the self-control to set the dishes down delicately on the counter, before stomping off to make fresh coffee.

By the time I'd finished the dishes, Chris had the coffee ready in a neat to-go cup from the cabinet. It was infuriating how hard it was for me to stay angry with him. I took the cup, my palm tingling with the warmth of it.

"Thank you…" Before I could add an apology, Chris crossed the room, heading for the door, and yanked it open for me.

He jutted his head toward the hallway. "Hurry. You'll be late for your curfew."

I studied him for a moment, trying to decide whether he was being protective or just eager to be rid of me. I frowned. It didn't matter. The message was the same: Go.

I scooped up my bag and walked out the door.

I arrived back at our room with minutes to spare. Erica was in the shower. Natalie and Allison were sucked into their phones, decaying on the couch.

"You just missed the bed check," Natalie muttered without looking up. "You're lucky Erica's mom is so clueless."

Ignoring Nat and Allison, I headed for the master bedroom. Patricia was flopped belly-down on our bed, scrolling through YouTube comments. I dropped my butt down beside her. "What are you doing?"

She gave me a weak smile as she looked up at me. "Sorry. I was rewatching the livestream to…you know…get ready for tonight."

I closed my eyes and inhaled deeply, then sighed. "Are you really going to make me take you, too?"

Patty's face fell ever so slightly.

Hurting Patricia was almost as awful as hurting Lacey. Cruel and sadistic at best. My heart dipped with guilt. "It's not that I don't want you there. It's just—Why do you want to come? You *hate* sneaking out. Breaking rules and stuff. It makes you, like, break out in hives."

Patricia pursed her lips into a small pout. "I don't break out in hives."

"You know what I mean. It's bad enough I have to baby-sit all these idiots…I don't want to have to worry about you, too."

Patty dropped her gaze, crestfallen. "I guess I'll stay here, then."

Relief washed over me like the lake across the mossy rocks. I smiled. "Thank you." I nudged her shoulder. "Hey, take it as a compliment. I don't care if Erica gets disemboweled by a ghost. It'd be good for views. But what would I do without Patricia White as my moral compass?"

She smiled at that.

"God, without you, I'd—

She leaned to her side and pulled her phone out of her pocket and slapped it on the bed like an offering. "Borrow someone else's phone for your redemption livestreams?"

I laughed. "That, too." I took her phone and tucked it into my bag.

Patricia nodded toward the laptop. "It's a good thing you're getting this over with. The trolling is getting scary."

"What do you mean?" My eyes moved to the screen.

Patty shut the computer before I could take a peek. "Just...get better footage this time."

I rolled my eyes. "Honestly, that's the last thing I'm worried about right now..."

Patricia turned on her side, propping her head up in her palm to stare up at me. "That's one thing I didn't understand."

"What?"

Patty sat up, then, and was quiet for a moment, struggling with how to word her question. She glanced at me, almost nervously.

My heart sank into my stomach. I knew what was coming. I gritted my teeth waiting for impact.

Patricia cleared her throat and then asked in nearly a whisper, "How come the first time you went in the woods, you got an incredible shot of her, but this time...tonight—the feed cut out?"

I shrugged. "I don't know, Patty."

She was quiet, then. And I didn't bother saying anything else. What else could I say?

My phone buzzed in my pocket, and I hurried to unlock it. It was the Inn's number. Chris was calling already. I answered it, my heart high in my throat. "Hello?"

"Lacey changed her mind," Chris's gruff voice answered. "When can I walk her over?"

"Give me ten minutes," I snapped back.

There was a silence that neither of us wanted to break, but neither of us wanted to end, either.

Then Chris blurted, "She had me order pizza."

I smiled despite myself.

His voice softened. "Do you want me to bring it?"

I bit my lip on a smile. "Sure."

I pocketed the phone, and bellowed loud enough for all the girls to hear: "*Who wants pizza?*"

EPISODE 20: THE BETTER TO BITE YOU

"So, you're telling me you seriously had an encounter with a ghost?" Erica wasted no time in drilling into Lacey for information.

Lacey, meanwhile, took another bite of pizza as she rubbed her bloodshot eyes and merely nodded.

Allison and Natalie exchanged looks as Lacey continued to devour slice after slice. Then Nat quipped, "I thought we were all going to get some..."

I scowled at them and nodded to the pieces in their hands. "You each have one, don't you? Everybody just eat, okay? We still have, like, an hour until midnight, and I would like to get at least a *nap* in before you make me go back out there."

We finished up the pizza, or rather, Lacey finished it. And we all got into bed. Luckily, Lacey was small enough that Patricia and I were able to sandwich her between us in the master bed with a few inches to spare on either side. Lacey was asleep instantly, but Patricia caught my eye across the bed and whispered, "Are you taking Lacey with you?"

I shook my head and whispered back, "I'm going to leave the number to my friend's room on the dresser in case you need help with her." I glanced at Lacey whose mouth hung open as she snored softly into the pillow. I smiled. "But I think she's in a food coma. You shouldn't have any problems."

Patty giggled. "That girl sure can eat. I've never seen anyone eat half a pizza that fast."

"Yeah..." The smile faded faintly from my face.

"What is it?" Patty prompted with a barely stifled yawn. Patty's eyes were half-closed, weighed down by sleepiness.

"Nothing." I smirked. I knew she wouldn't be able to stay up all night. "Go to sleep. I'll be right back."

"You're not leaving yet?"

"No. I just have to check something."

Patricia nodded through another yawn and rolled over, her back to Lacey. I scooted out of bed and went for my books and laptop. I stacked everything in my arms and slipped out the bedroom door, shutting it quietly behind me.

There was something about Lacey's appetite that wasn't right. And it wasn't ghost sickness. I dropped onto the loveseat and dumped the books onto the coffee table and flipped open the laptop and got to work.

A search on increased appetite after ghost encounters...yielded nothing.

I sat back in the cushions and rubbed my hands over my face. Okay. New angle. Supernatural hunger...that didn't even sound like a thing.

GHOSTFACEWASFRAMED

You're up late.

I rolled my eyes at Keirian's Ghostface avatar.

MYFR0ZENHEART

Research. Supernatural hunger. Any ideas?

GHOSTFACEWASFRAMED

Like what kind of hunger we talking? Eat your neighbor's heart out kind of hunger? Or eat out of the trash can hunger?

I snorted.

MYFROZENHEART

Sleepwalk and eat out of a burning hot pan hunger.

GHOSTFACEWASFRAMED

Easy. You know this one. Loup-garou.

Fear trickled over me, tracing goose bumps along the length of my arms and tickled at the back of my neck.

MYFROZENHEART

Doesn't track. Her family history is clear.

GHOSTFACEWASFRAMED

Then, no idea. But I gotta get to bed. Some of us actually have school...

MYFROZENHEART

Lol

But I wasn't. The word loup-garou glared at me on the screen.

GHOSTFACEWASFRAMED

Nice live by the way. You were you. Authentic and real. I'm proud of you. The boyfriend suits you, too.

I glared down at the screen. I didn't have time for this.

MYFROZENHEART

What are the tests for a loup-garou?

GHOSTFACEWASFRAMED

Eh...I don't know, Jax. They're so rare...

MYFROZENHEART

Can't trust any of the theories.

GHOSTFACEWASFRAMED

Exactly. Just—if it's final girl time? Fire.

Then he was gone.

I shut the laptop, my stomach sick and sour with nerves. It had to be something else. Loup-garou were originally found in Canada during the early settlement by the French. A Canadian witch, frustrated by the immorality of some of the filles du roi, created a blood curse in which the afflicted would age naturally as a human up until an eventual transform into a wolf-like monster consumed with a rabid, insatiable hunger which led to the consumption of their own young.

But Lacey wasn't a monster. She'd been infected by the ghost. I needed to focus. That was the key...what affects ghosts could have on people. I skimmed through the book on spirits and stopped at the section on encounters. It listed all the different ailments that one might develop following a spectral experience. Ghost sickness...no. Possession...no. Lacey'd been sleeping, not controlled by the witch. Haunting...no. Mirroring. I frowned and paused on that heading. *Mirroring: The infected displays symptoms similar to those in which the ghost experienced leading up to and during their death. Ex: if the ghost in question was stabbed, the infected could possibly present with unexplained stab wounds identical to those inflicted—*

A scream pierced my ears and sent me jumping up from the loveseat. Heart high in my chest, I ran for the master bedroom. The other girls must not have been sleeping, either, for all three of them tumbled out of their room. I held out my hand. "Get back in that room, or I will lock you in myself."

I don't know whether it was the words, the tone, or my face, but the three of them obeyed without comment and scrambled back into their room and shut the door.

I went for mine. With a deep gulp of air, I yanked open the door and froze.

Lacey was crouching on the bed, knees and arms bent, her mouth dripping black in the dark, her bloodshot eyes shining in the dark of the moonlit room as she stared at me.

My eyes quickly scanned the room for Patty. "Patricia?" I asked in as steady and low a voice as I could manage. I didn't want to spook Lacey, who was still crouched and posed to jump from the bed at any second.

A small squeak came from the floor on the opposite side of the bed.

I swallowed. All right. Patricia was at least conscious enough to respond. One down. I took a tentative step forward, testing my theory. "Lacey?"

She continued to stare as though she hadn't heard me. Just like before, she was sleeping. I ran for her, then, and seized her arm, yanking her butt back down onto the bed. "Lacey! Wake up!"

She went limp and then grabbed at me. Pulling at my arms. Panting hard and gasping as she roused from her nightmare. "Jacqueline! Jacqueline! It was awful! I was so hungry and then..." Her hold on me stiffened and then loosened.

"Lacey...don't—"

But she reached for her face, her fingers smearing the blood on her chin, and she dissolved into sobs. I hugged her tight, my heart breaking for her, and rocked her rapidly on the bed.

"Patty?"

A tearful mumble answered me from the floor.

My eyes blurred at the horror of the situation. One friend tormented, the other tortured. "Grab my bag and find the makeup kit. Pull out the bottle marked bungleweed and put it on your bite."

Patty rose unsteadily from behind the bed, clutching her shoulder as blood oozed from between her fingers. She stumbled for the bag and managed to find the bottle and dumped it on her gaping wound. Instantly, as before with Carol Anne, the blood began to clot, and the flesh began to heal.

Patricia gasped in wonder as she stared down at her shoulder, her fingers moving over the freshly formed skin. She ran for the light and switched it on. I blinked as my eyes adjusted to the harsh transition.

"Oh my God. I'm...I'm fine! It's—it's totally fine."

"Good. That's good, Patty..."

"Jacqueline, what's wrong with her...is she—"

"She's fine. She—she'll be fine. She—"

"Am I going to turn into a vampire or something?" Patricia demanded her voice rising high.

"No! No," I repeated firmly. "It's nothing like that, Patty. She —She was just having a nightmare...Patty, is there any potion left in the bottle?" I asked, trying to keep the annoyance out of my voice. If Lacey was going to keep on chomping chunks out of people, I'd need it. And it wasn't like I could get another bottle at the grocery store.

"Uhh...a little?" Patricia stoppered the tonic with a guilty wince. I gritted my teeth, struggling to maintain my patience and perspective. But it was hard. Patricia put the bottle down on the dresser and then positioned herself as far from Lacey and I as she could, watching the scene awkwardly.

"Lacey? I'm going to help you into the shower, and after we get you cleaned up, we're going to Cassandra's, okay?"

She didn't answer. Her little body simply shook with her tears. I took her silence as agreement and helped her off the bed and guided her toward the bathroom. "Patricia, call the number on the dresser and tell him to meet me out by my car. And make sure those girls stay put in their room until I get out."

I shut the bathroom door and sat Lacey on the edge of the garden tub. Then I started the shower, sticking my hand under to test the temperature. I looked back at Lacey. She was hugging herself and rocking back and forth, muttering softly.

I reached for a hand towel and soaked it with the fresh, steamy shower stream. Then I bent down at her feet and gingerly wiped away the blood from her chin and around her mouth. Lacey just stared ahead, her bloodshot eyes dull and glassy. My heart ached for her and guilt seeped into my stomach, making me sick. I never should have let her come to Wolf's Rock. I left her side, back for the sink. I needed to clean her mouth. I grabbed Patricia's toothpaste and a plastic cup from the counter and filled it with water. Then I held out the toothpaste for her inspection. "I'm going to squirt this in your mouth. You sip the water, and you can spit it back out after. Okay?"

Lacey eyed the toothpaste like I was offering her something poisonous. She shook her head furiously and then looked up at me. "I can't. I don't want it. I...Jacqueline, I'm so hungry."

I searched her reddened eyes, and my heart dropped. I lowered the toothpaste. She was afraid she'd eat it. The toothpaste. She was so hungry. I nodded my understanding, eyes blurring.

"That's okay, Lacey. That's okay. Here." I set the cup down on the tub and tossed the toothpaste back on the counter. Then I pulled her to her feet and toward the shower. Lacey stepped into the shower fully clothed, her clothes soaking and clingy to her tiny frame. She lifted her face up to the water and cried.

By the time I got Lacey cleaned and changed into fresh clothes borrowed from Patty, Chris had called twice. But even though I hadn't answered, he was waiting at my car just as I'd requested. When we approached him, me with an arm around Lacey, hugging her tight to my side, his face set in a hard mask. "What happened?"

I tossed the keys to him as I narrowed my eyes and shot him a warning glare with the smallest hint of a headshake. But Lacey was Lacey, and she answered softly but bluntly, "I was in the Dream Realm...and I tried to eat Jacqueline's friend."

I gave Lacey a squeeze and helped her into the back seat of my car and slid in beside her. Chris hopped in the driver's seat and revved up my car and sped us out of the Inn parking lot and down Apple Shore Drive toward the Rosecrest House.

When we pulled into the driveway of the creepy old Victorian, I eyed the house warily. We did not need any more paranormal problems tonight. As though reading my mind, Lacey murmured, "The mawkit's gone. You don't have to worry."

The mawkit—essentially a soul-eating mirror worm—had lurked in the mirrors of the Rosecrest for decades until Hannah Green had supposedly killed it. But I still didn't trust the house. We all got out of the car and headed for the back of the building and down the cellar to Cassandra's apartment. Before we could ring the doorbell, Cassandra threw the door open, casting us in the happy glow of her hundreds of candles.

"Huck said you wouldn't be here until the morning. What's happened? Oh, my gosh, Lacey, come in." Like some kind of scarlet-haired elven character from a renaissance fair, Cassandra Sawyer was a walking cliche. All she needed was the pointy ears.

Ignoring me, Cassandra practically flew to Lacey, the skirts and folds of her sapphire gown fanned about her as she descended on Lacey, nearly scooping her up into her arms and ushering her inside the apartment.

Chris hesitated in the doorway. I scowled and tugged him in after me. If I was going to have to put up with the woman, the least he could do was stand there and look pretty. And I muttered as much to him under my breath before hissing, "Watch out for the snake."

"What?!" Chris yelped, yanking himself from my grip.

I snatched him again and shoved him in front of me through the jungle of plants Cassandra kept all over her living room, and probably throughout the entirety of her apartment. It was impossible to see anything beyond the living room; the whole space was covered in leafy green. It reminded me of Lacey's cabin in that the furniture of Cassandra's place was wooden and cozy, but instead of lamps everywhere, there were candles: thick, short tapers, tall, skinny ones, all different shapes and sizes scattered about the place and peeking out from behind overhanging leaves.

Cassandra sat with Lacey down on the couch covered with too many mismatched cushions, cupping Lacey's head in her hand, cradling her against her bosom like a mother with a sick toddler. She stroked Lacey's damp hair and began to hum a soft melody as she rested her chin on Lacey's head.

"You're Jacqueline Charlebois, I take it?" Cassandra didn't bother looking at either of us, her attention was solely focused on Lacey. "Why don't you explain to me exactly what kind of situation we're dealing with here?"

I frowned at her tone.

Chris cleared his throat and started, "We were in the woods and—"

"Lacey had an encounter with the Scarlet Witch," I interrupted.

"The Scarlet Witch?" Cassandra's sharp green eyes shifted up to meet mine, but she didn't loosen her grip on Lacey. "You've found her? What is she?"

"No idea."

Cassandra scoffed. "So, the three of you went walking around looking for a centuries-old creature that for all you know could be an actual, *living*, wicked witch...with no idea of what might become of you?" Cassandra cursed under her breath and continued humming into Lacey's wet hair.

I scowled. "I know more about her than anybody. She's more than likely a ghost. Killed by a wolf and haunting Wolf's Rock looking for her grandmother. And I didn't go into it blindly; I know what I'm doing—"

"*Oh, it certainly seems—*"

Chris held up his hand between us. "Ladies, can we put away whatever grudge we have going on here and focus on Lacey, please?"

Cassandra looked at Chris for the first time. "You must be one of the Vantine twins. The eldest. You shoulder the weight of your father's expectations well. You have a good aura. Much better than that one. She's murky and cold. It'll take a true golden heart to warm her frozen one."

I blinked at her words, shifting uncomfortably where I stood, tugging at my tattered sweater.

Cassandra pulled back from Lacey so she could look deep into her eyes. She made a little gasping sigh before smoothing her thumb across Lacey's cheek. "Lacey, I'm guessing you don't remember the encounter?"

Lacey shook her head.

Cassandra nodded grimly. "She doesn't have ghost sickness. But her aura isn't hers. She's mirroring the ghost."

"What does that mean?" Chris asked quickly.

I rolled my eyes. "Mirroring is an *extremely* rare side-effect of an encounter—much more uncommon than ghost sickness, by the way—" I held up my finger to punctuate my point at the lunacy of the suggestion as I continued, "in which the affected suffers through the same symptoms that caused the ghost's death."

Chris's face crinkled with irritation and impatience. "But the Scarlet Witch was killed by a wolf, right? So..."

"Exactly. If Lacey was mirroring that—"

"And how do you know that's how the Witch died, Mr. Vantine?" Cassandra countered gently.

"—she'd have scratches and bite marks on her...not, like, *turn into* a wolf..." My voice trailed off, and my eyes went to Lacey. The connections were snapping in my brain as I slowly began to process what was happening. My heart pumped furiously against my chest, and my lungs tightened, constricting my air. There was no way...

But before I could catch a breath and organize my thoughts, Cassandra helped Lacey to a cup of tea and wrapped a heavy blanket around her, then with a flutter of her oversized sleeves, she practically shooed Chris and I to the door. "Lacey doesn't have much time. If I'm correct—which I am—she won't have long until her condition is fatal. And the only way to cure whatever aliment she contracted from the ghost for certain is to—"

"Kill the ghost," I blurted bluntly.

"—*pass it on*," Cassandra finished firmly. "I will keep Lacey safe and comfortable. You better handle this thing."

Chris started to protest his confusion, but Cassandra as good as shoved him out the door. "Hurry." Then she fixed her eyes on me. "You should know...your deceptive, deceitful personality isn't the only thing clouding up your aura, Miss Charlebois."

I blinked stupidly at her as I touched my head; it hurt too much to think straight, much less understand self-important, psychic mumbo jumbo. "What?"

"There's a taint in your aura. From a blood curse."

EPISODE 21: LIKE MONSTER, LIKE DAUGHTER

I laughed. "A blood curse?"

Cassandra nodded coolly. "After you deal with this ghost business and save Lacey, you come back here for her, and I'll see whether I can help you."

I shook my head in disgust. "You don't have to *threaten me* to save Lacey. I'm going to get this handled. You just make sure she doesn't hurt herself."

I turned on my heel and stomped up the stairs and into the night, with Chris hurrying up after me.

"I need to stop at my house first," I snapped over my shoulder as I marched around the Rosecrest, looming old and ominous overhead, toward my car.

Chris didn't object nor question the detour as we both wrenched open the car doors and dropped inside, the old junker bobbing slightly on its tires with the weight of us.

I was quiet in the ten-minute drive through the heart of the island, into the woods, and down the short, twisty dirt drive to my hovel of a home.

I slammed the car in park and sat for a moment. My eyes moving from Mom's car toward the house. Chris was an islander.

He knew where I lived. Otherwise, I'd be embarrassed. Instead, I was just bitter, because what he didn't know...or if he did, he pretended not, too, was what awaited me inside.

Whenever my mom was home...I would either walk into a quiet house punctuated by soft, gentle snores or some kind of emotional confrontation fueled by, and clouded with, alcohol fumes. I prayed for the former as I took a moment to steel myself against the latter.

Chris hadn't bothered me the whole ride there...probably to prevent me from reckless road rage...but after we were safely parked, and I was quiet for a moment, staring at my house, he cleared his throat and asked, "What's a blood curse? Is it like a disease or—"

"Oh, my God!" I twisted in the seat to glare at him. "Chris, that woman was just trying to scare me into helping Lacey. Which is insulting in and of itself." I rolled my eyes in disgust. "Of course, I'm going to help Lacey. Which means we need to deal with the ghost. That's why I have to stop here first...iron and salt, fire and holy water. White rose oil is best...but that's a lot more —" I bit my lip on the word expensive, and quickly cleared my throat. "Iron and salt to repel the spirit. Holy water and fire to burn the bones...or whatever it is that's tying her here..." I lowered my voice as I muttered more to myself than to Chris, "It *better* be her bones...like I need more women with emotional issues..." My eyes flicked to the radio clock and then back at my house. There was a low light glowing softly in the dark. Probably the oven. She'd better be asleep. I was in no mood to coddle her tonight.

Chris sat with me in the quiet another moment then tried again, "But what *is* a blood curse?"

I groaned high and loud, nearly shrieking at him in exasperation. "Oh, I don't know, Chris, what's it sound like? It's a curse on a family. On their bloodline. But according to what I've read, only witch families can have blood curses, and in case you haven't noticed—" I flung a hand down the length of my torso. "*Not a witch.*"

Chris hesitated. He opened his mouth and then shut it again, scowling thoughtfully.

I closed my eyes as I sighed, a low rumble in my chest. "What, Chris?"

"I thought your grandmother always told you that you *were*... isn't that the whole thing, that you're related to the Scarlet Witch?"

I glanced at him sideways, jutting my jaw to the side in frustration. It was like the attack on Lacey had kind of knocked my rose-colored glasses askew. "Chris...my grandmother says a lot of things. Just like I do. We like to believe we're special." I winced and squinted my eyes tight. Then I shrugged. "But we aren't. We just make things up to make us look interesting. The truth is, we're actually pretty boring—with perfectly ordinary smiles," I added spitefully as I glared back at the house. "Now, if you don't mind, I have a ghost to hunt. So, just wait here, and I'll be right back."

"But—"

I didn't wait. I slammed the door and stalked up the walk to my front porch and fumbled for my key to unlock the door. But as I stabbed the key toward the knob, the door pushed open. I closed my eyes as I groaned inwardly. She didn't even shut the door. Not a good sign.

I slipped inside and shut it quietly behind me.

And there she was.

Sitting at the tiny kitchen table, her head in her hands. She turned toward me slowly, still cradling her head as she stared at me with bloodshot eyes. Her cheeks, wet with saline, shined in the oven light as she blinked stupidly at me.

"Go to bed," I snapped coolly as I passed through the room toward my door without looking at her. I hated her drinking. She knew this. But she wouldn't stop. She just tried to hide it. Lie about it.

The chair scraped back as she scrambled up to grab ahold of my arm and pull me back. She twisted me around to face her, her hands gripping my arms tight, her nails digging into me like teeth. My nose crinkled at the stench of her, the alcohol seeping from her pores like sweat.

She gave me a hard shake that rattled my head as she staggered slightly with the motion. "*Did you do it?*"

I winced at her words...not because of their tone...but because of her voice. Her voice was never hers when she was drunk. The sound of it turned my stomach and made my skin itch. I glared at her. Unflinching in the face of her obvious distress. "Go to bed. You're drunk."

"What? I'm not." She tried to scoff and laugh it off, scrunching up her face like I was crazy and evidently forgetting her previous dismay. Covering the lie, saving face, was more important than anything else.

"Your lips are purple," I said in a voice cold and deadpan.

She licked them instinctively as she blinked, her face blank with feign innocence. "I was eating some of your bubblegum. You know, the grape kind...the kind that you get at the gas station; you love that kind—"

"Go to bed," I repeated, words wavering with hurt as my eyes blurred. And in that moment, I hated myself for breaking.

She stroked my arms lovingly as she smiled, her eyes ardent and wet with emotion. "No, no, sweetie, I'm fine. Let's sit and—"

"I'm working. *Go to bed.*" I made a move to turn, but she held fast, her nails biting into me once more.

"No!"

I looked at her, surprised by her outburst.

She shook me again, violently. Her expression darkened, marred with anger as tears flowed freely from her eyes. "No! No more of that! I'm putting a stop to it right now!"

My eyes narrowed as I searched her face. "What are you talking about?"

"*I know what you did*!" she shrieked in my face, spit and snot and tears sprinkling over me. "You filmed that dead girl and posted it on the internet!"

She might as well have slapped me. It hit the same. Anger heated behind my eyes, and I took a step toward her. "You don't know *anything* about *anything* I do," I said, my voice slow and cold.

"People are saying you killed that girl! Why are they saying that, Jacqueline?" she slurred, gasping desperately as though she couldn't remember how to breathe.

I rolled my eyes to the side and stared hard at the wine bottle half-hidden behind the kitchen chair, struggling between hurt and hate, disgust and pity. "It's true, Mom," I droned, dull with sarcasm. My eyes shifted back to give her a deadpan stare. "I'm a satanist, haven't you heard? I sacrificed one of the sweetest people on the island for the love of the Devil."

Anger and contempt contorted her face as her hands squeezed me harder still. "Don't you mock me. This is serious! Everyone is saying—"

"And that's all we care about, isn't it, Mommy? Keeping up appearances, the both of us. Make sure nobody sees us for what we are." I jutted my chin toward the kitchen. "Living in a shack. Barely speaking. Strangers more than anything else."

She blinked stupidly. "We're not strangers..."

"You're too busy swimming in your pain to look up and see what's going on with your own child." I scoffed, lip curled cruelly. "Instead of coming to me...*asking* me...talking to *me*, you take the word of the island gossip as truth and throw it in my face."

"I know all you care about is that stupid computer! You're on it for hours upon hours into the night! Who knows what you've gotten into? Internet chat rooms and dark web searches!"

I snorted at that. "I guess I need to change my passwords again, huh?"

"I don't know you anymore! Making videos of dead little girls for attention?! That's monstrous! You're a *monster*, Jacqueline!"

I laughed as though she were a joke. Because she was. We *both* were. She used booze, I used the internet...lying to ourselves, distracting ourselves from the painful truth that we weren't special. Not even a little bit. Not at all.

If we were, my dad wouldn't have left, would he?

Sure, maybe my logic was flawed. It'd been a long freaking day. But one thing was certain—unlike my mother, at least I was trying to change. I shoved her off me, and she stumbled back, more from the alcohol in her blood and her desperate need for dramatics than the actual force of my push. "Now, for the last time, go to bed."

I kicked open my bedroom door and grabbed my stuff and stalked back outside into the night. I yanked open the car door and dropped inside before slamming the door hard after me.

I felt Chris's eyes on me, but I stared pointedly ahead at my pathetic little shack, nestled in the gloom.

"Are you okay?"

"I'm going to need your boat."

EPISODE 22: LOW-BUDGET GHOST HUNT

We made plans to meet at the docks just like we had before, but this time I gave Chris a laundry list of things to grab while I headed back to the Inn to collect my stuff. After the Lacey situation, I'd left everything in the suite. And if I was going to actually hunt a ghost, I might as well record it at the same time.

But I tried not to think too much about it. *Hunting* a ghost was a lot different than *documenting* one. Of course, I'd heard of hunters, like Lacey's friend, Hannah...people that wasted their lives slaying monsters like it was the sixth century or something. And I had no interest in being one of them. I was happy to research, observe, take notes...but if it meant saving Lacey, of course, I would take care of it. And it doesn't take a genius to kill a ghost. Find out what's tying the ghost—hopefully the bones—and then cut the string. Or rather, burn it.

Easy.

Hopefully.

I slipped inside the suite, eyes squinted, praying the girls had all gone to bed...but of course, they hadn't. All three of them were sitting around the living room...but only Erica was fully dressed.

As soon as I entered the room, she stood up. "You owe me a ghost encounter. Are you ready? The boys are already waiting outside down by the firepits playing with Ted's firecrackers. Did you hear them?"

"No," I snapped as I stomped toward the master bedroom. Patricia was sleeping—which honestly didn't surprise me; she was always the first to crash at a sleepover—so, I did my best to be quiet as I organized my things and packed up my backpack. And did my best to ignore Erica, who lurked in the doorway, watching me.

"Plans have changed, Erica," I whispered as I loaded up my bag. "I can't take anybody."

"Why? Because your pizza-scarfing little freak of a friend attacked Patty?"

I rolled my eyes, but didn't take the bait.

"Yeah, we all heard. It took some time, but Patty cracked. Natalie and Allison are out, but I'm not."

I ignored her as I continued to pack.

"You are taking me," Erica snapped in a high-pitched whine.

I gritted my teeth tight until my jaw cracked. I double-checked everything. I was missing the bungleweed.

"Jackie! Hellooo! *You still have to take me*. I told you. I'll tell the Moms, and you'll—"

I slapped the bungleweed down into the depths of my bag as I looked at her sharply. "I don't care, Erica, okay?" I hissed. "Do whatever you want. But it's too dangerous to take anybody, and I need to get this done."

"If you don't take me—I'll tell the Moms now, and *they* will stop you for sure."

My hand froze just above the backpack. I lowered it to my side and turned slowly to stare at her with murder in my eyes. I stepped toward her, movements calm and deliberate, until I was nearly nose to nose with her. "If you try to stop me, I swear to God, Erica, I will—"

"Then Natalie will call the cops—"

I laughed. "You think I'm scared of the—"

"—and tell them that that dude you hang out with kidnapped you. He's over eighteen, isn't he? That means jail time, doesn't it? At least until they figure out what's what." She gave a careless one shouldered shrug.

My fists clenched at my sides. I wanted to hit her. Slap the smirk of her snooty face. God, I wanted to smash her stupid nose into her skull.

But I didn't.

"Fine." I took a step back with a little shrug. "I'll let the Scarlet Witch handle you."

I turned on my heel and went back to my backpack, but not before I saw the tremor of fear flicker across her face.

And I smiled.

We all met at my car and piled inside, but before I started it, I looked at all of them in turn. "Like I told you before—this ghost is bad, okay? Also, *like I explained before*—this ghost is centuries old. Which means she'll be pretty feral and nasty to deal with. And probably quick to kill if you look at her wrong. But there's something else you should know... This ghost doesn't just want to hurt you, it infects you with a paranormal illness. And if you catch it, it's fatal. So, last chance to back out. Because if you act stupid, I'm not going to save you..."

The boys laughed as they exchanged excited looks and then all buckled their seatbelts. Erica, who sat stifling in the passenger seat, eyed me coolly before snapping the buckle into place.

I gave a one-shouldered shrug before sticking the keys in the car and revving the engine. "Your funeral. And I'm not coming."

If Chris was surprised at the posse I had tagging along behind me, he didn't comment on it. But, by the tight line of his jaw and the darkness in his eyes, I knew he wasn't happy. By the time we moored on the shore of Wolf's Rock, everyone had gone quiet. The air of the place was even more menacing and creepy than it'd been in the purple and orange of twilight. The boys stood awkwardly on shore with Erica as the four of them continued to eye the woods anxiously.

I tugged Chris off to the side and out of earshot of them. "I'm sorry for the crowd. They threatened to call your daddy on you."

Chris snorted and shook his head. "Yeah, they don't look like the kind of kids that get told 'no' a lot."

I smiled. "Yeah, no." Then I bit my lip before launching into the plan. "You are the only one I trust to not only be helpful but to save my butt in a crisis."

Chris chuckled quietly. "Why, Jacqueline Charlebois, you flatter me."

I gave him a gentle nudge. "Well, you've got the whole white knight thing down," I teased. Then I cleared my throat and got serious. "But here's the idea—the dowsing rod will lead us to the Witch's bones. The closer we get to her bones, the more she's going to mess with us, and the worse it'll get." I reached into my bag and fished around for one of the three bottles of holy water. I pressed it in his hand. "Holy water. You sprinkle some of this on the bones. Salt them..." I handed him my second can of salt along with a lighter. "And burn them, just like your MRE."

Chris smirked as he tucked the offerings away in his ruck.

"In the event that I am dead, or otherwise incapacitated, it'll be up to *you* to end it. Okay? You are officially my second."

Chris started to argue, but I waved a careless hand. "Now...you have the crowbars I requested?"

Chris slapped a hand to his ruck. "I could only find three..."

"That'll do." I glanced at the co-op kids with a grimace. "All right. Come on..."

I headed for the huddle, and they fanned out to form a semi-circle around me.

First, I swung my backpack around, and I pulled out my old camcorder and passed it to Benji.

"Just like that film you guys did on skateboard culture. Think of it like a documentary."

Benji grinned at that. "Sure thing, boss babe." He switched on the night vision with expert accuracy and held it up to capture my eye roll. "Gotta love the retro tech."

I smiled. "Right?"

"She only has that because she's too poor to afford anything else," Erica mumbled under her breath as she fumbled in her purse for her phone.

Before she could unlock it and start her own stream, I snatched it out of her hands. "No video." I scanned the kids gathered around me like overeager puppies with a weary scowl. "No phones. I'm not kidding, and I'm not exaggerating just to freak you out—"

"Not lying, either?" Erica scoffed.

I ignored her and continued, my eyes moving from face to face and meeting each eye with a severity I hoped would hammer my message home, "Chances are...someone's going to get hurt. Ghosts don't like it when you try to kill them. And I'm not about to have one of you accidentally stream a snuff film or something."

"You mean like you did with that Rose girl?" Erica murmured icily.

I lunged for her, but Chris held me back. Before I could shove him off me, Chris nodded toward Erica, "Did you watch it? Did you watch the whole episode?"

Erica hesitated.

"There wasn't a sweeter person than Maddison Rose...and what was done to her..." Chris's hold on me tightened as he shook his head. "Maddie deserved recognition for what she did, and Jacqueline made sure she got it."

"What'd she do?"

Benji broke in then. "She sold her soul to the Devil to save her little sister."

Emboldened by his buddy, Kenneth added, quickly, "And everyone was saying Maddison was the reason for the crash that put her sister in the hospital, but if you actually watch the episode, you know that wasn't her fault, either."

Chris's hold on me loosened, and I shrugged him off.

"Uhh." Ted cleared his throat. "This is all interesting and everything, but can we go back to what you said before? We are going to kill it? The Witch...like, we're going in there to kill a ghost?"

I eyed Ted wearily. "Yes. We're going to kill it."

"I thought you were only about documenting, and—"

I sighed heavily. "I was, and I am. But not in this case. Things have changed. My friend Lacey was infected. And the only way to make sure she doesn't die is to kill the ghost first. So, if any of you have issues with that, wait in the boat." I didn't wait for their consensus. I turned to Chris, who was silent at my side, standing tall like a bodyguard. "We're limited on iron. So, Erica and Ted, between the two of you, decide who will be the defense. Benji and Kenneth. And Chris will be my muscle."

Wordlessly, Chris reached into his ruck and pulled out the crowbars and handed one to Ted, passing over Erica who scoffed in disgust at the sight of the crowbar, and then one to Benji who'd won a quick round of rock-paper-scissors. I watched Ted and Benji test the weight in their hands, Benji even stepped back to take a swing, as I explained, "One of the only things that will stop a ghost is iron. Hit her with it, and she'll vanish."

Erica crinkled her nose in dubious disgust. "So, that's all you have to do to kill a ghost? Bash it on the head with a crowbar?"

"No. The iron in the crowbar makes her *vanish*...believe me, she'll be back at you as soon as she can collect herself. To kill her, we have to find her bones. Salt, holy water, and burn the bones, it should send her spirit on."

"Should?" Benji asked as he passed the bar back and forth between his hands.

"Yes," I said simply without further elaboration. I was over this and ready to get it done. Sure—if I'd had white rose oil, we wouldn't need the salt, but with holy water as our only option for purification...salt was added insurance. And, as I said, it *should* work. I dug out what flashlights I had, passing one to Erica and one to Kenneth. "Stay quiet. Stay close. And, for the love of God, *do not be stupid*." I titled my head toward the woods. "Let's go."

EPISODE 23: INTO THE WOODS, PT. 2

"You expect to find some dead pioneer girl's remains in the dark with a magical stick?" Erica hissed, distain dripping like spittle from each word.

"She's not going to find anything if you keep distracting her," Chris muttered coolly, saving my breath. "So, why don't you be quiet and let her work?"

"Sure, Deputy Dewy, I'll get right on that." Erica fell back with the boys, as though melting back in the shadows.

I felt the tug on the end of the stick, and I moved slowly and deliberately with the motion of the rod.

"Don't forget to—"

"Pay attention to landmarks," Chris finished for me. "I got you, Charlebois. Just focus."

My cheeks warmed as my heart fluttered at his faith in me. He trusted me to make the dowsing rod work. And somehow, the pull on the rod got stronger, and my steps quicker.

There was a shift in the air as we moved deep into the woods, stumbling in the dark through the trees and roots and brambly bushes. Something stale and strange.

The twin flashlight beams shifted from in front of my feet toward the sides of us, the light losing itself in the trees.

"Ted, keep that thing pointed straight," Benji snapped low and harsh, casting furtive, uneasy glances around the dark gaps in between the trees all around us.

"Did you hear something?" Ted whispered, his voice hoarse and cracking with his nerves. He smacked my arm. "Did you see that?"

I elbowed him hard in the ribs. "Shut up, Ted. I need to—"

"Yeah, knock it off, Ted. You're freaking me out," Kenneth hissed.

"No, seriously. I saw—it was like yellow. And I watched every one of Jackie's videos. She says this girl got eaten by a wolf. Like Red Riding Hood style. That means there's gotta be—*what was that?*" He yanked me hard and whirled me to the right, half hiding me, half clinging to me, as he thrust the flashlight at the trees. "There! It was eyes. *It had to be eyes.*" Ted started tugging me back the way we'd come. "Jacqueline, I know you want to get a shot of this witch. But we need to go. Now. Wait until tomorrow."

"Ted, relax!"

"I forgot to grab my pocketknife! But I've—" He started slapping his pockets frantically. "I've got my mini blowtorch and some firecrackers! That'll help, I guess, if—wait, I thought I had more than—"

"Dude. Chill." Chris pulled me back out of Ted's grip and released me so I could stumble free and regain my footing. He snatched the flashlight out of Ted's hand and aimed the beam in the direction Ted was staring. "I didn't see anything. And there aren't wolves on this island. Even if there were, they wouldn't bother us. Plus, I have my gun. The only thing you need to worry about is the Scarlet Witch swooping down and giving you ghost cooties. But I'm only going to say this once—" Chris slowed his steps as he scanned the lot of them. "You all need to calm the heck down or head back to the freaking boat because I'm not about to start shooting at shadows." He clapped the flashlight into Ted's hand." That's how people get hurt."

Benji and Kenneth mumbled in agreement as Ted gulped the air and nodded furiously. "Yeah. Yeah. Sorry." He snapped his head back toward the woods. "I just was so sure…"

I rolled my eyes and muttered underneath my breath. "You know, this is a life-and-death situation. Despite what Erica may suggest, this isn't about my channel or subscribers or what anyone thinks of me. I need to get this done. And if you guys are gonna hide behind your skirts like a bunch of little girls—" I stopped short as my heart dropped. No. *No.* I snatched the flashlight from Ted. "Why do *you* have the flashlight?" I spun around on the spot, shoving the boys aside as though I might find her hiding behind them. "Where's Erica?" I demanded, shining the light in each of their faces in turn. "*Where's Erica?!*"

The boys all moved closer together in a clump as they cast darting glances around the darkness, seemingly closing in on all sides.

Chris took the flashlight from Kenneth and scanned the trees. "Erica!" His shout rang out through the woods, and, with nothing to bounce off, it was like his voice was lost along with her. "Erica!"

Benji grabbed Ted by the scruff of his hoodie and gave him a hard shake. "Dude, you were supposed to have her back!"

"She was right here!" Ted cried, his voice rising with his panic. "She swapped the bar for the flashlight just a second ago…"

Chris's groan vibrated in his chest like a growl as he shoved his way between them. "Hey! Hey! Knock it off. Not helping." Then he turned to me and whispered low enough so the boys couldn't hear, "Is this another Lacey situation?"

I gritted my teeth on an impatient grumble as I shook my head. "I need to get to those bones. Lacey—" I put a hand over my eyes and squeezed my temples. I needed to save Lacey. But I couldn't just leave Erica, however much I might want to…but how could we even begin to find her? My head started spinning, and I couldn't focus. Too much. It was too much.

Chris put a hand on my shoulder and squeezed. "Hey. Hey. Calm down. Take a breath. Tell me what you want to do."

I inhaled deeply and exhaled just as hard. "Okay. Lacey is priority. But obviously we can't just ditch Erica. She has her phone, right? We split up."

Chris snickered. "No way."

I rolled my eyes. "Chris, we don't have time to argue about this. I'm not putting Lacey at risk for a horrible witch like Erica. But we need to find her, too. And it's not like these idiots can be trusted to handle either assignment. So—"

Chris held up a hand. "Okay. You're right. You have your phone. The guys have phones. I'll take Ted and go find Erica. Then we'll call you when we have her and meet back up with you."

I shook my head, pinching my temples as I groaned. "No. I have to go after her. Because you don't know how to handle potential encounter effects. Everyone is different. But—

"Fine. I'm your second, like you said." Chris shrugged and held out his hand. "Give me the stick—"

"Dowsing rod…" I mumbled.

"Right. Give me the rod, tell me how to work it, and you call when you have her."

I squinted at him warily. In the dark, his eyes were black as he watched me. He inclined his head and reached for the rod. "Trust me."

I pressed it into his palm and explained the process. Then I stalked over to Benji and tugged the crowbar out of his hands. "You and Kenneth are going with Chris to find the Witch's bones. Ted and I are going to find Erica."

Chris held the rod out like a sword in the direction we'd been heading. All the boys were quiet as we waited. I bit my lip as I stared at the rod. I let out the breath I'd been holding when Chris took a tentative step forward. He'd connected.

Benji and Kenneth fell in step with him and the three of them disappeared through the trees and deeper into the dark. Satisfied, I turned on my heel and stomped over to Ted, slapped the flashlight into his chest, and grabbed him by the hood and yanked him back the way we'd come.

I dug my phone out of my bag and started calling Erica's number.

We moved quietly and carefully, listening for her ringtone or a rumble of a vibration.

"There!" Ted pointed the flashlight in the direction of the ring.

I continued to press her number. Redialing over and over. I choked up on the crowbar, my eyes moving from tree to tree as we passed through them. The flashlight bobbed with the rhythm of Ted's steps, hopping almost in time with the ringtone. Then we saw the glow of the phone as it lit up with the call. It was on the ground among the leaves and roots and fallen branches. Ted and I approached it almost cautiously, eying the darkness around us as we neared the phone.

There was a shine in the black, but it was gone in a blink. I squinted into the depths of the woods, but there was nothing. I kept my eyes moving and my head rotating as Ted bent down to scoop up her phone.

My ears prickled at the loud silence humming all around us. The leaves still left on the trees let out a long hiss and hush, and for one insane moment it seemed like the forest was breathing along with me. There was a creak and then another as the tree bark bent with the breeze.

"Jackie—"

I held up a hand, and he held his tongue. Didn't he feel it? Eyes. The weight of the watcher was unmistakable. I turned slowly, squinting hard into the dark.

Then something big charged at us from behind the tree with a feral shriek.

I swung the crowbar and connected. With bone.

There was another shriek, followed by whines of protest, as Erica crumpled to the ground.

I raised the crowbar again, certain she would jump up again ready to bite a chunk out of me just as Lacey had to Patricia...

But she didn't.

Instead, Erica threw her hands over her head. "It was a joke! It was just a joke!"

I lowered the bar, blinking stupidly down at her, cowering beneath the spotlight of Ted's flashlight beam. "A joke?" I repeated numbly.

Erica peeked up at me through her hands. Seeing the bar lowered and the danger over, she hobbled up to her feet, holding her side. "I think you broke my hip, you psycho!"

"A joke," I repeated again through gritted teeth. I dropped the crowbar and lunged for her, but Ted stepped in just before my fingers scratched out her azure eyes.

"Hey! Hey! Enough!" Ted grunted as he struggled to hold me back. But all I could see was Erica's smug smirk in the shadows of the flashlight, and I needed to tear it off her face.

"*You horrible, selfish, piece of—*" Each word, I punctuated with a lunge at her face, but Ted just barely managed to keep me out of reach.

"Stop! Jackie—we have to get back!" Ted gave me a final shove, sending me staggering back a few steps as Erica cackled gleefully behind him.

"Fine!" I screamed, close to tears. I pointed a finger at Erica over Ted's shoulder. "But if my friend dies because we didn't get this ghost in time, I'm buying a curse from the Nile Witch, and I don't care what it costs!"

"Ooo! I'm so scared!" Erica howled with laughter, and my cheeks burned with embarrassment and shame. Let her laugh. While she could.

"Who has my phone?" Erica held out her hand expectantly, and Ted slapped it into her palm.

I elbowed him out of the way and knocked into Erica's side as I stalked past her, sending her doubling over in pain.

"Keep up. And shut up," I pulled out my own phone as I stomped back the way we'd come. I sent Benji a text that we'd found her and asked him for his GPS coordinates. I didn't stop to wait. I kept moving, leading them through the woods. I couldn't stop, I was too furious. Plus, as we passed through the trees, weaving in between low hanging branches and scratch leaves, I kept seeing the glow of eyes in the darkness. And though I knew it was a trick of the moonlight...or the flashlight...all I could think about was wolves. Hungry. Ravenous. Feral.

We didn't get far before Ted started losing his nerve again. He came up to my side and whispered, "Did you hear that?"

I rolled my eyes and kept moving. "No, Ted."

Ted slowed his step, forcing me to wait with him. "Right there, you don't hear it?"

Exasperated, I took a deep breath and opened my mouth to tell him off, but then I heard it.

Erica stopped with us, looking from Ted to me. "What?"

"*Shut up*. Listen."

There was a soft, almost staticky, moan sounding from within our ranks. I frowned thoughtfully as my eyes searched the forest.

Then it changed. It—

"Wait, was that—"

Jaaaaaaccccckkkkkiiiiieeeeee

Instead of feeling scared, I was annoyed. I scrunched up my face as I turned my head trying to pinpoint the direction of the voice.

Ted grabbed my arm and gave it a violent shake. "It knows your name! It knows your—"

"What was that?!" Erica grabbed Ted and gave him a desperate shake.

Jaaaaaaacccccckkkkkiiiiiiiieeeeeeee

Everyone was quiet. The thin black strips of trees blurred together in the darkness as I scanned the woods all around us.

Then there was a bang that cracked through the forest like a gunshot. Ted and I ducked down into each other, Ted's body over mine like a shield, forcing me low to the ground as we bent over for cover. *What was happening?* Then another and another. Pop. Pop. Pop. Like the Scarlet Witch had grabbed a machine gun and started firing at us. My brain wouldn't focus. *What was going on?* Slowly, as the silence settled back around the woods, I squinted my eyes open and noticed the glow coming from the pocket of Erica's hoodie.

And heard the voice as it moaned, Jaaaacccckkkkkiiiiieeeee.

I lunged for her then, fingers like claws snatching at her hoodie as she squealed in protest. I ripped her phone out of her pocket and held it up for Ted to see.

Natalie's face winced on the screen. "Hey, guys..." I ended the video call and slapped the phone back into Erica's chest.

"Give Ted back his blowtorch and the rest of his firecrackers and the next thing you pull—I'm dragging you back to the boat by your hair."

Erica giggled as she fished out the stolen loot from her pockets and passed them back to Ted. "Oh, please, Jackie. Lighten up."

I muttered curses under my breath as I checked my phone for a text from Benji. Nothing. I texted again with a threat to call if he didn't respond in five. Then I turned on my heel and headed back in the general direction.

We were walking a minute at most before Erica started back up.

"Jackie...wait, slow down," Erica whined at my back. "Did you see that?"

I clenched my jaw tight and kept going at a rapid pace, barely containing the nasty retorts popping up in my mind.

"Jackie! I'm not kidding this time!" Erica tugged at my arm.

Her whine dropped an octave as she whispered harshly in my ear, "There's something out there."

And I stopped short, sending her colliding into my back. Ted stopped, too. And then it was like the whole autumn wood was plunged into winter. And then three of us stepped closer together as our breath came out in clouds.

"Ok...temperature drop. This is real, isn't it, Jackie?" Ted, his hand shaky, moved the flashlight slowly from tree to tree.

My arms prickled beneath my sweater as goose bumps raced down the length of them. I turned as a slow stream of wind whispered through the shadows and blew back my hair.

I squinted into the black. Erica was right. There was something. Hidden. Watching. Just out of sight.

And then, she was there.

A shimmer of white and blood red.

The Scarlet Witch.

EPISODE 24: THE HOTTEST GIRL BITES IT

In the beam of the shaking flashlight, just a few yards from us, flanked by tall gangly trees, stood a young woman plucked straight from the Revolution, her shoulders hunched as Lacey had been, a dark-red hood over her head obscuring her face, black hair blowing in a breeze that wasn't really there, her arms hanging limp at her sides.

Erica hugged tight to my arm, crunching my bones in her vise-like grip as she whispered so quietly I could hardly register her desperate apologies.

Ted seemed torn between hiding behind me and charging in front of me, so he did a little dodge step before ending up sidled against my other side.

I tried to shake Erica off me, with as little movement as possible, treating the Witch like an animal, because that's the closest thing to what she was: a feral creature ready to attack at the slightest provocation.

"Erica..." I breathed, my voice barely audible. "I need you to let go...so I can swing...and whatever you do...don't make her mad."

Erica whimpered but released me, slipping behind me with a squeak.

Slowly, I choked up on the crowbar, my eyes wide and unblinking as I stared at the Witch.

As if sensing my intention, the Scarlet Witch lifted her head. Her skin was stark white, sunken into her face, her eyes bulging black in her skull. They weren't bloodshot. My mind began to spin, desperately making connections as fast as I could process them. If Lacey was mirroring her, then the Witch's eyes should've been bloodshot. But they weren't. She inclined her head as she stared unblinking at the three of us. Then she flickered like static on an old television set. A glitch in a computer program. She was there, and then she was gone.

Erica's hand clamped down on my shoulder, her fingers digging into my collar bone. "Where'd she—"

She reappeared. Slightly closer.

Erica gasped.

Then the Witch disappeared.

Reappeared closer.

Like a light switch.

In rhythm with the pounding of my heart.

Every time she materialized just a bit closer. And her face slowly curled into a crazed grin, bigger and broader each time.

Erica moaned. Ted leaned into me.

And then the Witch popped up a foot from my face, and I swung. But she was quicker. She vanished of her own accord. I squinted my eyes, willing myself not to blink and miss again. But she didn't reappear. The three of us remained frozen, huddled and tense, ready for an attack that didn't come.

Erica released my shoulder and turned so we were back to back. "Is she gone? Did you scare her off?"

I shook my head, unable to speak. But, no. I definitely didn't scare her off. My eyes shifted through the darkness, like an unending abyss of nothing. She was playing with us. Trying to scare us. And it was working.

Then there was a nerve-splintering scream behind me. I

flinched and spun on my heel, crowbar ready, just in time to see the Witch grab Erica by the face. Her white hands curled like spider legs latching onto their prey. I sidestepped and swung. The crowbar cut through the Scarlet Witch, and she exploded in a burst of murky cold mist.

"Is she dead? Did you kill her?" Ted shouted in a panic.

I thrust the crowbar into Ted's free hand. "If you see her, pretend you're a man and swing like you mean it!"

I moved toward Erica, slow and delicate in my movements. "Ted, I need light." Ted lumbered over, juggling the crowbar and the flashlight, and pointed the light at her back. Erica's head had slumped forward just as Lacey's had. Her perfectly highlighted hair fell like a striped curtain, shielding the side of her face.

"Erica...Erica, it's Jackie..." Gingerly, I laid a hand on her shoulder, gently guiding her to turn toward me.

But she was rigid and unnaturally stiff. Then Erica's body began to twitch in violent, stilted jerks, shaking my hand off her. As my arm fell to my side, her body stilled. She lifted her head and turned slowly toward me, twisting like a doll.

I gasped at the sight of her. And she smiled at that, a wide manic grin with her bloodshot eyes bulging out of her head. "I'm sorry, Jackie—" She paused to lick her pale lips. "But I'm just so hungry..."

Then she lunged at me.

Her teeth came down on my shoulder. I shrieked in both pain and panic, before Ted knocked her hard on the head with the butt of the flashlight.

She didn't even flinch. Her pupils dilated, black in her bloodshot eyes, as her teeth continued to clamp down on different parts of my arm, biting down furiously, as I struggled against the weight of her, screaming as I fought to wrench my arm away from her. Ted whacked at Erica's legs with the crowbar, but he might as well have hit her with a pool noodle for all the good it did.

The weight of her body forced me down, and the both of us

fell to the ground. I pushed her neck with both my hands, but I couldn't manage to keep her back. Pain. So much pain. Pinches, hard and fast, all over.

"Ted! Please!" I screamed desperately.

"She's—she's rabid, I don't—Oh!" Ted fumbled in his pocket and pulled out his blowtorch and pack of firecrackers. He flicked it on, but before he could get the firecrackers lit, Erica's jaw slacked as the torch burst into flame.

"The fire! Ted, show her the fire!"

Ted shoved the blowing blue flame close to Erica's face, so close the air around my arm heated and I winced against the burn. Erica hissed and scrambled off me, shrinking away from him as he followed her with the fire. She crouched on her hands and feet and scrambled away into the depths of the forest like an animal. Ted just stood there, arm still suspended, thumb down on the gas of the blowtorch, staring into the darkness, shocked that he had been able to frighten away a monster.

I whimpered slightly, bruises and cuts from her teeth up and down the length of my arm. I rolled over and snatched the flashlight from the ground and shined it on my arm. Visible through the knitted gaps in my sweater, the worst bite of the bunch was already a purple bruise, a ring of tooth punctures oozing drops of blood. I winced at the gore and scrambled to my feet.

"You can switch it off, Ted," I murmured, my voice hoarse from screaming. "You did good."

He clicked off the torch but kept his arm high and extended. He turned toward me, dazed and confused. I thrust the flashlight at him and slapped his arm down. "Come on, we need to move. Before Erica or the Scarlet Witch comes back."

"But what about Erica? Is she...can we...fix her?" Ted bumbled.

"Yes, she'll be fine," I muttered coolly as I fished out my phone. "We kill the Witch, she should go back to her normal soul-sucking self once more."

I scrolled through the phone. Benji had sent several while Erica had gone rabid on my arm. I checked the messages quickly. He sent the coordinates, but then he sent another one right after.

BENJI

Witch touched Kenneth.

He's not doing so hot.

We're going to stop and wait for you.

He's hungry.

EPISODE 25: SCARLET HUNGER

My heart plummeted into the pit of my stomach. I pressed the call button and switched it to speaker, so I could switch on my data and punch in their coordinates at the same time. The path and compass popped up on the app. "Let's go, Ted."

And without question, Ted hurried after me and the two of us ran through the woods as fast as we could manage, dodging branches and tree roots and bumps and ditches. And all the while, Benji didn't answer his phone.

I cursed under my breath and kept calling. We weren't too far. As we moved through the trees, I kept feeling eyes. And a few times I swore I saw the same fluorescent glow. And thoughts of wolves kept slipping into the back of my mind. Occasionally, I glanced back to make sure Ted was still with me. Which wasn't necessary because he was a tall guy and not the quietest as he crashed through the branches behind me. As we got a few yards away, it was easy to see them because someone—probably Chris, had started a small campfire.

My heart relaxed. Ted and I burst through the last bit of brush and saw Chris standing guard with the crowbar, and Benji sitting with Kenneth on the ground beside Chris's ruck. Kenneth was shoveling trail mix into his mouth, fistful after giant fistful. His bloodshot eyes wide and staring through his shaggy mess of dark hair at the fire as it crackled and hissed at his feet.

Ted, hands on his knees, doubled over and out of breath, squinted over at Kenneth. "What's wrong with him?"

I yanked Ted up by the collar and dragged him up so my mouth was at his ear. "Don't say anything about Erica or I will set those firecrackers off in your shirt."

"Wait, what? Why—"

"Where's Erica?" Benji asked, looking back and forth between us. "You still couldn't find—"

"No talking! All three of you shut up for a minute." I caught Chris's eye and jutted my head to the side and the two of us moved away from their little camp and just out of earshot.

Chris's eyes went straight to the bite. He grabbed my arm and pulled me close. The loose webbing of my sweater did nothing to hide the nasty bruise of the bite. He could see everything. "Jesus, Jacqueline! What—"

I tried to shrug him off me, but he held fast as he dropped the crowbar and gingerly fingered the area around the bite and mumbled things about first aid in his ruck.

Eyes fused unblinking to the boys around the fire, I hissed, "It's not a big deal! Chris, this is important: you need to tell me exactly what happened."

"I don't know. We didn't see her. It just went really cold, and then Kenneth went like Lacey. Well, he didn't disappear, he just stopped walking, and we had to backtrack a couple yards to get him. He was hunched over like he was sleeping standing up. Then we snapped him out of it; his eyes were all bloodshot, but he seemed okay. We kept going for a bit until you sent your text, and we stopped to make camp until you found us." Chris through an exasperated arm in the boys' direction. "And he kept whining about being hungry, so I gave him the last bag of trail mix. Lacey'd already eaten the other one."

My mind was churning like black clouds in a storm, gathering and collecting all the information waiting for lightning to strike. Lacey. Erica. Kenneth.

"Now are you going to explain your arm? It looks almost as bad as Joey's leg when Cory's Shepherd snapped at him."

I scoffed at that, not fully hearing, and answered in rote fashion as my thoughts continued swirling, sorting through what was happening to everyone. It wasn't mirroring. "We saw her. The Witch. I think I made her mad when she saw the crowbar—" The Witch didn't have bloodshot eyes...but ghosts materialized in whatever version of themselves they saw themselves to be...they made their own reality...so, her appearance could just be her preference... "—She grabbed Erica's face. I sliced her with the bar—" But if the infected were mirroring her...she'd manifest as they did...yet she was...almost cursing them. Was it a curse? Could the ghosts of witches curse people? "Then Erica went rabid and chomped on my arm." My head ached. Too much. I pinched my temples between my thumb and fingers and squeezed. Hard.

Chris cursed under his breath as he eyed the bite. "At least, she didn't take a chunk like...well, you know."

Curse. Grandmother. I looked at Chris, eyes wide. "It's the Scarlet Hunger!"

Chris smirked down at me. "What?"

"The Scarlet Hunger! You remember that thing—that thing my grandmother always used to say when someone was really hungry. You know? Like, instead of she could eat a horse or something stupid like that she'd say, 'she's got the scarlet hunger!'"

Chris eyed me uncertainly, "Uhh...Jacqueline...I don't—"

"The *Scarlet* Witch! *Scarlet* Hunger! It has to be connected. Cassandra said my family has a blood curse—putting aside the fact that almost all self-proclaimed 'psychics' are all frauds with God complexes, and we aren't witches—what if the Scarlet

Witch *did* have a blood curse...related to some kind of crazed hunger..." My stomach heaved, and I swayed where I stood. "With bloodshot eyes. Oh, my God. Keirian called it." I grabbed Chris's arm for support, my nails digging into him. *"A loup-garou."*

Chris snorted despite himself. "What's a loup-garou?"

I waved an impatient hand as I explained while simultaneously trying to piece everything together. "It's a Canadian kind of were-wolf...but not. They don't infect others with their bite or anything. More like a human caterpillar. They grow up like normal people, but then as they reach adulthood, they develop a hunger. And eat and eat and eat, until they finally find themselves taking a bite out of another person. And once they bite a person, they begin the final stages of the change and turn into this mindless monster who can only think about eating. It's rumored that the loup-garou were created by blood curses. The first one being cast by this uptight Catholic Canadian witch who tried to wipe out immoral settlements. The loup-garou being the perfect monster to end bloodlines because—well, the loup-garou tend to eat their young, obviously..."

Chris scrunched up his face as he tried to follow. "So, you're saying you're a loup-garou?"

"No. I think I'd know whether my aunt was trying to take bites out of people," I snapped. Then Chris caught my eye as we both shared the thought of Memé. I groaned. "My grandmother has Alzheimer's, okay? She's not turning into a monster—"

"But Cassandra said you—"

I gave him a shove. *"Chris, we need to focus.* Forget about me! What I am saying is that somehow the Scarlet Witch has cursed Lacey, Erica, and now Kenneth. We need to find the Witch's bones and burn them before she curses all of us. Because the end of this metamorphosis is not pretty. Think Gollum-biting-off-fish-heads-and-Frodo's-finger kind of gross."

"But then what about the wolf?"

I remember the glow of eyes in the dark, and I looked at him sharply. "Did you see something?"

Chris raked a hand through his hair and rubbed the back of his neck. "I wouldn't say saw...but...I don't know, Jacqueline. It's weird."

I sighed. "Well, right now, I'd be more worried about Erica jumping out of the trees and giving you a hole for a hickey. Where's the dowsing rod? We need to get this done."

Chris passed me the rod. "So, what about Lacey?"

My heart dipped and my eyes blurred. "Yeah...I don't know."

"Since Erica took a bite out of you...does that mean she'll transform?"

I frowned and shook my head. "Honestly, I don't know. Like everything with this kind of stuff, it's guesswork. And the curse or whatever it is, hit her the fastest. But I think more than likely...if we don't burn the Witch's bones...she'll go on full loup-garou and then the only way to take her down is to set *her* on fire...and as much as I hate her, I'd rather not have her death on my conscience." I stopped there. The unspoken words ringing loudly in my ears: Or Lacey. All I could think of was Lacey. I didn't have Cassandra's number. Hopefully she was okay. I sniffed, squinted back my tears, and stuck out the rod.

"Round up the boys; I'll get our bearings..."

I guided the rod in a small circle as Chris headed back to the campfire.

And it was just like the orchard—time took a breath, as I waited for it to carry on.

Then, like the scratch of metal grinding against gears, a scream ripped through the woods and sliced into my eardrums.

I dropped the dowsing rod and clapped my hands against my ears, hunching down against the sound and gasping in pain as the noise seemed to scramble my brain, melting the matter.

Chris's hand was on my shoulder. How could he hold me when his ears were left unprotected?

I winced up at him as I collapsed to the ground and saw through the darkness and the dancing light from the campfire flames that Chris didn't seem to notice the shrieking wail tearing through the trees.

My mouth gaped open, silent and gasping at the stabbing in my ears. The sound was too much. The pain, too piercing. Too penetrating. Fighting consciousness as I sagged in Chris's arms, and the last thing I saw was a pair of glowing yellow eyes reflecting the gloom like an animal in the dark.

I woke up in a tent. In pain and moaning. The pressure in my ears was worse than a hundred ear infections. Immediately, my hands went to cover them as I groaned along with the throbbing ache.

Chris had a warm washcloth on my forehead, and he tried to smile down at me, but he could scarcely manage a wince. "Hey... you really freaked me out back there."

"What happened?" Ted demanded.

I made a face, nose scrunching in disgust. "Not so loud," I mumbled as low as I could register the sound. "It feels like my ears are bleeding." I squinted up at them as they exchanged wary glances over my bedside. "What?"

Chris swallowed, the knot in his throat bouncing with his gulp. "Well, they did. We were debating whether we *should* head back and try again in the morning. Get you to see Dr. Damiani."

I groaned in a frustrated mix of annoyance and pain. "No. We need to get this done. I don't need a doctor." Putting aside the fact that this was a life-or-death rescue mission—everyone but me seemed to actually grasp that fact—I didn't even have money for data, like I could afford a midnight trip to the doctor. "I just... need...a bottle of ibuprofen."

Chris flopped a first aid kit on the cot. "Here, maybe—"

"No. My backpack." I nodded vaguely toward the floor of the tent as though I knew where they'd put my bag.

Ted scooted to the corner. "Here!" He thrust it into Chris's lap.

"There's...a bottle...marked...corpectus." It was my emergency tonic from the Nile Witch. I never went out in the field without it.

Chris unstoppered the potion and arched a dubious eyebrow. He sniffed it suspiciously as only a freshly minted deputy would. "What is this stuff?"

I slapped at his hands and tugged the bottle from him and drank a careful mouthful. Then I passed it back to him and closed my eyes. "Just give me a minute." I'd never had to use it before. It was supposedly a cure-all for mild internal injuries. I just hoped this was mild.

My brain began to fog, and the pain ebbed away like water seeping through a crack in my mind. The wail. That only I could hear. She wasn't a ghost. Finally, I knew what she was. She'd betrayed herself with the scream sent just for me.

The Scarlet Witch was a banshee.

And if she was calling to me...it meant I was as good as dead.

EPISODE 26: BANSHEE

I had to think. Too many pieces that weren't cohesive. I sat up in the sleeping bag.

Chris put a hand on my shoulder, "Hey—you need to lay down!"

I rolled my eyes and grabbed my bag from his lap and pulled it onto mine. "I'm fine. I don't blow hundreds of dollars on that stuff just for kicks."

As I dug through the backpack, Chris stared at me. "So, your ears are okay?"

"Mhmm," I murmured distractedly as I pulled out the books I'd brought.

"You brought books with you?" Ted snickered, his earlier terror momentarily forgotten. "Typical Jackie."

"Shh!" I paused on a page and looked up at Chris. "Where's Kenneth? And Benji?"

Chris's face hardened, but Ted only laughed. "Kenneth is going through the last of the jerky. Dude won't stop eating. He's like my sister—eats the whole pantry when she's stressed."

I looked at Chris. "You should be out there with them!"

"You were priority. And Benji knows what to look for."

"You told him?"

"He's handling it." Chris nodded stiffly and shifted his eyes to Ted and back to me with a pointed stare. Apparently, he hadn't told Ted. Which was wise, considering his courage tended to be touch and go.

"Ted, why don't you go help Benji keep an eye on Kenneth."

"But what about the ghost?" Ted cast a furtive glance toward the door of the tent.

Before I could think of something reassuring to say, Chris answered, "I put a salt circle around the campsite. Just don't cross it. You'll be fine."

I bit back the smile sneaking onto my face. Well, look at him. Christopher Vantine, paranormal investigator. Had a nice ring to it.

Ted looked to me for confirmation. I nodded. "Don't step outside the circle."

Reluctant to leave the safety of either me or the tent, Ted slowly pushed back up on his knees and crawled out of the tent.

I glanced sideways at Chris. "Nice work, Vantine."

Chris grinned. The glow of the lantern glittered in his cobalt eyes. "I learned from the best."

I held up a hand. "Hey, I didn't tell you anything about salt rings. Just salt. That's good thinking right there."

Chris shrugged with an easy smile. "I'm not just a pretty face, you know."

I scoffed with a roll of my eyes and went back to the books. I thunked the one on spirits into Chris's chest. "Here, look for 'banshee.'"

"Why?" Chris plopped the book open and started scanning the index. "What's a banshee?"

I cracked open the book on monsters, thumbing through the pages for the section on humanoids. "The Scarlet Witch isn't a ghost. She's a banshee."

"Which is—" Chris prompted as he turned pages.

"A banshee is a dead witch."

Chris smirked without looking up. "So, a ghost."

I gritted my teeth on a sigh. "No. A ghost is a spirit that clung to Earth and refused to pass on due to some form of unresolved emotional tie. A banshee is—"

"'*A banshee is the spirit of a witch that serves as a warning to her House. She will roam the Earth, wailing a warning to her descendants of their impending doom.*'" Chris looked up from the book with a smirk. "So, a ghost."

I groaned. "No! It's—"

"Wait." Chris's face fell. "You heard her. That's why your ears bled."

I stared pointed down at the book in my hands, trying to read the words but not processing anything.

"'*If a person hears the banshee's shriek, death is typically imminent within hours.*'"

I smacked the book in front of me as I let out an exasperated sigh. "Chris, I know all that. Would you look for the part that says how we kill her? I'm pretty sure it's the same way you kill a regular ghost, but we have to be sure."

"Uhh, so you're just going to ignore the fact that according to this you're just going to up and die in a few hours?"

"Yes," I snapped venomously. "One problem at a time!"

Chris fixed me with a hard stare, his mouth set in a grim line.

I couldn't hold his gaze, my resolve weakening under the weight of it as I looked back down at the book in my hands and spoke slowly and pointedly, "If we don't kill her, there is literally no chance at all to cure Lacey and Erica and Kenneth...at least, I don't think. And honestly, I don't even know if *that* will save them." I let out a groan and raked my hands through my hair. "Just read, please."

Chris struggled for a moment before turning back to the book in his hands. While he researched banshees, I had to look up the loup-garou. Things were coming together in my head. And I needed to know more about them than just how to kill them. (Fire.) I needed to know how to *cure* them once they completed the transformation from human to monster. *If* there was anyway... for a lot of reasons...but the main one being: if killing the banshee didn't work, what would I do about Lacey?

It was almost impossible to focus on the reading. Intrusive thoughts of a monstrous Lacey hunting down Cassandra Sawyer through her jungle of plants and chomping on her jugular kept penetrating my mind as I struggled to process paragraph after paragraph of droning filler. I tried to remember to breathe, but I kept forgetting as my eyes pored over the pages, the breath lodged in my chest, caged tight.

It was disheartening and depressing, as I essentially reread everything I already knew: the loup-garou is a monster created by a witch's blood curse. Sometimes it skips generations. Once the infected reaches adulthood, their hunger increases to unnatural appetites, until they become so consumed by the hunger that they attack a fellow human. Once human flesh is consumed, the transformation begins. In the end, the monster loses all rational thinking and essentially devolves into a mindless human-munching machine. Fire is the only way to kill them. And there is no known cure.

I got to the end of the section, nibbling my bottom lip as I considered the facts. Supernatural lore was always incomplete, with countless exceptions and caveats and undiscovered truths, because unlike the natural world in which scientific studies and decades of research and money were invested into learning, the paranormal was underground, hidden, and scorned as make-believe. So, anything stated should always be tested...but I didn't have time to mess around.

It was a blood curse. I should go back to generalizations. I tossed the monster book aside and dug out the book on supernatural maladies and injuries. As I began scanning the pages, Chris cleared his throat. "So, it looks like to kill a banshee, you anoint, salt, and burn their bones...just like a regular ghost."

"Does it say anything about banshees cursing people?" I mumbled distractedly as I flipped to the section on blood curses.

"Eh, it was kind of vague on their abilities...because banshees are rare. They are born of violent deaths. And, at the time of their death, have an intense fear for the wellbeing of their family members. It mentioned that a lot of banshees were formed during ancient pandemics. Which kind of makes sense, if one of the criteria for their creation is a concern for their family. But anyway, so—centuries later, when people came in contact with the banshees, they up and died from the black death and other random medieval illnesses. Although, it *did* say that isn't always the case. A lot of times, banshees just float around waiting to scream at their grandchildren. In general, it seems like a banshee is a warning."

"So, she's warning everyone about loup-garou?" I shook my head as I mumbled the words aloud, "'*A blood curse can only be cured by shedding the blood of original sin.*'" I scowled down at the page, before glaring up at Chris like it was his fault. "What does that mean?"

He inclined his head, his forehead crinkled in confusion. "What? Read it again?"

"'*A blood curse can only be cured by shedding the blood of original sin. To reverse the curse, the inverse of the ailment must be applied?*'" I scoffed in disgust and flipped the book to read the cover. "Who wrote this pretentious garbage?!" I rolled my eyes at the author. "Michel Whayland. I bet he's some crusty old shut-in who reads his own books out loud just to hear himself talk around in circles." I opened the book back to the page and glanced sideways at Chris. "Any idea as to what that might mean?"

Chris scrunched up his face as he reread the passage for himself. Then he shook his head with a one-shoulder shrug. "Maybe it means you have to kill the person who cursed you? Original sin? Right?"

I frowned. "I don't know...maybe." I reread the passage a few times. Then I pulled out my phone and took a picture of the page for later.

"So, are we going to talk about how according to the banshee, you're going to die?"

"No," I snapped coolly. There was a lot more to it than that... but Chris hadn't connected that yet.

Chris chuckled darkly. "Well, at least we know she's not going to kill *you*...she wants to keep you safe."

I snorted. "Right. Until I pull out the blowtorch. See how much she cares about me then when I cook up her remains."

Suddenly a shout bellowed angrily from outside the tent. Chris and I looked at each other, eyes wide, before we scrambled for the tent door.

Chris slapped through the canvas as he ducked out first, then straightened and froze just outside the opening. I had to sidestep him to see what was happening, but Chris flung out his arm to keep me from passing him.

Benji had Kenneth in a headlock, squeezing tight as Kenneth struggled and gasped for breath. Ted, meanwhile, was bouncing from foot to foot trying to argue with Benji to let Kenneth go.

"Hey! Hey!" Chris's shout clipped them quiet, and all three of them shifted their eyes toward him. "What happened?"

Ted pointed at Benji, his finger shaky and his expression unsure. "Kenneth kept saying he saw eyes. And he wouldn't stop, so Benji—" He waved his hand at the two of them to illustrate what he couldn't seem to find the words to describe.

"He wouldn't shut up!" Benji grunted defensively as he held Kenneth tightly to his chest. "He was freaking out, and I wasn't about to have him go psycho on us because he was seeing things!"

Chris let out a low growl of frustration and stomped across the campsite to separate the two boys. He shoved Benji onto his butt and yanked Kenneth to a standing position. "You good?"

Kenneth nodded as he massaged his neck and shot a wary glance at Benji. "Yeah..."

Benji scoffed furiously. "If you would've just shut up—!"

"I freaking saw it, man! There were eyes! It's out there watching us! Who killed the Witch in the first place?! A wolf! Who's to say they aren't still out there!" Kenneth shook his head as his voice cracked with his panic. Then he nudged Chris. "You got any more jerky?"

Chris put a hand to his forehead, and I stopped listening to them argue about provisions. My eyes were on the darkened trees beyond the campsite. I'd seen eyes before I'd passed out...and now Kenneth had seen them, too. My gaze shifted the perimeter of the camp as I stepped close to the edge, mindful of the salt ring which glowed a light blue tint in the black of night. Nothing. No flashes of fluorescent eyes watching in the depths of the woods. I turned back to the boys and approached Chris.

"We need to move..."

Chris nodded in agreement as he continued to scowl at the boys now arguing over the last stash of jerky.

My heart dipped, and I inhaled deeply. "Please, tell me you grabbed the dowsing rod when I fell..."

Chris looked at me sharply. Then his face scrunched in an apologetic wince. "Uhhh..."

I groaned inwardly and forced a smile. "It's fine. I have an idea of where it went...just..." I hazarded a glance at the boys. "Watch them..."

Chris bent down and picked up his crowbar. "Here."

I accepted the bar with a nod of thanks and headed back in the general direction I'd been when I'd fallen. I hesitated only briefly before stepping over the salt. It was strange. Just by passing over the line, I felt immediately more exposed. Like at any moment, something would lunge at me from the dark.

I switched on the flashlight of my phone and searched the ground, occasionally casting glances back at the fire to judge where I'd been when I'd fallen. I'd found the spot. There was no question because I could see several spots where sticks had snapped when Chris had bent down to help me.

But it was gone. The idea of the dowsing rod vanishing sent little prickles of panic up and down my arms. Either the Scarlet Witch snagged it, or Erica took it. I couldn't decide which was more frightening, a banshee sabotage or a loup-garou cheerleader skittering around the campsite. I switched off the phone light so my eyes could adjust to the dark and make out the shapes in the shadows surrounding me. I spun slowly in a circle, every quiet creak of the trees and scratch of the dead leaves overhead sent my heart wincing. How was I going to find the Witch's bones without the rod? I covered my face in my hand for a moment, my grip on the crowbar slackened, as I tried to think. I could call Keirian and ask whether he knew another way to find remains? Or...

"*Jacqueliiiinnne...*"

I jumped to the left, my hand dropped to a fist at my side, and I choked up on the bar as I raised it high. I twisted in a tight circle. There was no one. No loup-garou. No banshee. No hidden phone. Nobody. Yet *something* had whispered into my ear, so low I could still feel the tickle of my name against my neck. My eyes shifted as I turned around and around, my muscles tight and ready for an attack. But none came.

"*Jacqueliiinnne...*"

I slapped at my ear with my free hand, sidestepped and swung hard through the air. Nothing. Chest heaving up and down with my ragged breath, I swallowed thickly as my blood pounded in my ears.

It wasn't the banshee. She'd make my ears bleed again with her wails. And it wasn't Erica. She didn't have the self-control to teasingly terrorize me. Not anymore.

What else was out here?

Then I saw it.

The yellow shine of wild eyes.

And slowly, a giant white wolf, the size of a lion, stepped out from the shadows.

Mouth parted in awe at her size, I blinked stupidly as my arm sagged with the weight of the crowbar, useless at my side. Her eyes glowed with a strange brightness to them, as though they were made of light. And I could hear her voice in my head, my ears prickling as though the wolf whispered at my side. "*Come.*"

I didn't hesitate. Crowbar still slack in hand, without question, I took a step forward, and the wolf took off into the dark. And I followed. It was like my brain had fogged, clouding my judgment and critical thinking. And suddenly it seemed perfectly reasonable to follow a super-sized, supernatural wolf with glowing eyes deeper into the woods. Without a word to Chris. And without fear.

I was moving through the woods after her dark shadow without much conscious effort. It was more instinct than it was independent action. I couldn't say how far we made it into the woods before we came upon a clearing in the trees; an overgrown circle of high grass and weeds tangled all around the space, and in the center of the clearing, was a large log cabin, circa 1600. Two stories, four front windows, and a broken front door.

I stood at the edge of the trees, staring at the cabin unable to process the sight of it. The whole thing was gray and weathered from time and the elements; it seemed to bow inwards, caving in on itself, but, miraculously, mostly still standing, at least in the front from what I could see. I looked around for the wolf, but she was gone. Again, at least from what I could see. I hadn't even had time to think of what kind of creature she could be...and my head hurt trying to think.

My phone rumbled angrily in my pocket. Oops.

I pulled it out and switched on the data for my GPS coordinates and texted them in response to Chris's repeated calls from Benji's phone.

He texted back.

BENJI

Don't move.

I snorted in response. Yeah, okay, Chris. I tucked the phone back into my butt pocket and slowly walked the perimeter of the property. The side of the house was broken, like a tree had fallen through it...or something had smashed into it. Around the back, there was a covered porch, but the awning drooped so low it literally covered the porch like a curtain draped over it. There was a modest stable off to the side of the cabin, which looked big enough for at least two horses. I approached it cautiously as I pulled out my phone and shined the light around the enclosure. It was empty, and the paddock was busted from the inside. The horses kept here had probably broken loose hundreds of years ago.

I stepped back from the stable and continued my trek around the property, occasionally casting glances around me at the woodline. I wasn't afraid of the cabin. The most we'd find inside would be bones. But the woods held Erica, rabid from her loup-garou transformation, and the banshee. When I made it back to the spot I'd started, I watched the woods for signs of the boys. I checked my phone. It'd been a while, and I was wasting time waiting for them. I had what I needed to end this, and somehow I knew the remains of the Scarlet Witch were inside that cabin. I hitched my backpack straighter on my shoulders and headed for the house.

The closer I got to the cabin, the more my conviction lessened. I had no idea what was in the cabin. And how did I find it? An unknown paranormal entity capable of mind whispering. It seemed a bit risky to enter a busted up building on the instruction of a supernatural being...at least somewhat associated with a banshee.

I stopped at the entryway, my eyes scanning the cabin and squinting into the darkness seeping through the broken boards of the door, cracked in half. A breeze pressed against me, caressing my face, tugging my hair, before creaking and groaning through the house. I glanced back at the woods behind me. Still no boys. I turned back to the cabin. If her bones were inside...as soon as I started to soak them in the holy water, the banshee would appear. And if she screamed loud enough, she could kill me. But I'd already heard her scream...so, I was dead anyway. And I couldn't think of a better way to go than by chasing down the Scarlet

Witch. I pulled out my phone. And honestly, I wouldn't be me if I didn't catch it all on film. So, I turned on the flashlight, camera, and started to record.

I squinted slightly into the glare of the light as I held the camera up to my face. "I've been hiking through the woods of an abandoned island for hours. The Scarlet Witch has made herself known, and it is now clear she is in fact no ordinary ghost. She is a banshee." I cocked my eyebrow for the audience. "How do I know this? Well, I heard her scream." A cocky smirk slid into place on my face, before I jutted my chin toward the camera, adding, "And for all of you true followers of my channel, you know what that means. Not only am I a descendant of the Scarlet Witch—as I've contended for years—but I am also going to die within a day, save for some kind of divine action. And I decided, if I'm going to die, I might as well die with my camera rolling and teach you all something."

A gave a little cheeky wink, before I flipped the camera toward the woodline in the distance, the moon, high and halved, hung just above the branches in a dusting of stars casting a blue-tint over the clearing as I panned around the property. "Centuries ago, when the islanders banished the Perrault family from town for being witches, legend had it they went into the woods." I held up a finger in caution with a small smile. "But the piece of the story that was lost along the ages, the small little detail that had, up until now, made the Scarlet Witch literally impossible to find—was that they'd settled in the woods of a smaller surrounding isle. Not on Martin Isle, herself." I turned the camera toward the house, moving over the busted entrance. "This cabin is presumably the home that Charles Perrault built for his family after their exile from Martin Isle, So, we should see signs of a family of five. Father, mother, grandmother, and two daughters."

I held the camera up as I carefully climbed through the cracked door and moved the phone around the place—what had been seemingly the kitchen. It was covered in thick layers of cobwebs, dirt, and grime, which was to be expected, the blue moonlight streaming in through the windows, illuminating the dust floating through the air like slow-motion snow, but there *was* something odd about the state of the room: the kitchen table and chairs were knocked over, scattered around the place, and the hutch that'd held the china was busted and there were shards of broken dishes all over. Even the staircase positioned against the left wall, opposite the fireplace, had its railing bashed in several places. It looked as though someone had raged around the room and trashed everything. This I knew from experience. Our kitchen had looked similar the night my dad left. Men like him, they tended to break everything before they left. As though the broken hearts and spirits of their loved ones weren't enough.

I moved the light up the stairs, half expecting some creepy little girl with way too much hair to be looming at the top, but it was empty. Then I moved the light carefully back around the kitchen and then down at the floor as I walked slowly farther into the room. But as soon as I crossed the threshold, a scream tore through my eardrums.

EPISODE 28: THE CABIN

I dropped the phone, clamping one hand over my ear and blindly swinging the crowbar around me in a circle with the other. Nothing. I only swiped through the air. My brain felt like it was melting, the piercing vibration of the unending scream shaking my mind to mush. Banshee. Banshee. I tried to think. What did I know? I couldn't think. My eyes leaked with a stream of tears, and my face contorted with the pain. *What did I know about banshees?* Banshees. Ireland. Brigid. Fertility. Fire. Ash.

Ash.

I dropped the crowbar and scrambled for the old fireplace. Desperate and down on all fours, I dug at the hearth and stuffed the dirt in my ears, now wet with blood which, with a swirl of the soot, mixed into a compact mud. Instantly, the scream died away to a dull wail. I let out a little moan of relief as I bent my head forward in thanks. The alleviation was overwhelming. I had to take a moment.

I was okay.

I was alive.

Oh, my ears.

I scowled down at the dirty floor beneath my hands. That's it. Findings now proven to be fact, the official stance of the Inside My Frozen Heart channel was now as follows: Banshees were the most stupid supernatural creatures in all of existence. '*Oh, I love my family so much I want to warn them of their imminent death by killing them first!*' I rolled my eyes and gritted my teeth as the wail moaned softly in the back of my mind like someone had tried to turn the radio off but missed a few notches. Annoying.

I blinked furiously, clearing my vision of unshed tears and grabbed another fistful of soot from the fireplace and stuffed it in my pocket. This time I would be prepared.

I sat back on my heels ready to start my search for the remains, but before I could stand, my heart stopped, and I had to gasp for a breath.

One by one, naked footprints pressed themselves into the dirty floor, leaving the kitchen and turning left through the darkened doorway across the room. Like footprints in the ash. The Scarlet Witch.

Somehow, it was much more terrifying to have her physically present. As a ghostly creature, she was horrifying, but as a sound she was just plain annoying.

I eyed the doorway warily. I had to go deeper into the house if I was going to find remains...but honestly the idea of following ghost footprints would make anyone take a pause. I wiped my filthy hands on my pants and then stood quickly, shifting my back-pack straighter on my shoulders. Time to get this done.

I looked around the kitchen for my phone, but it was so dark and dirty inside the only way I found it was the low rumble of a text. I reached underneath the turned-over chair and snatched up the phone.

Chris's text was bright on the screen.

BENJI

You went into the creepy cabin, didn't you?

I smiled slightly as I pictured Chris's surly scowl. But before I could type a sassy response, another text bubbled on the screen.

Hide

Erica

My eyes darted instinctively toward the broken front door. Any second, she would crash through, ready to eat my face off. I looked around the room. There was no place to hide. I looked toward the doorway and then over at the staircase, and like every other *dumb* blonde in every single slasher film—I ran up the freaking stairs.

The second my foot creaked the first step, I regretted my choice, but I had to commit, there wasn't time to correct my mistake. As light as I could, praying the stairs would hold, I tiptoed up the staircase at a furious pace. By the time I reached the top, there was a smash down in the kitchen that shook the whole cabin. I flinched and struggled to get my bearings, shining the phone around me. I was in a small square hallway. Two doors. There were two doors on opposite sides of the box-like space. I had to choose. Left. I pushed the door open and slipped inside. I leaned my back against the door and latched it quietly with the flimsy little hook latch. I scrunched up my face at the feeble protection, before shining the phone around the room, wincing, ready for an attack.

Like the kitchen, it was covered in cobwebs and coated in dust, but unlike the kitchen, it hadn't been vandalized. It was a simple bedroom with two twin beds lining the length of the wall, a girl's room judging by the doll propped up in the rocking chair by the fireplace. But it was the beds that caught my attention...although one was neatly made and put together, the other was...odd. The blankets of the bed were darkened in the middle. Stained. I stepped closer, my heart tight in my chest. The phone light shined on the browned blankets. They weren't just stained. They were shredded in places. I moved the light up the length of the bed as my heart pumped loud in my packed ears. And I let out a little cry and shuffled back away from the bed at the sight of the skeleton, tucked partially in bed. I swallowed, my tongue thick in my dry mouth, and struggled to calm my heart. I stepped closer. She died in bed. The young woman died in bed. But how?

My mind started spinning again. The wolf left me here to find the Scarlet Witch's remains...but if she had been killed by a wolf on her way back from Nile, why would she be tucked in—

My phone rumbled in my hand as another text popped up on the screen.

BENJI

Erica is in there. Where are you? We're going in.

ME

Upstairs. Left room. Don't forget—fire.

I went to the door and lifted the flimsy latch. I strained my ears against the soot packed inside, listening for their footfalls on the stairs. Rhythmic creaking groaned in the bones of the cabin. Then there was only muffled silence. I waited. Maybe they went in the wrong room. I cracked the door just a bit.

Erica's grotesque grinning face greeted me.

The transformation was complete. Her smile was too wide, spreading the length of her face, and revealed rows of gigantic teeth. Her nose, once perfectly petite and upturned, was now the size of a potato—lumpy and bulbous, her oversized nostrils twitching at the smell of fresh meat. Her beautiful azure eyes, now black and bloodshot, were huge in her head, swollen and bulging out of their sockets like baseballs. Her ears stuck out from her head, batty and pointed, like fleshy pig's ears protruding from her highlighted hair which was now stringy and falling out, judging by the random naked patches all over her skull. But it was her skin that truly turned my stomach.

Her skin had torn. It was cracked with purple stretch marks, scrawled all over and peeling, as though her distorted features had pulled the organ's elasticity way past its capacity. It looked like she was ripping right out of herself.

I blinked through my tears as I flinched away from her, while still bracing the door with my knee. She was monstrous in every sense of the word. And I was as good as eaten.

She chomped her oversized jaws in the crack of the door, and I pressed all my weight against it. But I might as well have stepped aside, because with a simple shove, Erica smashed her way through, sending the door slamming into me and crushing me against the wall. I held the door tight against me like a shield, hiding myself from her. I closed my eyes and willed my breathing to slow and my heart to calm. According to the loup-garou lore, although her senses would improve, her intelligence would suffer. And as long as she didn't hear me...or smell me...or see me...she'd probably be stupid enough to think I'd disappeared. Or forget I was here altogether.

My ears prickled at the muffled sound of Erica rooting through the room, lumbering around it like an idiot in her search for me. There was a shout near my ear and I winced away from the crack in the door.

Chris. There was a roar of a blowtorch and a whine like a dog being kicked and then a smash of glass as someone (hopefully Erica) went through the window.

I took a gulp of air and pushed the door away from me just enough to see the broken window. Benji and Kenneth ran for the sill and stared out across the clearing below. Somewhere in the room, hidden from view, Ted started shouting about the sleeping dead girl. I closed the door quietly and, my back still against the wall, I watched Chris drop to his knees beside the bed. He pressed his head to the ground without any concern for the grime and slapped up the blankets to peek underneath.

"You really think I'd hide under there?"

Benji and Kenneth flinched at my voice and grabbed each other.

Ted nearly fell over onto the bed, then yelped and scooted to the far corner of the room, farthest away from the dead girl.

Chris scrambled to his feet and rushed at me. He pulled me into a crushing hug, his arms tight against my back. He pressed his cheek against the top of my head as his hold on me constricted. Then he pushed me away from him and held me at arm's length.

"Are you okay?" His eyes searched my face as his thumb rubbed against whatever smear was on my face. Dirt or blood, I didn't know. "What's wrong with your ears?"

"Ash. It blocks her shrieking just enough to be annoying." I shrugged, increasingly aware that his hand was still cupping my face and the boys were watching.

And at least one of them was snickering.

My face burned.

And Chris felt it. He smiled, a mischievous crinkle in the corners of his eyes. But instead of doing something stupid, he let me go, so abruptly I stumbled a bit. Chris shook his head in mocking disappointment. "I can't believe you ran upstairs."

I rolled my eyes to the ceiling. "I know! I know!" My gaze rested on Kenneth. He didn't look good. His face was pale and his bloodshot eyes were shifty beneath the strands of shaggy dark hair hanging in his face. I jutted my chin in his direction. "Kenny, how are you feeling?"

"Hungry," Kenneth snapped, his voice raspy and raw.

Benji gave his shoulder a smack. "He's good. Holding strong."

"And once you kill the ghost, he should go back to normal, right?" Ted asked, eying his friend suspiciously.

I nodded, my mouth in a grim line as I stared down at the bones in the bed. "We've got to burn these bones now. It's our best chance to cure everyone."

"Best chance?" Kenneth demanded, taking a step closer. "What do you mean, 'best chance'?"

"Wait—Jacqueline…"

"What?" I looked sharply at Chris, bristling with impatience.

Chris met my stare with a calm, steady one of his own. "How do you know this is her?"

I tossed a hand toward the remains. "How many skeletons do you think are hanging around this place?"

"We've found two others, so far…"

I blinked. I shifted where I stood and inclined my head in confusion. "Two? Where?"

"Erica was coming up the stairs. I ducked right, trying to lure her away from you, but—"

"I opened the door…" I finished, my brain spinning with skeletons. "So, there are two other bodies?"

"Yup. Tucked in bed, just like this one." Chris scowled down at the dead girl. "It's weird. The stains are the same, too."

"Like blood," Ted blurted, a tremor in his voice. "*Like they were butchered to death in their beds.*"

I raked a hand through my hair. "We'll have to burn them all. Just in case. And then we'll have to search the rest of the house…"

"How many dead people do you think you'll find?"

"Well, the Scarlet Witch lived with her parents…her sister…and her grandmother. Her sister—"

"*Your* great-grandmother."

"—supposedly made it off the island and back to Nile. So, that'd be four bodies…"

Benji frowned, his forehead crinkled in thoughtful confusion. "But, Jacqueline, why—"

I groaned, my impatience getting the better of me. "Later, okay? We can piece together the facts *after* we get this done. Burn these bones and get the rest, before Erica comes back, or Kenneth can't hold out any longer and—" I stopped myself. No need to put the thought in his head. I bit my lip and waved a hand as though clearing the air of the awkward pause. "You know, before he makes a mistake." I jutted my chin toward Chris as I slipped my backpack off my shoulders and dug through it. "Let's go."

"I'll take care of the couple." Chris swung his ruck in front of him and hugged it with one arm as he rummaged for the holy water and the salt can. "Anoint, salt, burn?"

I nodded. "Just a sprinkle of the holy water. You'll know if you did it right. The fire will burn with white light." I pulled out the salt can and then pointed it at Ted. "You go with him. She comes at him, you hit her with the crowbar. Can you handle that?"

Ted gulped so deep his Adam's apple bobbed up and down. He jerked his head in confirmation and held up the crowbar like a hitter going up to bat and followed Chris out of the room.

I tucked the salt under my armpit, and pulled out the holy water and the blowtorch. I left my bag on the floor and approached the bed. I unstoppered the water and held it over the bones. "Be ready." I glanced at the boys each in turn. "Chances are, she's not going to like this..."

"Wait!" Benji held up his hand, before digging my camcorder out of his bag. He switched it on and aimed it at me.

I smiled slightly as the little red light winked at me. Then I turned my attention back to business, and sprinkled the holy water onto her skull and all down her skeleton, reverently with pointed precision. It felt like I was anointing her for burial, and technically I was. The weight of it, the solemn importance of putting a soul to rest overwhelmed me. I finished with the holy water and put the stopper back in place. Eyes on the bones, I dropped the bottle into my bag still open on the floor at my feet.

I shifted the salt can from under my arm into my hands, but I didn't move to open it. The stains and the shredded blankets. Ted was right. She was butchered in her bed. I popped the metal top on the salt.

Instantly, her scream ripped through the ash still packed in my ears. I gripped the salt tighter as I jabbed my shoulder into my ear and covered the other with my free hand.

"In coming!" Kenneth bellowed as he charged forward.

Benji kept filming, the camera held firmly up to his face.

I twisted around just in time to see the Scarlet Witch flying at me, her arms outstretched and white hands curled like gnarled claws. Her eyes bulging and her mouth sneering as she shrieked. I flinched away from her as Kenneth slashed at her with the crowbar. But she vanished before he could connect. He stumbled a bit as he stopped short, bar raised and ready to defend me.

I blinked stupidly as my ears continued to ring.

"Go on!" Kenneth shouted, his bloodshot eyes scanning the room, ready for her to reappear. "Finish it!"

I poured the salt all over the bones and the bed. But before I could bend down for the blowtorch, her scream pierced through the ash and pricked into my eardrums and doubled over in pain.

Kenneth looked down on me, panicked and bewildered. "What? Jacqueline! What's wrong?"

They couldn't hear her. They didn't know.

I tried to speak, but I couldn't focus enough to form words.

Then she appeared. The bright red hood framing her black hair as it blew in a breeze that wasn't there, her black eyes huge in her sunken face, white skin stretched across her skull, and mouth so wide her jaw seemed to unhinge as she screamed.

She extended her arms, one hand curled toward Kenneth and the other curled toward Benji. Then she crushed her fingers into tight fists. Benji dropped the camera, Kenneth dropped the crowbar, and both of them clawed at their necks, mouths gaping for air.

She was squeezing their throats with her power. Suffocating them. And she laughed, a high, shrieking cackle that hurt worse than any of her screams.

Chris. *Where was Chris?* I tried to reach for the crowbar, but I couldn't make myself move. Hands pressed hard against my ears, I curled up into a tight ball on the filthy floor and sobbed as her screams scratched against my eardrums and melted my mind.

Warmth seeped through my fingers, as blood oozed from my ears. Eyes shut tight, dizzy in the darkness, I couldn't hold onto consciousness through the throb and stab of the pain.

And the last thing I thought of was the wolf from the woods, and one word whispered, "Help."

Silence.

It was quiet.

My eyes flew open, and I struggled to my feet. I blinked slowly, mind muddled and ears aching, and looked around the room. Benji and Ted were holding the door, braced together like a human barricade. The door bumped violently against them.

I inclined my head, completely confounded.

There should've been sound.

A pound or a bang as the door thumped hard against them, threatening to burst open. I blinked stupidly as I watched them struggling to hold the door. I couldn't make my brain work. Chris? I needed Chris. Where was Chris?

As if in answer, there was a muffled grunting in my head, the sound lost somewhere in my ear canal. I turned toward the window. Chris held Kenneth in a tight headlock as Kenneth gnashed his teeth and clawed at his arms, fighting to get free.

Chris's mouth was moving. Shouting at me. Brow furrowed, I focused on his lips. I couldn't make it out, he was moving too much as Kenneth jerked violently in his arms.

I had to do something.

That was it.

Do something.

Slowly, my brain started to clear, and I scanned the floor. There. Disoriented and stumbling, I went for the blowtorch. I held the switch and the flame whooshed to life.

Then the Scarlet Witch appeared scratchy like static and glitching like a channel change. Her black eyes bore into mine, and her face contorted in a furious sneer. She slapped a hand against my cheek, her nails digging into my skin, tearing into my flesh.

But before she could melt my brain with her scream, I held the fire to the white skull resting on the bed.

The bones burst into white flames, wild, furious, and hot. And in front of me, the Scarlet Witch did the same. She clawed at herself as her whole body began to burn. The fire roared across the length of her as her face contorted in a shriek I couldn't hear, and then she burst into an explosion of blinding light.

Then she was gone.

As though she'd never been there.

I stumbled back from the bedside as the fire disappeared, leaving the bed just as it was before—minus the skeleton. I stared blankly at the empty blankets.

A hand rested on my shoulder. Chris. He passed me the corpectus bottle. He didn't speak, perhaps he didn't think I could hear, but probably because he was too tired from fighting a loup-garou.

Kenneth. I looked around the room as I gulped down the last of the corpectus. Kenneth was passed out on the floor, but his face was human. Benji and Ted had stepped back from the door. And after exchanging furtive glances, they cautiously opened the door. Erica, features normalized but dark hair still patchy and thin, was crumpled unconscious in the doorway. And all I could think of was Lacey. Lacey would be fine.

The potion was just as fast as before. The pain vanished, my hearing returned, and my head cleared. I took the corner of my shirt and swirled out the ash and blood from my ears. Chris squeezed my shoulder and gave it a gentle shake. "You did it, Charlebois. All cured."

I didn't smile.

Something was left.

Something I hadn't put together yet.

Chris touched the tip of his finger to my cheek. "Do you have anything for these? They look pretty angry."

I winced at the sting of the Witch's scratch slapped across my face. "Yeah...I'm not worried about..."

I was missing something.

What was it?

I looked up at Chris. The night was dying, and in the hazy, purple twilight of morning, his eyes were a brilliant violet. I searched his face as though I might find the answers there. And honestly, I found a few. But none I was ready to acknowledge. I inclined my head curiously. "What took you so long?"

Chris winced almost guiltily. "Erica attacked us." He held up his hand, and I recoiled in horror. His thumb was wrapped with a shred of his blue checkered shirt. But I could see through the crude, dirty bandaging, his finger was split in half. The ivory bone at the top of his thumb was peeking through the bloody tourniquet.

"Oh, my God! Chris! Here." I scrambled for my bag and slapped around for the bungleweed bottle. My heart dropped. Patty had used all of it. I cursed under my breath and chucked the bottle back into the bag. I straightened and took his hand in mine. "We'll fix it. Miraculum will heal it good as new." I held back the fact that the potion was extremely expensive, and I had no idea when the Nile Witch would be back in Nile.

Chris pulled his hand back and shrugged. "Just a few stitches, and I'll be fine."

I frowned, my eyes on his hand.

"But...Jacqueline...something weird happened."

At that, I met his gaze, but he avoided mine. "What do you mean?"

He rubbed his neck with his good hand. "Well, Erica had us. Ted was completely useless, and Erica was on me. I could barely keep her away from my face. There was no way we were getting out of there without help. And then there was this flash of white light. Like a smoke screen. And Erica was thrown off me. She must've hit her head because she was out for like a minute. Then..."

"What? Chris, spit it out. It's not like I'll have trouble believing you," I snapped as I threw my hands up in frustration, fighting the urge to stamp my foot.

"There was this wolf."

"A gigantic wolf? With yellow eyes?"

"She just appeared in the white smoke as it cleared."

"She? How'd you—"

"Her voice. I could, like, *hear* her in my head. But it was weird because it was *your* voice."

"What did I say?" I demanded.

"'Help.'"

My arms prickled as he echoed the word I'd said before I lost consciousness. I put my head in my hands and rubbed them down my face and massaged my cheeks.

"It's a familiar," I murmured as my heart began to pound in time to the pieces snapping into place in my mind.

"You've seen it before?"

I shook my head as I shoved my hand through my hair and stepped back to study the empty bed. "No. The wolf is a familiar. A witch's companion. The Scarlet Witch's, specifically." I looked back at Chris. "That's why the wolf... The wolf brought me here. She helped me find the cabin. And that's why she helped you save me. She wanted me to put her mistress to rest."

"And you did it!" Chris gave me a playful nudge and cocky

grin. "I can't wait to watch this episode. Benji better have caught that bit where I burst in and tackled Kenneth." Chris chuckled at himself.

I wasn't listening. Everything was crashing into place.

I shook my head, eyes blurring with hot tears, as I breathed, "Chris, we have to get out of here."

"Sure." Chris gave a lazy one-shouldered shrug. "We just get Kenneth and Erica back on their feet and head back to the Inn."

I swallowed, barely able to breathe. I put my hand in his good one and squeezed hard. "No. I mean, *we have to get out of here*."

Chris bent his head closer to mine, his brow crinkled in concern. His eyes searched mine as he lowered his voice to match mine. "What do you mean?"

"The Scarlet Witch was warning us." I looked around at the state of our group. Kenneth and Erica still passed out, and Benji and Ted collapsed into each other, shell-shocked and still catching their breath. "She was warning all of us."

Chris tugged on my hand and caught my eye. "Jacqueline..."

I winced and whispered hoarsely, "It's her grandmother."

He cocked an eyebrow. "Her grandmother?"

I swallowed again as my fear lodged tight in my throat. "It wasn't the wolf that killed the Scarlet Witch. It was a loup-garou."

"But—?"

"Her grandmother was sick. So, the Scarlet Witch and her sister went into town for medicine. But it didn't help because it was a blood curse. She wasn't killed by a wolf. She was killed by a loup-garou. *Her grandmother*."

His eyes narrowed as he started to make sense of what I was saying. "So—"

I closed my eyes briefly, spilling tears down my face. "So, the only thing that can kill a loup-garou is fire."

"Hey, calm down." Chris's hand cupped my face, and I let out a little gasp. "You're okay, Jacqueline Jay. Breathe." His thumb smoothed away the saline from my cheekbones. "What is it? I still don't understand…"

"She's here in the house. Chris, she's still *alive*." I choked on a sob. "And that's why the Scarlet Witch was warning me. Her grandmother is going to kill me."

EPISODE 30: FIFTH

"You need to get them out of here." I stared blankly from Erica to Kenneth. Benji and Ted were moving between the two of them, helping them to sit up against the wall and giving them sips of water from Chris's CamelBak.

"What? I'm not—"

"The loup-garou hasn't eaten in hundreds of years," I murmured almost robotically, coming to terms with the reality of the truth. "She'll be in some kind of hibernation state. You and Benji are the only ones strong enough to help those two. And Ted tagging along would only be a hindrance to me. Get me killed before I finish."

"Jacqueline—"

"You lead them to the boat and—"

Chris grabbed my arm and shook me hard. "No. Not happening. Why wouldn't you come with us? If it's hibernating, then we all just sneak out. You're not making sense."

I inhaled deeply, steeling myself with as much strength and courage as I could muster. I fixed Chris with a firm stare. "I heard the banshee. Barring some act of divine intervention...I'm dead today, Chris. And if you don't leave with them, then everybody is..."

Chris scoffed with a sarcastic smile that didn't reach his eyes. "Just because a banshee told you so?"

I didn't answer.

And in the weight of my silence, his confidence faltered. He shifted his stance like he didn't know what to do with his body, and he inclined his head in question. He held up his hand and then lowered it with a one-shouldered shrug. He frowned, his cobalt eyes, violet in the morning twilight, shining with hurt. "You're just going to fall on your sword? Just give up?"

He wouldn't understand.

He *didn't* understand.

And it was better that way...but I wasn't lying anymore. Certainly, I wasn't going to have the last thing I said to him be a lie. So, I chose my words as carefully as I could manage. "I'm not giving up, Chris. *I'm finishing this.* We can't leave her here." I bit my lip, holding back. For all my self-righteousness, I still couldn't bear to admit the whole truth. That would be on my gravestone. Jacqueline Charlebois, Liar, Pretender, Afraid of Her Shadow.

And Chris read it all over my face. "What aren't you telling me?"

I scowled and looked away, eyelashes fluttering and sprinkling tears down my cheeks as my emotions caught in my throat. I coughed to clear it.

Chris snatched my chin and forced me to look up at him. The sudden violent outburst, sent a hot mix of vexation and inexplicable interest. I glared up at him, matching his fury with hazel eyes hardened with anger of my own. I took in the sight of his tight jaw, flaring nostrils, and narrowed eyes, several strains of his hair falling into them. He reminded me of Maddie's manga art, and I had to fight a smirk.

"Jacqueline..." He leaned in closer to my ear as he breathed my name, low and nearly threatening, hot against my cheek. His grip on my chin tightened. "For some reason, you seem to think that I'm some kind of moral hero. But believe me, I'm not."

The primal fear flooded me. But not fear of him. Fear of what I was feeling for him. Instinctively, I fought against him, but he held me fast. And somehow, the fact that he wouldn't let me go...it soothed a hurt place in my heart. And I grew still. Calm. Then I leaned in to him. And I listened to him.

"You think I'd put all these kids before you? Well, *forget* that. I need *you* to be okay, Jacqueline. Forget everyone else. You aren't dying today. Got it?"

I struggled against a rueful smile, biting my lip to keep it from trembling. Eyelashes fluttering, splashing tears, I blinked up at him through shining eyes. Overcome with the unspoken truth behind his words.

And then he said it aloud: "I'm not going anywhere. So, tell me what you need me to do."

We moved them all to the woods with careful instructions to wait no more than an hour. If we didn't show up, call Joey with the GPS coordinates. As Chris ensured everyone was stable and understood the plan, I checked my phone for the tenth time.

I was lost in the screen when Chris came up behind me.

"You ready?"

I flinched and shoved my phone into my pocket with a guilty wince. "Yes. You have the blowtorch?"

Chris held it up and gave it a wave. But my eyes were on his bandaged thumb.

He followed my gaze and lowered his hand. "Stop. It's not a big deal." He gave me a nudge with his arm. "Let's go."

"Hey, Jacqueline!"

I looked over at Benji, startled.

He held up the camcorder. "You should film it. Shut them all up forever."

I smiled with a soft scoff. And I shook my head. "Somehow, I really don't care what any of them think anymore."

Benji grinned at that and tossed the camcorder back onto Chris's ruck.

Then with a weak wave to the boys, I walked with Chris back across the clearing toward the house, pale gray and almost ordinary in the dawn, but with a quiet insidiousness buried inside. The ominous, creepiness of the cabin had faded away with the darkness of night, but what was left was harsh and cruel in the light of morning. Somehow, that made it all the more frightening.

Chris's hand found mine. He gave me a comforting squeeze, his hand warm and safe, encircling my own. And he didn't let go. So, I squeezed him back. And we walked hand in hand to the cabin.

At the door, we paused for a moment. I looked up at him, tall at my side, and I smiled slightly. Searching his face, I hoped he understood how much it meant to me. How much *he* meant to me.

But before I could even attempt to speak, Chris laughed, his cobalt eyes crinkling. "Let's get this over with, before you go all girly and fall in love with me."

I blinked at him in surprise, cheeks burning as I gaped at him, completely speechless.

Chris smirked. "Come on, Charlebois. We'll have plenty of time to make out later."

He ducked through the crack with a side-cocked grin and a cheeky wink, leaving me standing on the doorstep fuming. I scoffed and hurried after him with a harried hiss, "*Wait a minute!*"

He stopped short, turning just in time for me to bump into his chest. I stumbled back a step, and he steadied me with his good hand. He bent his head, so we were nearly eye level. "Yes?"

I scowled darkly, regaining my composure.

Chris snickered, his eyes searching mine. "Well, well, well... look at that."

"What?" I snapped, still unable to sort out my thoughts fast enough to come up with a coherent statement.

Chris grinned with a slight shake of his head and then he jutted his chin toward me. "What's the plan, Jacqueline Jay?"

My heart fluttered. I licked my lips and regained control. But it was hard not to give in to insanity, when the end of this was so bloody.

"Just—just follow me. Can you handle that?" I snapped, bristling and bothered. I shoved passed him and took the lead.

But as I pushed by him, he whispered, "Can *you*?"

I gritted my teeth at his teasing and charged through the kitchen. It was the sight of the overturned table that jarred me back to reality. She had torn through the kitchen when the hunger had overtaken her...and then, what? Had she found her way upstairs and eaten them all, one by one, while they slept? My eyes averted from the chaotic state of the room and rested on the doorway.

There was no backing out now. I had to do this. It would end with me. One way or another. I passed the length of the kitchen and turned left down the hallway. I didn't even bother going right. The Scarlet Witch's footprints in the ash had gone left. She had shown me the way. And I followed.

The hallway was extremely tight and narrow, so much so if I tried to lift my arms, my elbows would hit the walls. There was only one door at the end of the corridor. This was it. I stopped in front of it and pulled out my phone to check once more. Just to be sure. It was a guess either way, but I wanted it to be as educated as possible. As I stared down at the screen, I whispered to Chris, "As soon as we walk through the door, she'll probably start to wake up. The smell of our blood pumping...it'll most likely rouse her—"

"Okay. Wait, Jacqueline, what are you doing?" He nodded toward the phone in my hand.

"—You need to hold back. No matter what happens, Chris.

You don't light the torch until I tell you, or I'm dead." I locked my phone and met his eyes for the first time since I'd started speaking. "Got it?"

Chris made a face. "Uh, no. And why—" He snatched my phone before I could put it away.

I gasped. "Chris—"

"—why would I *wait* to light her on fire?"

I moved for my phone, but he held it out of reach as he read. He scrunched up his face as he tried to understand.

"Chris—"

He lowered the phone as he began to comprehend the situation. He looked at me, stricken and hurt. He held my phone up for me to see with a cool air of accusation. His brow furrowed as he looked at me, like he was trying to reconcile the betrayal he felt. His face relaxed for a moment as though bewildered, he couldn't process it. Then his forehead crinkled with anger again as he tried to find his words. "Explain."

I sighed heavily and took the phone in my hands. "I heard the Scarlet Witch's warning because she's my great-aunt. *Her* grandmother—so, *my* grandmother—was cursed by another witch. A blood curse that skips a generation."

Chris blinked furiously, his eyes shining. He frowned and shook his head. He folded his lips together, shook his head again, and then swallowed. He gestured to me vaguely. "So, what? You're saying—"

"The curse is on my family, Chris. My blood is cursed. So, eventually, somewhere down the line, I'll start to get hungry. Inhumanly hungry—"

"No. No, Jacqueline. You can't know that for sure."

"—until I can't fight it anymore. And I take a bite out of someone I love." I averted my eyes at the word, awkward and embarrassed, and I focused back on the phone. I zoomed in on the passage I'd photographed earlier in the tent. The passage on blood curses. "Because that's the point of blood curses. To end families in the most horrific ways possible. And this one, ends with parents eating their children. But," I pushed the phone back into his hand and tapped the screen. "I meant what I said earlier. I'm not falling on my sword. I think I can cure this."

Chris looked up from the phone and stared at me hard. "You can?" His voice broke, and he bent closer so we were a breath away once more, his eyes searching mine for confirmation.

I nodded, lip quivering as I struggled to stiffen my courage, but the care and concern in the corners of his eyes, the desperation in his question broke me, and I answered, words thick and watery with emotion to match, "I think I can break the blood curse on my family."

He locked the phone and gently pressed it into my palm. He didn't speak. His silence made my anxiety rise. I needed him to agree. I needed him to consent to the plan. I pressed my lips tight, then I tried again. "You want me to trust you to stay. I need you to trust me to come back."

Then his hand cupped my cheek, and he gave me a rueful smile. "I'm here. Whatever you need."

I gasped, overwhelmed with gratitude and something else I couldn't name. And if I could, I wouldn't. "Thank you," I whispered. Then I grinned through the tears. "I told you. That white knight complex will get you into trouble."

"I've been in trouble since I saw you catching champlets with Lacey in fifth grade."

"Fifth?"

"Fifth."

I bit my lip, holding back the last thing I wanted to tell him. I inclined my head toward the door. "Let's go."

He took my hand and held me back. "Wait. Jacqueline...how? How are you going to break the curse?"

"'A blood curse can only be cured by shedding the blood of original sin,'" I recited the text. I'd reread it so many times in the past hour, I had it memorized. "'To reverse the curse, the inverse of the ailment must be applied.'"

Chris frowned at my nonanswer. "Which means what, Jacqueline Jay?"

I still didn't answer. And I wouldn't.

No more lies.

I pushed open the door and stepped inside.

EPISODE 31: THE BETTER TO EAT YOU

The first thing I noticed was the smell. A rotting, festering stench that stabbed through my nostrils, singed the follicles, and stung the nerves. I recoiled, disgust marring my face as I pinched my nose tight against the stink.

But then I could taste it—and that was infinitely worse.

My stomach heaved as I released my nose with a gag and inhaled deeply, nostrils flaring. My eyes watered as I glanced back at Chris.

His nose crinkled and he scowled darkly around the room as he entered after me. He nodded toward the far corner. My eyes moved along the room slowly, taking in the scene. It was a bedroom, just as dirty and dusty as the rest of the cabin, but the thing that caught my eye—even before the ancient monster tucked in bed like a zombie in an apocalyptic nursing home—was the iPhone on the bedside table.

With a Captain America case.

It was Chris's.

And beside it was the dowsing rod.

And those weren't the only things on the nightstand. There were a few other items left there, coated in dust, like little souvenirs from across the ages: an old worn leather wallet, small Victorian hand mirror, a tarnished silver pocket watch, a tiny tackle box, and a moth-eaten sailor's cap.

Offerings from the Scarlet Witch. Collected over the centuries from people unfortunate enough to cross her path.

Gifts from a granddaughter to her grandmother.

I would've thought it sweet if I wasn't so terrified...and if the Scarlet Witch hadn't melted my brain more times than I'd like to recount.

My eyes shifted from the nightstand to the bed.

And there she was...a grotesque mummified creature; her facial features swollen and distorted just as Erica's and Kenneth's had been, her body naked, sallow, and sunken into the bed as she wasted away, decaying and rotting.

My stomach lurched, and I couldn't seem to catch my breath over the pace of my heart. I knew what I had to do. But actually doing it...would I be able to? I held out a hand and motioned for Chris to stay back. I locked eyes with him, cobalt to hazel and mouthed, "Wait."

Chris nodded, his face set and stoic, the blowtorch raised and ready in his good hand.

I took in the image of him. His narrowed eyes sharp and alert, his head bent slightly forward in deference, his muscles visibly taut and at the ready. Literally backing me up, strong and steady, trusting me and my judgment. A good man in every sense of the word. Always there. But would he be after this? After he bore witness to an execrable affront to humanity.

I swallowed thickly, my tongue dry and scratchy in my mouth as I turned back to the monster in the bed. I took a tentative step toward her. The loup-garou's bulbous nose twitched. I froze, heart stalled in my chest, as I took a moment to calm myself. She could smell my blood pumping. She was starting to wake up now.

I had to do it fast.

There was no guarantee, but I had to try.

Otherwise, her fate was mine.

I'd finally figured out what I wanted my life to be. And I had plans to live it.

I moved closer and closer.

With each step, the loup-garou began to stir, twitching, shivering movements that made me flinch.

I was at the edge of the bed when her mouth began to open and close. Like a hideous hatchling snapping for a rodent, too weak to leave the nest.

My eyes burned as they blurred and overflowed with tears of repulsion and disgust as I watched this pathetic, revolting *thing* squirm to life in the bed.

It was abhorrent.

How could I do it?

Especially when I didn't even know if it would work?

My heart hammered against the wall of my chest as I began to panic.

It might not work.

How could I commit such a gruesome act?

"Hey..." Chris murmured softly at my back.

I looked at him quickly, eyes wide with my rising hysteria.

Chris bent his head toward me in a small nod of encouragement. "You can do this."

I blinked rapidly, tears spilling, and I nodded stiffly. I inhaled deep and purposeful, trying to slow my heart, steady my breathing, stop myself from slipping into shock. Then, I jerked my head back to the loup-garou. Her glassy gray eyes, bloodshot and cloudy, were open now. The sight of me seemed to excite her: her twitches became jerks, her eyes dilated and seemed to grow bigger, and she opened her mouth wider as though I might just stick my hand inside for her.

Now.

I let out a little gasp and whimper of dissent.

Then I shoved her head to the side, crushing my hand into her cheek, pressing her hard against the pillow.

And I fell upon her.

Teeth bared.

Mouth wide.

And I bit down into the leathery skin of her neck, tearing and ripping at her hide.

Hot tears poured down my face. My body shook as I sobbed, moaning through my gritted, grinding teeth as I tasted the saline spilling onto my lips. I needed to break her skin. I needed to taste her blood.

As I struggled to rip into her throat, she made a raspy grunting noise of protest and started to thrash. I couldn't hold her down and bite at the same time. I forced her into the pillow and pulled even harder with my teeth. But she was bucking against me. I was losing control. As soon as I lost my grip on her, she'd rip into me within seconds. She'd cut into me as easily as Dog shreds into a mouse. And the blood curse would be complete.

The matriarch would murder the heir.

Maternal filicide.

But then he was there.

Chris leaned into her head, slamming her down hard on the bed. "You can do this, Jacqueline. Finish it!"

It was all I needed. I tore at her, yanking my head back with as much force as I could focus, and her skin gave way. The rubbering texture of it was almost too much. My stomach heaved and I had to put all my will into keeping my mouth shut and jaw chewing.

"Now?"

I shook my head as I worked the hide in between my teeth. The metallic bitterness of her blood sent my stomach churning, and hot sour bile bubbled up my throat as I continued to chew through clenched jaws.

The slimy slip of her blood coated my tongue as I struggled to force it down my throat. I needed to swallow it.

But it was stuck. I couldn't chew it.

I had to gulp it down whole.

I closed my eyes, allowed my mouth to fill with spit, and I swallowed it down.

I couldn't speak, only nod. There was no way I'd risk opening my mouth and throwing it all back up.

But I couldn't say what Chris did next.

Whether he even saw my signal to light her on fire.

Because the moment the bloody chunk of skin slipped down my throat into my stomach, there was a ringing in my ears, a steady hum like an ethereal chime, as a flash of white light exploded in my eyes and it was all I could see.

And then I wasn't me anymore...

Disembodied. Omniscient. Evanescent.

A voice low and muffled murmured softly in my head as the speaker slowly came into focus, along with the rest of the room. A short woman with long black hair hanging down past the shoulders of her peasants gown, casting uneasy glances around the kitchen toward the window and door of the cabin, stood beside a stooped, old woman with stark white hair roped in a braid down the length of her curved back. The old woman, bent over the cauldron hung in the fireplace, gripped the ladle with gnarled hands and stirred the contents slowly but deliberately, in strong, steady strokes. The dark haired woman placed a hand on the old crone and spoke in a voice sharp and almost urgent, "High Priestess Grey isn't happy about the bones, Winifred."

Winifred scoffed. "Oh, please, Morrigan. They're just calves. A few missing cows never hurt anyone." Then she cackled. "Is the House of Grey so fragile they cannot withstand a common House like that of mine? Perraults are nothing to them. Stool, wedged in the hooves of their horses. Why would Amarilla Grey trouble herself with my doings?"

"Respect her name," Morrigan hissed her eyes darted back to the door. "High Priestess Grey says you dabble too far into the depths of darkness. Drawing attention to us. The House of Grey fears a European response.”

Winifred waved away Morrigan’s concern with a disrespectful snicker. “Oh, please. This is the New World. Freedom. New thinking. We’d never see anything like burnings here in the Colonies.”

“The islanders are already showing their distrust, Winifred. You told me you weren’t responsible for the children...you said they were—”

“They *are*. And I’m *not*.” Winifred rolled her eyes. “The islanders love me. They pay us well for my bone scrying.”

Morrigan frowned. “And what do you think their attitudes will be when there is a harsh winter? Or if more children continue to disappear? The Greys have been here much longer than we. They’ve been in the Colonies since the white rose of York bled red. They *know* these Martin Isle people. They have lived beside them since the founding. And I think we should heed High Priestess Grey’s warning—”

“Oh, nonsense, Morrigan. They think that just because they are a Hallowed House that means something.”

“The Son of God blessed their matriarch...I’d say that means—”

“Apparently it doesn’t mean much if the House of Perrault, lowly cobblers and bone scryers, can upset their delicate balance. You yourself know how little they think of us...why, your own House disowned you when you married my son! Now enough of this—”

There was a soft knock on the door and both women turned, startled.

“*How did she pass through my warding?*” Winifred breathed.

“Because she’s Amarilla Grey,” Morrigan grumbled over her shoulder as she hurried to open the door for their uninvited guest. Morrigan bowed deeply, her nose nearly touching her knees. “Good morrow, High Priestess Grey. What do we owe the pleasure of your visit?”

The woman's presence seemed to fill the room as much as her dramatic height. The silk gown beneath her black velvet, fur-trimmed robe shimmered and shined like molten silver and sharpened the shade of her striking gray eyes as they shifted passed the simpering Morrigan to Winifred, who was neither welcoming nor warm in her regard for the High Priestess. On the contrary, she held her whiskered chin high so that her pudgy nose pointed in the air, and she looked down the bridge of it at the High Priestess with all the defiance of a stubborn mule. And with all the intelligence to match. For if anyone knew anything of the women of the House of Grey, it was that they were not ones to stand for disrespect.

Time creates a gulf of distance between the past and the present. Distance makes it harder to see. And when you can't see things, you forget them. And mistakes are made as historical errors are repeated. And Winifred Perrault had forgotten the vicious vendetta of the Grey women. How Elizabeth Grey's eldest daughter, white rose and York princess, had laid a blood curse upon her own mother-law, thus cursing her own heirs, for the murder of her little brothers...knowing full well it wasn't her mother-in-law who was directly responsible. Just the fact that the mother-in-law had benefited from and cheered their death was enough. What would Amarilla Grey do, now that Winifred Perrault was, in her opinion, endangering the safety of their entire House?

"You've heard from my messengers, Witch Perrault?" Amarilla asked, her striking silver eyes gathering strength like clouds before the storm.

"The cardinals? Psh. I'm an old woman. I can't read well these days. My eyes aren't what they used to be, you know." Winifred shrugged and folded her arms across her chest out of defensive habit.

"But you've heard from my cousins..." Amarilla Grey murmured almost pensively as her eyes moved around the tiny kitchen. "The Blackwells were clear in their interactions with you..."

At this, Morrigan looked at Winifred, her face blanched with fear. Winifred lowered her arms and began to fidget with her apron. "High Priestess, I—"

"They explained the severity of the situation to you, and you behaved quite beastly toward them...or so I'm told." Amarilla Grey's eyes darkened as they rested back upon Winifred.

"I didn't mean no offense, I just—we just needed to make ends meet..."

"The islanders chased you off the island. And still, from this little rock, a stone's throw from the shore, you still cannot help but carry on with your dark practices and put our entire race at risk."

"This...it's the *Colonies*...you don't need to worry about burnings like back home..." Winifred rambled as beads of sweat lined her brow.

Amarilla Grey's eyes narrowed and for the first time, she stepped fully into the room. Her impressive height and imposing presence filled the kitchen, and Morrigan and Winifred instinctively grew closer together, shrinking beneath her silent fury.

"It has already begun. There have been whispers of mistrust as far as Massachusetts. Because of witches like you and yours who think themselves novelties of the normal world. Parading about the towns like peacocks when you're no more special than barn pigeons."

"We...we have settled here on this rock. Away from Martin Isle. As you requested. We won't—

"My niece, Jemima Blackwell, was stoned in the town square this morning. Did you know?" Amarilla Grey murmured in a soft, matter-of-fact way that made Morrigan swallow audibly.

There was an icy quiet that settled about the room, ominous and sinister.

"A group of island men dragged Jemima out of the bookshop by her hair. And stoned her to death in the dirt like a dog," Amarilla continued, her voice hardening with each word, her lip curling in disgust.

Winifred gaped. "Why—why didn't she defend—"

Amarilla Grey took a step closer to the old crone. "Because Jemima Blackwell, at just twelve years of age, understood something that up until now you have refused to acknowledge. *No witch is safe if our sorcery is not secret.*"

"God help us," Morrigan murmured as she crossed herself, eyes wide and fused to Amarilla Grey.

"And do you know *why* they went after her, Witch Perrault?" Amarilla Grey took another threatening step toward her.

Winifred blinked rapidly. She dabbed at her forehead with her apron. "I wouldn't know...I—"

"You lie as you breathe, hag," Amarilla Grey spat, slowly losing her patience.

Winifred scowled at that. "I truly don't know what—"

"Because of the children..." Amarilla Grey's face darkened as she hissed, "*The island children you've been butchering for bones... your absence didn't stop the deaths...and Jemima Blackwell just happened to be friends with the last little girl you flayed.*"

Winifred's eyes bulged wide, and she shook her head, opening and closing her mouth in muted protest as Amarilla Grey drew closer.

Morrigan gasped as she stared, horrified at her mother-in-law. "*Winifred, you didn't? You haven't!*" Her eyes darted toward the cauldron and for the first time she saw the ivory bones, small and thin, for what they truly were as they protruded from the bubbles of the broth.

"Because of your wickedness and your pedicide, you will pay in blood for the death of my sweet niece."

"No, no, please. I won't—I swear—no more, I promise— please, High Priestess!" Winifred cried, backing up into the stove.

Morrigan released her mother-in-law and inched away into the corner of the kitchen by the hearth as she watched in horror as Amarilla Grey neared Winifred, the High Priestess's hand raised as though to bless the wicked old crone. "Please, High Priestess, I have daughters," Morrigan breathed. "Two *good* daughters. They are innocent of their grandmother's evil. Please, have mercy."

Amarilla Grey smiled solemnly. "It will be a mercy. Upon the world. The end of the House of Perrault."

She placed a gentle hand upon Winifred's cheek as she screamed, long and tortuous.

White light flashed, blinding me to the scene.

EPISODE 32: THE TRUTH IN THE LEGEND

I was standing in a blank world. White, stark and cold, all around me.

And then there was the wolf. Her voice was soft in my head.

"I thank you, Jacqueline Charlebois. You set my mistress free and have healed the generational trauma and broken the blood curse upon your line."

I tried to speak. But my incorporeality made sound impossible. All I had left of my being was thought. And that, the wolf heard.

"My name is Cerridwen. And I claim you as my witch."

What? *Claim* me? I'm not a witch.

"You are correct in a sense. It is true, a witch wouldn't recognize you as one of them. Your house has all but died out. But as a familiar, I can sense your bloodline. And you are the true heir of my mistress, Epona. And you have set her spirit free. Beyond that, you ended the suffering of her grandmother, the one she loved most. I have seen into your heart, and I claim you as mine."

No. I don't want anything to do with any of it. Amarilla Grey was right. The Perraults deserved to die out. Flaying little Nile children for their bones deserved nothing less. I'm not a witch. And I don't want a familiar.

The wolf blinked her golden eyes and bowed her head. "I've marked you as mine. If ever you change your mind...the bond is yours to make. And I am yours to command."

No. I don't want it. I want to go back. Take me back.

The wolf bowed again.

There was another flash of blinding white.

And I was solid. Real. Human.

I fluttered my eyes open as I worked to make sense of my surroundings.

Chris had me cradled in his lap in the grass. It was damp with morning dew and cool from the October cold, but somehow there was impossible heat, dry and suffocating. And then I smelt the smoke.

My eyes found Chris's, my forehead crinkled in question.

His hand went to my face. "Hey...Benji took everyone back to the boat. I told them to take the left. Walk until they can't anymore. Even Ted can handle that. They should be back to the Inn by now. I hope you don't mind...I dug your phone out of your pants and called Nicky. He's waiting for us on the shore."

"Fire?"

Chris smiled sheepishly as his thumb smoothed my cheek. "You said fire cleanses, right? I hope I made the right call...just figured, burn the whole place to the ground..."

"Yeah. Right call." I tried to keep the bitterness from my voice, but it was hard. They were monsters. Amarilla Grey was right to curse them. That's where I came from. That was my inheritance. Burn them all. Even so, my heart ached with the painful truth of it.

Chris's eyes searched mine. "Are you feeling okay?"

"Eh. It feels like it's my *veins* that are on fire."

Chris glanced over me at the burning house. "I should probably call Joey and get the boys over here to put it out before the whole—"

"What happened?"

Chris looked down at me, his hold on me tightening. "Well... you...you know. You gave me the signal, but before I could light the torch, that *thing* went limp in my arms. It laid back on the pillow as it bled out on the bed. Then there was this hum, this sound, like—

"Chimes?"

"Yeah, you heard it?" Chris cocked an eyebrow, surprised.

"Just keep going," I prompted, struggling out of his lap and pushing myself up. "Did she change back? To more...human-like?"

"No, it was just the sound, and then it—she—just kind of... died. So, I lit her on fire like you said. She kind of exploded. It was like I'd set fire to a gallon of gasoline. The whole room went up. And when I turned back to you, well, you were kind of zombified."

I scoffed with a laugh. "Nice, Chris."

"Well, I don't know how to describe it," he mumbled defensively. He waved his words away almost impatiently and continued, "Anyway, you were standing there. Eyes wide and staring. I couldn't get you to snap out of it, so I carried you out of the house."

I cocked an eyebrow. "Very white knight of you. I feel like a princess."

Chris gave me a cheeky wink. "You better. It's not everyday I carry a girl across the threshold." His confident cocky grin, piercing a dimple in his left cheek, slipped a bit as uncertainty creased his brow. "I gave you the few drops I could shake out of the corpectus bottle and some holy water...I hope that was okay?"

I smiled, warm with pride in his resourcefulness, but couldn't make it reach my eyes. "You did good, Vantine. Now let's check on Lacey."

. . .

We were quiet on the boat ride home, like soldiers haggard and shell-shocked from war. Nicky eyed us awkwardly as he steered us toward the shore through the gold quiet of early morning, the gray water churning quietly beneath the hull. "Bad date?"

Chris scoffed as he stared out across the lake.

I saw the frustration lining his face and regret washed over me like whitecaps. I'd wasted so much time holding him back, keeping him at arm's length, when I really should have been pulling him closer.

I looked at Nicky as I took Chris's hand. "It was the best date I've ever had."

Chris glanced back at me in surprise as Nicky laughed.

When we finally docked and drove to the Rosecrest House, I parked the car and stared up at the old Victorian house, quiet and crumbling in the gray light of morning.

"You okay?"

I inhaled deeply as I blinked back into focus. "Yes. Just preparing myself." I turned and gave him a small smile. Still too weak to reach my eyes.

Chris inclined his head in question. "For what? Erica and Kenneth turned back all right. What makes you think Lacey wouldn't, too?"

It wasn't that. But I shrugged it off. "I don't know. You're right. Let's go make sure Lacey isn't a bloated man-eating monster."

"Jacque—"

I didn't wait. "Let's go, White Knight." I scooped up my bag, kicked open the door, and shut it behind me.

Chris hurried after me, but I was already around the back of the house by the time he caught up. I led the way down the stairs without looking back despite his protests.

"Jacqueline, what is it? You—"

"Shhh," I snapped as I rapped loudly at the door and jammed my finger into the doorbell.

The chain scraped across the lock, and Cassandra threw open the door mid-doorbell assault. She looked like we looked: battle-worn. Her thick braided red hair was messy and in complete disarray with strands sticking out of it every which way like a frayed rope. And her sapphire gown was torn at the sleeves. But her smile was radiant and that of a conqueror. She pulled me into the apartment and into a tight, crushing hug.

"Thank you," Cassandra breathed into my ear. "Thank you, Jacqueline. She is more precious than you could possibly know."

I stiffened at that. Offended by the implication that I didn't value the most innocent of all my friends. "I want to see her." I stepped back, out of the warmth of her embrace.

Cassandra pushed stray strands of red out of her face as she studied me. "You've cured more than Lacey, I see..."

I gritted my teeth. Her freaky, psychic, superman vision was invasive and annoying. I pushed past her into the living room.

"She's had a long night...she needs to rest," Cassandra cautioned with a slight bite to her words.

And so she was—Lacey was curled up on the couch beneath a furry white throw blanket fast asleep. If she was still a loup-garou, she wouldn't be able to sleep with fresh meat walking around the place. And her face was calm and her features normal, but I wanted to make sure. I had to make sure.

"I haven't explained anything to her, yet," Cassandra snapped at my back as I approached the couch. "She doesn't remember the change...don't remind her."

I rolled my eyes. As if I didn't know when to lie.

Ignoring Cassandra, I bent down beside Lacey and smoothed a hand across her cheek. "Lacey?"

Her eyelashes fluttered and her eyes opened, revealing the rarest of hazel eyes that rivaled my own. In that moment, they were the most beautiful eyes I'd ever seen.

I smiled as mine blurred. "Lacey, I just wanted to tell you...*thank you*," I breathed my voice low and watery with emotion. "I finally found her. The Scarlet Witch. I found her, and I put her to rest. And I couldn't have done it without you."

Lacey gave me a sleepy, simple smile. "I'm proud of you, Jacqueline."

The praise made my heart ache. I smoothed her lily-blonde hair from her brow. "Go back to sleep."

"I'll find you for lunch." Lacey yawned and snuggled deeper into the blankets. "But don't worry. I don't want to eat you."

I laughed at that and tried to hold on to the happiness while I could. Because in less than an hour, I'd never feel that kind of joy again.

EPISODE 33: ARE YOU THERE, GRANDMA? IT'S ME, JACQUELINE

Chris was quiet the whole ride to Charlebois Manor. But as soon as I put the car in park, he started in on me.

"And what is it that you aren't telling me this time?" He didn't even bother keeping the annoyed clip from the timbre of his voice.

I sighed despite myself. "I'm going in to check on Memé. In case you've forgotten, she had a hard day yesterday." I nodded toward Aunt April's car sitting smug and shiny in the driveway beside my beat up old rust bucket. "And my aunt is here. She'll need a bit of a pick-me-up, I'm sure. Especially considering Carol Anne probably quit. Her routine will be all messed up. I won't be more than twenty minutes—" I held up a hand to keep him from arguing. "I say 'twenty' only because sometimes she needs me to sit with her a moment before she's okay with me leaving."

Chris wasn't convinced. He frowned, cobalt eyes narrowed. "That's great. But what is it that you aren't saying?"

I swallowed and licked my lips. Tasting the lies one by one as they came to me. I didn't want to lie anymore. Especially not to Chris.

But I needed him to wait for me. I couldn't have him follow me inside.

I inhaled deeply, nostrils flaring. My temper was rising with my impatience. This was hard enough, I didn't need to be dealing with his white knight, savior complex on top of it. "Fine. You're right. There *is* something I'm not saying. But I'll talk to you about as soon as I get out, okay? I can't think straight right now."

Chris pursed his lips to the side as he studied me hard. "Fine."

I let out the breath I'd been holding and grinned.

My whole body filled with warmth as a mixture of relief and something else flooded through me. And acting on impulse and savoring the feelings fluttering in my heart, I threw my arms around him and pulled him into a tight hug. He squeezed me back hard. Then I shifted away just enough to face him, my hands still locked around his neck. I searched his eyes with mine. "You're something else, Christopher Vantine."

"It's about time you noticed." A sly smirk pinched a dimple into his left cheek. Then he kissed me.

And for a moment, I forgot that I was dead in about five minutes. Because, though *Chris* had forgotten, the banshee had sung for me. And that meant my fate was sealed.

I didn't bother to knock. I slipped silently through the door, my jaw clenched, muscles taut, ready to face her.

But my eyes went to the macabre mess in the middle of the blood soaked carpet.

Aunt April.

Like the Nile children, she'd been flayed down to skeletal remains; nothing left but a few stringy tendons, some connective tissue, and bone.

I blinked as my stomach heaved, the room spinning slightly as I struggled not to faint. Then I saw the loup-garou, in my memé's dressing gown, pacing the length of the bookshelf as though searching for something to read. Her skin was scarred with purple stretch marks. Her features swollen and grotesque, her eyes bulging bloodshot from their sockets. Her mouth sagged as her teeth protruded from her jaw.

She had the scarlet hunger.

And her appetite would never be sated.

She'd tried to warn me, but she'd waited too long.

She'd tried to start the fire, but it'd been too late.

And now it was on me.

Her nose began to twitch. She smelled me.

I had to act fast.

I moved with swift, silent steps toward the table beside her reading chair and grabbed our book of Nile fairy tales along with her Afghan.

She turned, and her eyes crinkled with a horrific, gruesome grin.

And it was another one of those moments, where time takes a breath.

We looked at each other.

My eyes stung with tears as they spilled down my cheeks, my lip trembling with emotion I couldn't contain.

How could I burn her? How could I set her ablaze?

My memé had done nothing to earn this fate. It hadn't been her lies and pedicide that had warranted this curse. She didn't deserve it. None of it.

But she wasn't my memé anymore. There wasn't any question in my mind. The truth was staring back at me with huge, hungry eyes, set in a swollen head with big, twitching ears and giant bloody teeth protruding from it.

Then the loup-garou's old, weathered hands, stained scarlet and dripping with daughter's blood, curled like claws, and she ran at me.

And I froze.

I couldn't hear.

I couldn't see.

I hugged the book and blanket tight to my chest, closed my eyes, and braced for the pain. Tearing and blood. But nothing came save for a hot hiss.

I squinted my eyes open.

Chris, blow torch burning blue, stood between me and the loup-garou.

The creature chittered and ducked its head down, scurrying backward into the wall.

I blinked stupidly trying to process the scene.

Chris yanked me to the side, keeping me behind him, as he backed us up toward the door, setting the couch and carpet ablaze as he went. Then he blocked me from the view, his body filling the doorway, as he watched and waited for the room to catch.

"Wait outside, Jacqueline."

I let out a little sob as the tears streamed down my face. The loup-garou's shrieks, chirping from the depths of the room, hurt worse than the banshee's screams.

I didn't argue.

And this time, I ran.

Chris found me sitting in my car, the book and blanket on my lap, staring blindly ahead, tears still flowing silently down my cheeks like rain down the windshield. He tugged open the passenger door, which creaked loudly in protest. I winced as he shut it. I didn't look at him. I couldn't. I just continued to stare, unseeing, straight ahead as my eyes leaked.

"It's done," he murmured gently. "And I put out the fire... after... After," he finished firmly.

Jaw clenched tight, I gave him a shaky nod to confirm my understanding. I didn't trust myself to speak. If I tried...the flood-gates would open, and I'd never be able to close them. I'd drown in my sobs. I was sure of it.

"Called it in…everyone'll be here soon." His eyes flicked back toward the Manor up on the hill. "And spin it like you say we do…"

I spoke then, in a dead, dry, monotone. "And everyone will think my senile memé set her house on fire…and murdered her daughter…and that'll be the story. Not that she'd been a victim of a witch's curse, a punishment that wasn't hers to bear. Not that she'd been doing her best to warn me for months about it. Not that she'd tried to set *herself* on fire to save us from her." I cursed under my breath. I was tired. Too tired to say anymore. To think anymore. But I had to know. I took a quick breath. "Chris, I heard the banshee." I looked at him then, searching his face. "I should be dead. How did—?"

"First, you tell me. I thought when you bit into the old broad back on Wolf's Rock that you broke your family's blood curse? Cassandra even said—"

I closed my eyes, irritation itching away my heartache. "I did break the blood curse."

Chris scowled at that.

I inhaled deeply as I searched for an explanation to satiate him. "But if you remember…Memé bit Carol Anne before we even went to Wolf's Rock." I fixed him with a hard stare.

Chris nodded slowly as he raked a hand through his cropped hair. "Okay, so she'd already transformed—but, so had Lacey and—"

I sighed in exasperation. It felt like teaching a baby to read. Impossible and stupid to try. "Lacey, Erica, and Kenneth were cursed by the Scarlet Witch as a warning. Just like those banshees you read about giving everyone the plague. So, they were cured when we burned her bones and—"

Chris slapped a hand over his eyes and ran it down the length of his face. "Right, okay. Sorry. Not blood curse related." He inclined his head as he asked again, "But *your* blood curse is broken?"

"Yes." I answered easily. "The curse I'd carried in my blood is broken. So," I nodded toward him, eyebrows raised expectantly. "how did you know—"

"Divine intervention, right? The wolf."

I looked at him sharply, leaking eyes narrowed in question.

Chris nodded toward the entrance of Charlebois Manor. "She appeared on the doorstep, and I heard her in my head. Clear as day. 'Save her.'"

Brow furrowed I looked from Chris to the double doors of the Manor and back again. "But—"

Chris shrugged. "Don't ask me. I'm over all this supernatural stuff. Makes my head hurt."

I scoffed on a small laugh of disbelief. "Well, too bad…because apparently I'm descended from witches…and have a wolf familiar acting as guardian angel, so, I don't know what to tell you."

"What do you mean?"

"Paranormal activity is something you'll just have to get used to—" I sniffed and dabbed at my wet face with my tattered sweater sleeve. Then I met his eyes with a rueful smile. "—if I'm going to be your girlfriend…"

Chris grinned, his cobalt eyes crinkled with mischief. "Are you asking to be my girlfriend, Jacqueline Charlebois?"

I smirked. "You know you want me."

Chris bit his lip on his smile. "That I do."

I giggled at that with a small shake of my head. "You're too good for me."

Chris's brow furrowed as he searched my eyes. "You still don't see you. But that's okay. Because I do."

I took a breath, but before I could argue, he held up a finger. "Hold it." He pointed it at me, his eyes narrowed in mock seriousness. "I'll only be your boyfriend on one condition…"

I simpered with a coy flutter of my lashes. "And what's that, Corporal?"

"You gotta promise you won't turn into a loup-garou on me because that would be the worst break-up ever."

I laughed at that and kissed him like it would be our last.

And when I broke away, heart hammering and head dizzy in love. I licked his kiss off my lips and smiled. "I promise."

But what Chris didn't understand is that although the blood curse was broken...that meant for future heirs.

Not for me.

So, when I promised him I wouldn't turn...

I lied.

Thank you so much for reading.

This story saved my soul.

I wrote it during one of the darkest times of my life, and it helped me survive the devastating horror of heartbreak.

Twisted takes on classic fairy tales are my favorite things to write, and *Scarlet Hunger* is a teaser into an upcoming series of spooky Nile fairy tales featuring our favorite Nile girls.

While this book processes through a lot of my pain and hurt, I hope you still enjoyed Jacqueline's story and finished it feeling uplifted.

If you did, let everyone know when you leave a review!
Share your thoughts on Goodreads and/or your preferred book seller.

WELCOME TO THE NILE UNIVERSE

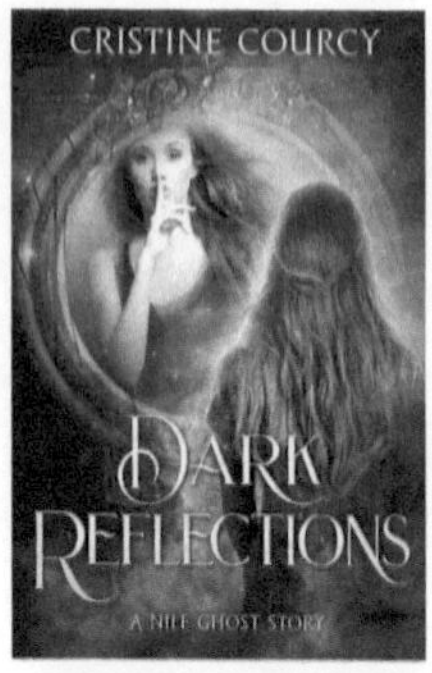

Dark Reflections: A Nile Ghost Story

Available Now

There is no such thing as ghosts. No one knows this better than Hannah Green. But after moving to Nile, the most haunted town in America, Hannah's finding it hard to keep her head...

The Sacrifice of Maddison Rose

A Grey Sisters Saga Novella

Coming Soon

This book shares the untold story of Maddison Rose. Everyone has heard the rumors...but no one knows the truth. What really happened to Maddison Rose?

Sign up for the Courcy Camp newsletter for exclusive (free) access to *The First Hunt of Phoenix Grey* at

cristinecourcy.com/newsletter

But if newsletters (or eBooks) aren't your thing, order *The First Hunt of Phoenix Grey* at **www. cristinecourcy.com/exclusive-releases** or your preferred book seller!

Seraphina Grey Summons a Demon

Book One of the Grey Sisters Saga

AVAILABLE NOW

A witch without magic. A demon out for blood. A dark family secret. How can teenage witch, Seraphina, solve the mystery and hunt down the demon when she can't even do magic?

Phoenix Grey and the Blood Farm

Book Two of the Grey Sisters Saga

AVAILABLE NOW

Kidnapped kids...butchered babysitters...and a trace of dark magic. Is this a case even Logan can't solve? Phoenix sure thinks so...

And finally...

Seraphina Grey and the Carnival of Nightmares

Book Three of the Grey Sisters Saga

COMING SOON

ABOUT THE AUTHOR

Hi, I'm Cristine!
I love old sitcoms and slasher films.
When I'm not writing, I'm playing Animal Crossing or Harvest Moon 64.
When I am writing, I like to write dark fantasy with a light heart.
This means I want to disturb you without leaving you feeling yucky at the end of the story. In short, I'm inventing a new genre I like to call 'cozy dark fantasy.'
My books are heavily influenced by my experiences growing up wild on an island in the middle of the lake.
Almost all the things I write about are inspired by real life...but for legal purposes— that's a lie.
To read more lies and see photos of the things that *did not* inspire my writing, sign up for my newsletter at cristinecourcy.com/newsletter.

Connect with me online:
WWW.CRISTINECOURCY.COM

goodreads.com/cristinecourcy

facebook.com/cristinecourcy

instagram.com/cristinecourcy

threads.net/@cristinecourcy

youtube.com/@cristinecourcy

x.com/cristinecourcy

tiktok.com/@cristinecourcy

amazon.com/author/cristinecourcy

www.ingramcontent.com/pod-product-compliance
Lightning Source LLC
Chambersburg PA
CBHW031031310726
48969CB00007B/1943